ABACUS

Abacus

Chris McGowan

Euphausia Press

Library and Archives Canada Cataloguing in Publication

McGowan, C., 1942–
   Abacus / Chris McGowan.

ISBN 978-0-9810831-0-0 (paperback)
ISBN 978-0-9810831-1-7 (hardcover)

1. Science—Experiments—Juvenile literature. I. Title.

PS8625.G67A63 2010 jC813'.6 C2009-904096-4

Summary: Thrown together with her science-geek kid brother AP, Kate travels through time, stalked by a sinister attacker. True events are historically correct and readers can repeat AP's experiments.

Design and Composition: Jay Tee Graphics Ltd.
Printed in the United States and in England

To Emma, Carter, Miles, Raquel and Nathan,
with love.

Acknowledgments

First and foremost I want to thank a legion of youngsters who read an early draft of *Abacus*, giving me such valuable feedback. In alphabetical order they are: Caden Armstrong, Emily Betteridge, Laura Blackmore, Devin Cassidy, Michael David, Whitney Gemmill, Cory Green, Justine Kavanagh, Chloe Lavington, Eloise Lavington, Emily Lostchuck, Adam Nickerson and Kyle Niece. Without your enthusiastic help, this book would never have happened.

When I anxiously approached John Lester, Principal of Regency Acres Public School, Aurora, with my unusual request to have *Abacus* critically reviewed by some of his pupils, he was immediately supportive. I thank him for his time and trouble in setting up the at-arm's-length reviews, and for arranging for me to meet with the youngsters after the fact to discuss their comments. I also thank him for his continued interest in the project. Kevin McHenry, Headmaster of St. Andrews College, Aurora, kindly arranged for a similar review of the manuscript in the Upper School of his institution. I thank him for organizing the reviews and for monitoring the process throughout. Jennifer Wills of St. Marguerite d'Youville School, Ottawa, read *Abacus* with a group of her Grade Five students. I thank her for her valuable comments and enthusiastic endorsement.

I am sincerely grateful to Doron Ben-Ami for his superb cover art. Working with such a gifted artist has been a privilege and a most enjoyable experience. I thank him too for his encouragement and inspiration at times when these were most needed.

Sandy Bogart Johnston provided encouragement and guidance during the early stages of this project, for which I warmly thank her. My thanks also to Mary Macchiusi for her valuable advice and support.

I am truly grateful to Dimitra Chronopoulos for the meticulous care she took in copy editing the final draft of the manuscript. What a great joy it has been working with such a professional. My thanks also to Caroline Kaiser for her careful attention to detail in proofreading.

I thank two veterans of the book business, Eleanor Le Fave of Mabel's Fables and Erin O'Conner, for sharing their valuable insights into the world of

ACKNOWLEDGMENTS

children's books. I am also grateful to Morris Rosenthal for his advice and wise council, and to Mary Gnetz for her patient help. My thanks also to Julian Mulock for his generous help.

Catherine Pouliot designed the book, giving me a new understanding and appreciation for the subtle nuances that make a printed page more pleasing to the eye. I thank her for her talents and skills.

I am very fortunate in that my publisher secured the services of Judy Brunsek, with her extensive experience in the world of publishing. Judy is a hard taskmaster, but I needed organizing and am truly indebted to her. I also wish to thank Michaela Cornell, my publicist, for her focused professionalism in bringing this book to peoples' attention.

Pat Morrison, my big sister, has been enthusiastic about *Abacus* since she read the first draft many years ago. Feisty like Kate, she has been pushing for its publication ever since, for which I am truly grateful.

Some years ago, Liz, my sea-anchor, sat in silence on a long drive north to our friends' cottage, as I charted the storyline of *Abacus*. I thought she would advise me to stick to non-fiction, but instead she encouraged me to put pen to paper. Aside from her support through the ups and downs of this project, she has used her professional book background with sage advice, proofing and correcting. I am blessed in having such a supportive wife.

Last, I thank my two lovely daughters, Claire and Angie, for their support and encouragement, and for blessing me with the wonderful grandchildren to whom *Abacus* is dedicated.

Contents

ONE
Past Times   1

TWO
Lost in the Forest   10

THREE
Castles in the Air   26

FOUR
The Young Warrior   37

FIVE
Floating Phantoms   49

SIX
Battle Plans   56

SEVEN
The Vipers' Nest   60

EIGHT
Marooned   69

NINE
A Poisonous Plot   80

CONTENTS

TEN
Counting the Seconds 89

ELEVEN
The Old Routine 92

TWELVE
Buffalo! 97

THIRTEEN
Talking Cloud 107

FOURTEEN
Robert Drew 119

FIFTEEN
Counting Coup 123

SIXTEEN
The Sacred Hills 131

SEVENTEEN
Ho-Ka Hey! 141

EIGHTEEN
Wagons Roll 149

NINETEEN
Tracking Trouble 154

TWENTY
Joining the Army 158

TWENTY ONE
Cocky Custer 166

TWENTY TWO
Signs in the Sand 173

TWENTY THREE
The Battle of the Little Bighorn 176

CONTENTS

TWENTY FOUR
Watch Out!   183

TWENTY FIVE
Future Shock   187

TWENTY SIX
Anyone for the Sun?   191

TWENTY SEVEN
Wab World   203

TWENTY EIGHT
Mummies   212

TWENTY NINE
Conjuring up Magic   223

THIRTY
Ramesses the Great   237

THIRTY ONE
Black Magnet   247

THIRTY TWO
Tomb Robber   256

THIRTY THREE
Fleeing the Pharaoh   267

FURTHER READING
279

NOTES
285

HOW TO REPEAT THE EXPERIMENTS IN THE BOOK
289

1

Past Times

Kate stared out the window as the cabin crew demonstrated the safety features of the Boeing 767. They were about to take off from Boston's Logan International Airport.

"It's not fair," she grumbled. She was quite capable of looking after herself while the rest of the family went to England. Summer was almost over, and Kate wanted to spend the last of it with her friends. She'd be missing baseball too, and she was one of the best players on her team. Sure, Uncle Miles had died suddenly, but her parents could sort out his things without her help. And the last thing she wanted was to spend the next two weeks with her twelve-year-old brother.

"Have you buckled up?" asked her father, turning around from the seat in front.

"Do you want some gum to stop your ears popping?" added her mother beside him.

"My buckle's done up," Kate snapped. "And no, I don't want any gum. I am fifteen, remember, not three." Heaving a loud sigh, she turned toward the window again. Her fair hair reflected in the glass like gold—she'd spent ages getting it just right.

"How about you, AP?" asked Mr. Littleton.

"I'm good," his son replied, glancing up from his book. He was excited about visiting England again. "I put on my seat belt when I sat down."

"You're *so* perfect," sneered his sister. "Lucky me to be sitting with a *world* traveler."

AP, ignoring the taunt, continued reading.

Like father, like son—Mr. Littleton had his nose in a book too. His wife, Samantha, began chatting with the woman across the aisle.

"Are you folks traveling back home to England?" asked the woman, detecting Mrs. Littleton's English accent.

"No. We're from England originally, but we live in the States now." She nodded toward her husband. "Ken got a job at Woods Hole—the Oceanographic Institution. He's a marine biologist."

"That covers a wide area," said the woman, thinking of everything from plankton to whales. "What's his specialty?"

"Large open-sea fishes, like sharks and tunas," replied Mrs. Littleton, surprised at the question—most people had little idea what marine biology was about. "I think that's where AP, our son, gets his love of science."

"AP?" queried the woman. "That's your son's *name*?"

"No, not exactly. Those are just his initials." She lowered her voice and leaned closer. "He can't *stand* his real names—Arthur Percival. Ken chose them. We agreed that I'd name our first child and he'd name the second. He's always been interested in the Arthurian legend."

"Arthur Percival," repeated the woman, looking puzzled.

"You know, King Arthur and Sir Percival."

The woman smiled vaguely.

2

"Sir Percival was one of the Knights of the Round Table. Ken's read a lot about them. Of course, there's no evidence King Arthur ever existed—writers made up the legend during the Middle Ages. Anyway, that's how our son became AP." Samantha smiled. "Kate's lucky she was born first. Otherwise she'd have been named Guinevere!"

The woman nodded. If she'd been christened Arthur Percival, she would have kept it quiet too.

"Look at that, Kate," said AP, pointing out the window as their airplane gained height. "See the mist above the wing?" Being short for his age, he had to stretch up to see properly. "Millions of tiny water droplets, condensed from the moist air. It's caused by..."

Kate cut him off. "I don't want one of your dumb lectures. Science is boring, and you're even worse." With that, she popped in her ear buds and turned her iPod to full volume. AP returned to his book, *Basic Aerodynamics for Inquisitive Flyers.*

After the in-flight supper, AP read for a while and then nodded off. Kate, unable to text her friends, flipped through the magazine she'd bought. An article on career choices caught her attention. Then she filled out a quiz on music groups.

She glanced at her sleeping brother. Between science and his schoolwork, she doubted he could name a single band. She nibbled on some pretzels, watched two movies and stayed awake all night.

Their plane landed at London's Heathrow Airport at 10 o'clock the next morning. The Littletons trudged over to the baggage claim area with the other jet-lagged passengers. With the time difference between England and Boston, it was only 5 a.m. as far as their bodies were concerned.

❀   ❀   ❀

"How far is it to Uncle Miles's place?" moaned Kate.

"Two or three hours," said her mother, settling into the passenger seat of their rental car. "Try catching up on your sleep."

"I would if I had any room back here!" she growled. "How come England has no decent-sized cars?" She banged her hand against the door to emphasize the point.

"I'll move my seat," said her father, inching forward until his knees almost touched the dashboard. "How's that?"

"Better. At least I can breathe again. As for you, shrimp..." She glowered at AP, who was minding his own business. "Keep your distance!"

"For goodness' sake, leave your brother alone!" snapped her mother. "Don't spoil this trip for everybody."

Mr. Littleton started the engine for what promised to be a long journey. AP buried himself in another book: *A Field Guide to British Birds.*

Soon they were on the highway, leaving London. As Mr. Littleton got used to the new car and driving on the left side of the road, he started to relax.

"Neither of you knew Uncle Miles," he began. "Nor did I, really—he was much older than me. Strange too."

"You shouldn't talk about your brother like that," admonished his wife. "Especially now he's dead."

"Well, he *was* odd. He had no friends—never married."

"How odd?" asked Kate, taking a sudden interest.

"He lived a solitary life," replied her father. "He never seemed to want—or need—other people."

"Like someone else we know!" said Kate, nudging her brother in the ribs. "Was he into books and science too?" AP refused to take the bait.

"Not so much books," continued Mr. Littleton. "His big thing was antiques—antiques and travel. He lived in many different parts of the world."

"Wasn't he in Africa for the last few years?" asked AP.

"Yes, until his health began to fail. He caught malaria on an earlier trip there. Goodness knows what else he picked up."

"How long did he have his antique shop?" asked AP, fending off Kate's attempt to claim more of the back seat.

"A couple of years. Long enough to fill the place with all his stuff. Plus the antiques that were already there."

"So it was an antique shop before Uncle Miles took it over?" asked AP.

"Past Times has been an antique shop for as long as anyone in Saxton Burleigh can remember," replied his father. "And it's several hundred years old, like the rest of the village."

AP sat back, visualizing thatched roofs and timber-framed walls. Kate, already bored with the conversation, opened her magazine.

They left the highway soon after stopping for lunch and were now driving down country lanes. The conversation between Mrs. Littleton, who was trying to read the map, and her husband, who was trying to follow her instructions, showed they were lost. "We should have paid the extra and rented the GPS," said Mr. Littleton.

"Give me the map," snapped Kate. "I'll navigate."

Kate's sense of direction was legendary in the Littleton family. After studying the map, she glanced at the afternoon sun. "We're heading southeast and Saxton Burleigh is southwest," said Kate confidently. "Make a right at the next intersection."

Her father knew from experience that she would be right.

The trees on either side of the lane arched overhead, concealing the sky and making the Littletons feel as if they were driving though a living green tunnel. Minutes later the lane opened up into a road just wide enough for two cars to pass each other.

"This is *it*?" gasped Kate. "Saxton Burleigh?"

A medieval church stood on one side of the road, overlooking a cluster of thatched cottages. Strung along the other side were a post office and a row of small stores. And there, at the end, was the antique shop. Mr. Littleton parked outside and fumbled for the spare key. "Here we are," he announced. "Let's go and check it out."

Past Times was just as AP had imagined it. Everything was old and musty, from the creaking floorboards to the low-beamed ceilings. Antiques and curios filled every space. There were rickety chairs with spindly legs, grandfather clocks, stuffed birds, flintlock pistols, African masks, Chinese vases, shelves of books, darkened oil paintings and a suit of armor with one leg missing.

"Wow," gasped AP, staring around him. "This place is *amazing*."

"I'll say," muttered Mr. Littleton. Taking care of Uncle Miles's affairs included the enormous task of listing everything in the shop. "Where do we start?"

"This *is* a big job," agreed his wife. "But it'll be easier once we get organized."

They found a small kitchen at the back of the shop, with a sink, stove and tiny fridge. Upstairs were Uncle Miles's living quarters. A small dining table with four chairs stood in the front room, with a threadbare sofa and television in one corner. Dominating the room was an antique cabinet, its polished top cluttered with old TV guides and unopened bills. The drawers, crammed with papers, were too much of a temptation for AP.

"Hey!" snapped Kate. "Stop poking in other people's things!"

"Carry on, AP," said his father decisively. He rarely lost his temper, and Kate, hearing the anger in his voice, was smart enough to back off.

"Kate, see if there's anything on TV," suggested her mother. "English television's different from ours."

Kate fiddled with the knobs and tried changing the channels, but all she got was snow. Exasperated, she went downstairs to see if there were any cold drinks in the fridge.

"Look what I just found!" AP was waving a black book in his hand. "A diary that Uncle Miles wrote in Africa. The bottom drawer's jammed full with them."

"Let's see," said his father.

While they scanned the diaries, Mrs. Littleton examined two wooden crates, which were taking up most of the floor space. The shipping labels showed they were from Kenya —Uncle Miles's last address before returning to England. Both had been opened. One was empty, aside from a single wooden mask lying on the bottom. With its enormous forehead and long morbid face, the carving looked ominous. The other crate was still full.

Mr. and Mrs. Littleton wanted to complete their list before an antique dealer came to price everything the following week. But they knew nothing would get done unless Kate could be kept occupied, so Mrs. Littleton slipped downstairs to tell her about the crate.

"All sorts of treasures might lurk inside," she began. "You could unpack while AP makes a list."

Reluctantly, Kate agreed—maybe she would find some neat jewelry among all that stuff.

Kate turned on the radio and, to her surprise, found a station with "real" music.

"Look at the size of that elephant!" exclaimed AP minutes later as his sister unwrapped another animal carving. "The biggest so far." He patted the rich red wood. "Which do you like—the rosewood or the ebony ones?" He picked up a small rhino that was as black as night and surprisingly heavy.

"Red, black, wildebeest, warthog—who cares?"

Kate found a variety of bracelets and necklaces made from colored beads, and tried several on. Some animal pendants, threaded on thin leather cords, caught her eye too. Then she came across one that was unique—a finger-length rectangular frame with nine vertical rows of beads.

"Here, try this," she said, slipping it over AP's head.

"Hey, it's an abacus. A tiny one. But why is it with all this stuff? The abacus came from the east, not Africa."

"An abacus?"

"You know, an ancient calculator. I used to have one when I was little, remember? Mine was way bigger though. I played with it for hours."

"You would!"

"This one works the same way mine did, except the rods are vertical instead of horizontal—that's the 'traditional' way of making them."

"So how does it work?"

"See the beads in this row?" He pointed to the far right. "They each count as one unit."

"Okay," said Kate.

"Each row has ten beads. If I move one of these beads to the top, that counts as one." The beads fitted the rods tightly, so they stayed in place when he moved them. "Now, if I add four more beads, I've got five. Each of the beads in the next row counts for ten. So if I move three of them up to the top of their rod, I've got thirty. Thirty plus the others makes thirty-five."

"Brilliant! What would we do without an abacus?"

"It gets harder. The third-row beads are each worth one hundred, then one thousand…"

Kate stifled a yawn.

"With nine rows of beads, you can count up to hundreds of millions."

She sighed.

"Watch this," he continued, pushing the beads in the two rows on the right back to the bottom again. "Say you wanted to enter 1524—a random number. You start with the fourth row from the right and move one of the beads to the top of its rod. That's the one thousand." He then moved five beads to the top of the third rod. "That's the five hundred." Next, he moved two beads to the top on the second rod, finishing off by sliding four beads to the top of the right-hand rod. "And that's the twenty-four. See? It's easy."

"If you say so."

Crowded Planet's latest hit, "High Water," blared from the radio.

"What's that tiny black button at the bottom for?" Leaning on his shoulder, Kate reached down and pushed it with her finger. Suddenly, the room filled with brilliant blue light, silhouetting AP and his sister like shadows.

Then they disappeared.

2

Lost in the Forest

AP and Kate found themselves lying on the ground, dazed and in the dark.

"Where are we?" Kate whispered. AP felt the ground—it was hard and bumpy. When he looked up, he saw branches. Beyond them were stars and a magnificent full moon.

"We're in a forest!" he exclaimed. "This makes *no* sense. What's happened?"

AP tried pinching himself. Sure enough, it hurt. Then he pinched Kate. "Stop it!" she snapped. So they were not dreaming. They really were in a forest. But where? And how did they get there?

"This isn't funny," said Kate, as if it were all AP's fault. "I want to go back, right now."

"We can't go anywhere until it gets light. We don't even know where we are." He shook his head as if to clear it. "I'm feeling so dizzy I don't think I can stand, let alone walk."

Kate was groggy too.

"Let's stay here till morning," AP suggested. "Maybe we can sleep it off."

"Right here, on the ground, in the middle of nowhere? You must be joking!"

"Do we have any choice?"

Kate groaned.

"Look, we can make a mattress out of dry leaves." He began raking up armfuls. "And cover ourselves if we get cold."

"Great!" Kate muttered, and grudgingly followed his example.

Forests can be scary, especially at night. AP reasoned this was because dangerous animals could sneak up on a person without being seen. Fortunately, Britain's animals were harmless. Luckily, this wasn't happening back in North America, where there were bears and wolves to worry about.

Just as they were getting comfortable, a bloodcurdling screech ripped through the silence.

"What's that?" gasped Kate.

"Only an owl—I think. Let's forget it and try to sleep. I'm exhausted."

They both slept fitfully. At one point AP sat bolt upright, convinced he'd just seen a bear ambling through the trees. But bears didn't exist in England. He lay down again, closed his eyes, and tried blotting out the forest.

When they awoke the following morning and discovered how they were dressed, Kate was horrified.

"What am I doing in *this*?" she shrieked. A drab blue dress hung shapelessly from her shoulders to her ankles. "It's *so* gross." She wore flat-soled shoes of soft leather, like moccasins. They reached up to her ankles and were tied with leather strips.

"What about me?" AP groaned, sounding equally offended, though he had no interest in clothes.

His long-sleeved tunic was knee-length and made of coarse brown material, like the burlap used to wrap shrubs in the fall. A wide leather belt with a heavy buckle held up his pants.

"You look good for a change," she quipped, unable to suppress a grin.

Suddenly remembering the African crate, AP put a hand to his chest. The abacus was still there. Surely this all had to do with the pendant. Pulling it out from beneath his tunic, he started turning it over in his hands. He could only see the beads from one side and the back looked like a plain rectangle of wood. Then, for the first time, he noticed a tiny white button. "Hey, look at this! Should I give it a try?"

"Sure. Whatever."

As soon as AP pressed the button, the abacus lit up with a map of the world, each country outlined in brilliant blue.

Both stared down with gaping mouths.

"How does it *do* that?" asked Kate incredulously. "And how come the map's tiny, yet we can see each country in detail, like an enlargement?"

"No idea," admitted AP, shaking his head.

"And what's all that?" She pointed to the bottom of the map where the South Pacific was filled with numbers. The first was 2010, the year, but she didn't recognize the second.

"That's the number I picked to show how an abacus works." A red circle in front of the 1524 had a flashing minus sign inside.

Ignoring this for the moment, he pointed to the numbers beneath it:

$$s = 2,551,442.9s.$$

"Looks like some sort of equation. But I can't figure it out." Then AP had an idea. "Look," he said, tapping the flashing sign in front of the number 1524. Each time he did so, it changed from plus to minus. "The map's a touch-screen."

Then he noticed a flashing red dot over England, surrounded by a circle. When he tried touching this, nothing happened. But when he slid his finger along the map, the dot followed. He parked the spot on Sweden and it stayed there, but stopped flashing. When he moved it back to its circle over England, it began flashing again.

"I know what's happened," AP began. "This is some sort of time machine and we've been—"

Suddenly the sound of voices drifted through the forest.

"Quick!" whispered AP, grabbing Kate's arm. "Get behind that tree."

Safely hidden from view, they watched in silence as a small procession made its way along a well-worn foot-path. Thirty or forty people walked by—men, women and children—dressed in simple clothes like Kate's and AP's. Most carried wicker baskets on their backs, filled with vegetables, apples, loaves of bread, sacks of grain and balls of coarse wool. Two of the men carried a live pig, slung from a pole between its tethered feet.

"Come on," said AP when the procession was out of sight, "let's follow them."

"Follow them?" Kate repeated. "Why would we do that?"

"Well, we can't stay here with nothing to eat or drink. It's a matter of survival!"

In exasperation, Kate agreed and they set off.

Walking through the forest, well out of earshot, they discussed their predicament.

"You can't seriously think we've traveled back in time," Kate challenged. "Sure, the number on the abacus is 1524, but those people aren't dressed for the Middle Ages. Henry VIII never looked like that!"

"We haven't traveled back *to* the year 1524. I think we've traveled back 1,524 *years*. That explains the minus sign in front of the number. And the flashing spot over England shows where we are."

He held out the abacus and pressed the white button again. "See? We've gone back 1,524 years from the year 2010. He did a quick calculation. "So this must be the year 486!"

"Oh no!" he exclaimed, in horror. "That *was* a bear I saw in the forest last night." Kate looked puzzled. "Bears existed in Britain during medieval times. Wolves and wild boars too."

"What?" bawled Kate. "Reset that thing and take us back to the present! This place is dangerous."

AP thought about it for a moment. "Okay, that should be simple. The number on the abacus is still set for 1524." He changed the minus to a plus. "Then if we press the black button, we should be back in Saxton Burleigh in the present. Hold tight, you don't want to be left behind."

Grabbing his arm she closed her eyes, expecting everything to return to normal. "What are you waiting for?" she snapped. "Press the button!"

"I did," he shot back. "Nothing's happening."

"Oh, great. Perfect! We're *stuck* in 486. I have no friends and nothing to wear but this—rag." She tugged at the formless dress. "We have no phone, no iPod, no computer, no shower, no toilet...there's NOTHING HERE!"

"Look on the bright side," said AP grinning. "You've got me!"

They walked on for much of the morning, through gently sloping countryside. The forest was far behind now, and there were few trees for cover. Keeping to the higher ground, they kept a watchful eye on the travelers below. "How long have we been following them?" she asked, keeping her voice low to avoid being overheard.

"A couple of hours, maybe."

"Feels more like seven or eight to me," she grumbled.

Eventually, the procession came to a halt beside a large lake. Putting down their loads, the people began preparing a meal. AP and Kate stared longingly from behind a lone willow—starving.

Although feeling safely hidden from sight, something must have given them away, and they watched in horror as people began pointing up at the tree. Then some of the strangers started calling and gesturing for them to come down. They seemed friendly enough, so after much hesitation, Kate and AP left their safe haven and descended to the lake.

Most of the men were clean-shaven, with neatly trimmed hair. Some had beards and shoulder-length locks. All the women had long hair, worn loosely or in braids. Fair hair predominated, with a sprinkling of redheads, including a wild-looking man with a mane like a lion. Kate, with her blond hair, and AP, with his blue eyes, fit right in.

Kate and AP learned that the people lived in a far-off village and had been traveling for two days. As they chatted with the villagers, something remarkable dawned on them —they were both speaking in an ancient form of English they wouldn't have understood in their modern world. How had the abacus transported them through time *and* transformed them to blend in so perfectly?

"It's a bit like a computer," suggested AP when nobody was listening. "I can hook up a new device to my laptop, and the software makes it work properly."

Kate gave him one of her blank stares.

"The abacus does the same thing," he continued, "changing the way we look and speak to match our surroundings."

"How does it do *that*?"

"Maybe it rearranges the molecules of our clothing and reprograms the speech part of our brain."

Kate was about to ask him what that all meant when some of the children came to say hello.

The villagers invited them to share their meal. They began with flatbread, which looked like a pancake.

"Chewy," said AP, taking his first bite. "Like a day-old bagel."

When pencil-sized sticks were handed around, Kate exchanged puzzled looks with her brother. Taking a cautious nibble, AP rolled it around in his mouth. Salty, like beef jerky, he realized it was dried meat and took some more. Kate tried some too and was surprised at how good it tasted.

Then someone passed Kate a string bag containing a creamy white ball the size of a grapefruit. Some pieces had already been cut off, giving her a clue what to do with it. Most villagers wore a dagger in their belt, and seeing that Kate didn't have one, a man handed her his. Wanting to fit in, she hacked off a generous slice, put it on a piece of bread, and took a bite. It tasted worse than sour milk, but she pretended to enjoy it. She figured it was some kind of cheese. They offered her more.

"No thank you. It's *so* good, but I want to leave some for my brother." She took one last bite, followed by lots of bread.

"You'll like this." Kate smiled. "Here, I'll cut you a piece." She speared a hunk on the end of the knife and handed it to him. AP was suspicious—Kate never looked that happy when she was doing him a favor.

All eyes switched from Kate to AP.

AP guessed the stuff would taste terrible, so he made a snap decision and rammed the whole thing into his mouth. Without any doubt, this was the most disgusting thing AP had ever eaten. He had to put on a brave face though, partly to convince the villagers, but mostly to fool his sister. So he smiled, patted his stomach and rolled his eyes. Even Kate was taken in by his performance.

Everyone except the youngest children drank beer, served from earthenware bottles into pottery goblets. AP remembered reading that beer was the everyday drink during medieval times. He disliked the bitterness, but after the white stuff, it tasted good. Kate, who had tried beer a few times, didn't like it, even though she boasted otherwise to her friends. They finished off the meal with freshly picked apples, the first crop of summer.

After packing away the food, the people gathered in small groups, occasionally glancing out across the lake. By piecing together snippets of overheard conversations, Kate and AP realized the people were awaiting the arrival of someone important. And it was for him and his cause that they had brought all the goods. But who was he? Nobody had told Kate and AP because everybody assumed they knew.

They waited beside the lake for most of the day. AP and Kate began wondering whether anyone would ever show up. Many of the villagers were stretched out in the sun, asleep. Some of the men spent their time whittling wood, and one was making a bow. He worked with skilled hands—the kind that develop from years of practice. As AP watched, the craftsman beckoned him over for a closer look.

"Don't boys know how to make bows where you come from?" he asked.

"Um, no," replied AP, trying hard to think of a likely explanation. "Only the boys chosen to become master bow-makers are taught." Feeling pleased with his effort, he added, "The rest of us miss the chance."

"That's a pity because there are so many interesting things to learn." The man patted the half-formed bow with an enormous hand. "This is yew," he continued. "We always use that because of its natural springiness." He ran his hands along the length of the wood. "The grain's good and straight from one end to the other. You must choose your wood carefully."

AP stroked the bow, admiring its gentle curvature.

"The curve will be greater when the bow's been strung," the man continued. "See those notches at either end of the bow?"

AP nodded.

"We tie a loop at each end of a string, making sure it's shorter than the distance between the notches." He traced an imaginary line between the two ends of the bow. "Next, you lean down on the bow and slip the loops into the notches."

AP knew how bows worked: pulling back the string made the bow arch more, storing energy in the wood like a spring. When the string was released, the energy was transferred to the arrow, causing it to fly.

"I made this one for hunting," said the man, picking up a second bow. "Here, try it."

AP found it hard to pull the string all the way back, but his instructor said that didn't matter. "The important thing is your aim."

AP practiced on a nearby tree. Kate looked on, amused, as he kept missing.

"Anyone could do better than that!" she taunted. "Try an easier target."

"Such as?" he snapped.

"How about the lake?"

"Funny. Let's see if you can do better." He handed her the bow.

Her first arrow stuck into the ground nearby. The second one flew over the tree. The third arrow skimmed the ground, but missed by a long way. Kate, frustrated, returned the bow.

AP continued practicing for about an hour, by which time he was hitting the target with almost every arrow. His instructor told him he had all the makings of a marksman, providing he kept practicing. Meanwhile, Kate, who got on well with youngsters, had been having fun with some of the children. They'd shown her their games, involving sticks, wooden balls and pieces of string. Kate, in turn, taught them how to play baseball. They enjoyed them-selves so much they would have continued all afternoon. Feeling hot and tired, Kate called a time-out and wandered down to the lake for a drink. AP went along too.

"How's our being here going to affect the people?" she asked her brother. Kate was especially thinking of the chil-dren. "I've just shown them how to play baseball, more than a thousand years before the game's been invented. Will there be major-league baseball in England in the Mid-dle Ages?"

AP shook his head. "Nothing we do here in the past will have any lasting effect. As soon as we're gone, everything we did will disappear with us."

"Why?"

"That's part of the time-travel paradox. I read about it once."

"So, let's hear it."

"Say you've got a time machine set up in your house. You've just got up. It's 7:30 on a Saturday morning."

"Who gets up *that* early on the weekend?" Kate interrupted.

"Do you want me to explain or not?"

"Sorry. Keep going. I'm all ears."

"Okay, so you have some pancakes and check your e-mails. Then it's time to go traveling. You look at your watch and it's now 9 a.m." He glanced down at his bare wrist. "You enter your time machine and set it for one hour earlier."

"That's 8 a.m. Saturday morning?" she asked, to clarify.

"Exactly. So you set the time, press the button, the machine activates, then you step outside and it's 8 a.m. again."

Kate nodded.

"You can smell the pancakes. You look into the kitchen and see yourself eating. Then you delete all your messages, which stops you reading your e-mails. But you already know you read them before you entered the time machine."

"That makes no sense!" Kate exclaimed.

"Of course it doesn't. That's the whole point of the time-travel paradox."

He paused for a moment.

"After you erased your e-mails, suppose you tied yourself up. That'd stop you getting into the time machine you just stepped out of a few minutes earlier."

"That's impossible!"

"Which is why it's called a paradox. A paradox is something completely contradictory."

"Okay, so what's the point?"

"The time-travel paradox is the reason most people think time travel's impossible. They say that if people could travel back to the past they could change the future, which is not feasible. The alternative is that time travel *is* possible, but doing anything in the past which changes the future is *not* possible. You and I both know time travel is real, so we can be equally sure that altering the past is impossible.

"So when we return to the future—if we ever do—it'll be just as if we were never here—no baseball, and everybody will have forgotten we came."

"Exactly. We won't ever have existed in these times."

Kate let it all sink in, slowly. AP idly tossed a stone into the water.

"How do you know all this stuff?" she asked. "It's *so* weird."

"Books." AP shrugged. "I like to read."

Kate broke the silence that followed.

"When *are* we going back to our own time?" She sounded anxious. "Why didn't the abacus work when we tried it?"

"I don't know—maybe it needed time to recharge its batteries."

"So it could work right now?"

"We can try," he said.

Glancing around to make sure nobody was watching, he pulled out the abacus and turned on the screen. Instantly, the map lit up, along with the numbers 2010 and 1524. A plus sign was still in front of the number 1524.

"Everything's set. Ready?"

Kate linked an arm through his and nodded.

He pressed the black button. Nothing happened. Again. Nothing. "Forget it."

"Is it broken?"

"Not sure. The screen's still working, so it's probably okay."

"We've *got* to get home," she blurted. "I want to see Mum and Dad, and everyone else again…" Her eyes filled with tears.

"We will," he said, laying an arm across her shoulders. "I promise. Let's give it a rest for now, and try again later."

The water looked so inviting in the afternoon sun. If only the time travelers had bathing suits and towels, but they had to be content with getting just their feet wet.

"There'd be no risk of hitting your head diving into this lake," said AP, staring down at the sandy bottom. "See how it slopes away? It must be fairly deep."

"Isn't it weird that nobody goes swimming, not even the children?" said Kate. "And the ones who stripped off to bathe keep close to the water's edge. Maybe it's too deep."

"Or they're afraid of water."

❋ ❋ ❋

A shout from the shore broke the tranquility of the late afternoon. Boats had been spotted. Sleepers were woken, babies were gathered up and children ran down to the shore. Everyone was buzzing with excitement and shading their eyes to catch a first glimpse.

Kate and AP, wanting to keep a low profile, strolled a short distance away. Both wondered what sort of a man inspired such an enthusiastic and loyal following.

AP expected a fleet of longboats with dragon-head prows and square sails, like the Vikings used. But the four rowing boats that came into sight looked unspectacular. They were large, with three rowers on each side and space in between for cargo. As they neared shore, the occupants raised oars, threw lines across and prepared to land.

Standing at the prow of the lead boat was a tall, muscular man with broad shoulders, neatly-trimmed long hair and a well-clipped beard. An impressive figure, he was obviously their leader, given the way the men jumped to his orders. As he leaned forward, something slipped from his belt and fell overboard. Judging from the commotion that followed, it was something valuable.

One of the men tried to reach the object with an oar, but this was too unwieldy, and it would take forever to nudge the object into the shallows. Amidst the shouting and arguing, nobody seemed to know what to do.

"This is crazy!" exclaimed AP. "Why doesn't somebody just jump in and get it?"

Within seconds he'd slipped off his clothes and dived into the water. Taking a deep breath, he headed for the leader's boat.

When the people saw AP cutting through the water, they gasped in astonishment. Then he reached the boat and disappeared beneath the surface. Shouts of confusion came from those standing on shore, but those in the boats could see him streaking to the bottom.

By now, Kate realized the people had never seen anyone swimming before. She guessed swimming hadn't been invented yet, at least not in Britain. "Come on, AP," she murmured to herself. "You can do it."

AP felt the pressure against his ears, like being in the deep end of a swimming pool. In the crystal clear water, he easily spotted the object, glinting against the sandy bottom. It was a dagger! AP's fingers closed upon the hilt.

Minutes later AP, wet and dripping, was standing on shore, surrounded by the men from the boats. The villagers watched in hushed anticipation as AP handed the ornate weapon back to its owner. The leader took it from him in silence, and then he spoke.

"This dagger is sacred," he began, facing the crowd. He held it high for all to see. The gold handle was inlaid with rubies, which burned in the sun. "My father's father gave it to me." Then, turning to AP, "And who have I the honor of thanking?"

AP, hardly feeling honorable in his baggy undergarments, drew himself up to his full height of four feet ten and three-quarters inches. "Arthur," he announced solemnly, though it was pronounced "Artorius" in the ancient tongue he was speaking. His proper name seemed to fit the occasion.

"What a coincidence," replied the leader with a broad smile. "That's my name too." He waved the dagger above his head and the crowd roared their approval. Then, with a flourish, he slipped it back into the scabbard on his belt. From that moment Arthur—who would be known in legend as King Arthur—held AP and his sister in the highest regard.

"Please honor me by traveling back to my home," said the leader. "You will be special guests in the most beautiful place on this verdant isle."

The villagers spent almost an hour exchanging news with Arthur. They were pleased to report that all was peaceful and quiet in their part of the land. Then the men began loading the goods into the boats. By the time they had finished, the sun was low on the horizon. The warmth of the day had been replaced by an early evening chill, and Arthur was anxious to get underway. Kate and AP made their hurried farewells and clambered aboard. Then the expedition set off, leaving the villagers to set up camp for the night.

Several miles away, a hooded figure hunched over a small fire, watching the flames lick the fading daylight. A black cloak was pulled tightly about his bony frame, concealing everything but his sharply pointed nose and piercing eyes. He was about to spend his second night alone in the forest—lost. Like Kate and AP, he had traveled through time, but not by accident. Although unaware of their identity, he knew *someone* had activated the abacus. He also knew they must be close by. Whatever it took, he would track them down and recover the device. He desperately wanted to get his hands on it and would stop at nothing to do so.

3

Castles in the Air

How much *farther*?" Kate whispered as they picked their way through the trees. Almost an hour had passed since their arrival on the other side of the lake. Soon darkness would prevent them from seeing where they were going. She was tired, hungry and longing for a proper toilet and shower.

"Enough!" roared their leader from the head of the column. For a moment Kate thought he was shouting at her. "We'll camp here for the night."

Dropping their heavy baskets of supplies, Arthur's men set to work. The two who had been carrying the pig dumped it down like a sack of potatoes, without a second thought for the animal's comfort. They didn't even bother removing the pole from between its tethered legs.

"Poor thing," said Kate as the pig struggled to get onto its haunches. "Are they just going to leave it there all night?"

"I guess so," said AP, equally concerned. "The least they could do is give it some water." They found a bowl and filled it. The pig was so thirsty it almost knocked the water from Kate's hand.

While some of the men gathered armfuls of fresh ferns, others collected wood. Soon a fire was blazing, sending sparks high into the night sky.

"What do we use for a sleeping bag?" asked Kate.

"That's what the ferns are for." AP pointed toward one of the men who was making them into a pile. When it was about knee-high, he patted it, as if testing a mattress.

"We should do the same," said Kate, looking around at the dense undergrowth. "Before it gets too dark."

"Where's my namesake?" bellowed Arthur as everyone sat around the campfire after the meal. "Come over here, boy! Bring your sister too. I want to tell you things."

AP and Kate made their way around the circle, feeling the heat from the flames upon their faces. The men, over twenty in number, smiled as they went past, their own reflections glowing in the firelight.

"Tomorrow, before the sun goes down, you shall see my kingdom," announced Arthur.

"Camelot?" asked Kate enthusiastically. Arthur's magnetism made people want to listen when he spoke.

"Camelot?" queried Arthur. "What is that?"

"The castle," she replied.

When Arthur still looked puzzled, Kate explained it was a building to defend against attackers. He beamed and nodded.

"Yes, you'll see my *castle*," he said, using the unfamiliar word. "And I promise, you will be astonished." Then, turning to his band of followers, he said, "It's a special place, isn't it?"

A great cheer erupted.

"The valleys are greener than any in the land," he continued. "The rivers teem with fishes."

"Huge ones!" shouted a voice from the other side of the fire.

"Aye, bigger than you, young Arthur!" offered another. They all laughed together—AP was used to jokes about his size.

As the evening wore on, the stories of Arthur's domain grew ever larger. By the time they were ready for sleep, Kate was convinced that Camelot was as wondrous as legend had painted. AP had his doubts.

"Time for bed," said Arthur, stifling a yawn. "Tomorrow's a long day."

More firewood was added to keep the blaze burning all night, and everyone settled down.

"Stay near the fire," Arthur warned his young companions. "Bears and wolves prowl these woods."

Kate hardly slept, even though she and AP had moved their fern piles closer to the fire. Seeing her brother slumbering soundly made her feel even worse.

❀ ❀ ❀

By the following afternoon, the flat countryside had given way to rolling hills of pink heather.

"At the top of that next rise," said Arthur, pointing ahead, "you're in for a surprise."

"Your castle?" asked Kate enthusiastically.

AP shot her a puzzled look. All day long she'd been complaining about sore feet and feeling grubby. Maybe she was hoping for a big improvement when they reached Camelot. But from what he'd read about sanitary conditions in castles, she was in for a disappointment.

"Close your eyes," said Arthur as they neared the top.

When they reached the summit, he told them to look.

"Well?" he asked, folding his arms and staring down proudly. "What do you think?"

Kate expected to see a castle with towers and turrets, surrounded by a moat. Instead, all she saw was a sprawl of wooden buildings enclosed by a big wooden fence—like the forts the U.S. army built out west during the Indian Wars, when they were fighting the native peoples of North America.

"It's—nice," she began, after an uncomfortable silence. "I—can't wait to get there."

Camelot looked even worse up close.

To AP, the best part was the fence. Made from tree trunks driven into the ground, each post was so close to its neighbor you could barely squeeze a finger between the gaps. A heavy wooden gate—guarded at all times—barred unwanted entry.

Sentries on the fence recognized the approaching column and shouted orders to open the gate. Hinges creaking, it slowly swung back. Once everyone was inside, it was closed and bolted.

Kate gazed in dismay at the run-down buildings and grime. Garbage, piled high against the fence, reeked. "Why not leave their waste on the other side of the fence?" whispered Kate.

"They probably want to open the gate as little as possible."

Dozens of log buildings dotted an area the size of a football field. Most were no bigger than a shed. Some were falling apart—nobody seemed bothered to do repairs.

"That's the longhouse," Arthur proclaimed, pointing to the largest building. "My headquarters. I live there with my wife."

The longhouse—though nothing like Kate's image of Camelot—was still an impressive building. It was one enormous room, crowned by a huge pointed roof. There were only a few small windows, so it took time for their eyes to adjust to the dim light. A pig was roasting over an open fireplace at one end, filling the room with a wonderful aroma that made Kate and AP realize how hungry they were. Glancing up, Kate saw the smoke curling through a large hole in the roof.

"When it's cold we keep both fires burning day and night," Arthur explained, pointing to the fireplace at the opposite end. "And we shutter the windows to keep out the winter air."

Suddenly, a cloaked figure appeared from nowhere, moving toward them like a phantom. Kate instinctively shifted closer to her brother. The person was dressed in black and had long, flowing white hair. Was this the legendary Guinevere? As the mysterious individual drew closer, they saw it was an old man. He was small, with a large hooked nose and bushy eyebrows the same color as his hair.

"Medoc!" greeted Arthur. "I'd like you to meet my two honored guests. This is young Arthur, and his sister Kate."

The old man smiled, lowering his head in a majestic bow. After exchanging greetings, he listened intently as Arthur recounted the story of AP's miraculous recovery of the dagger.

"I tell you, Medoc," Arthur said, beaming, "this boy's powers are as strong as yours!"

The old man agreed this was a most extraordinary feat. He seemed friendly enough, but Kate caught his suspicious glance at AP when he thought nobody was looking.

That night Arthur hosted a small feast for his guests. He sat AP on one side of him and Kate on the other, next to his wife. Kate was surprised to discover Gwendolyn was only a few years older than herself. Gwendolyn had petite features—high cheekbones, a small upturned nose and mystical brown eyes. She wore her long brunette hair tied in a knot. The two instantly liked each other and chatted all evening.

People ate with their hands, occasionally using knives to cut slices of meat and gobbets of fat with the crispy gold skin they relished. Kate picked halfheartedly at the leanest parts of her meat, while AP wolfed his down.

Medoc, sitting beside AP, spoke little during the meal. When Arthur commented on this, the old man said he was unwell. "It's probably just a touch of the ague."

"Perhaps you should take one of your potions," Arthur suggested. "You always force foul concoctions on us when we're sick!" The others guffawed, nodding their heads. Medoc smiled politely.

Eight other men attended the feast, accompanied by their wives. Arthur had introduced them as his commanders—his most loyal and trusted men, and the members of his council. AP remembered two, Hector and Gavin, from the journey across the lake. When Arthur retold the story of how his young namesake had retrieved the bejeweled dagger, his audience listened in silence.

The topic then changed from daggers to dangers as one of the commanders reported a raid on a nearby village during Arthur's absence.

"Who's doing the attacking?" asked AP innocently. Several people stared, puzzled by his question. Surely everyone knew the likely culprits.

"Young Arthur comes from far away," Arthur explained.

"Where exactly?" asked Medoc, suddenly interested in the conversation.

Kate glanced at AP, wondering how he would handle the question. Knowing her brother, he'd think of something smart to say.

"Far up north," he replied, figuring this was a safe bet.

"On which side of the wall?" Medoc continued.

Having once read a book about ancient Britain, AP guessed Medoc was referring to Hadrian's Wall, built by the Romans to keep out aggressive northern tribes.

"The other side," AP said. He almost added "in Scotland" but remembered it was not named until later.

"How far north?" Medoc persisted.

"Enough of this!" Arthur interrupted, holding up his hand and smiling. "Our guests will think you're a nosy old man!"

The whole table burst into laughter. Medoc smiled as if he was enjoying the joke too, though his eyes revealed otherwise.

"In answer to your question, young Arthur," their leader began again, "the attackers could have been local brigands, or members of a hostile tribe like the Iceni or the Trinovantes. Perhaps they were marauders from across the sea. These are dangerous times. More foes than friends live out there." He waved an arm toward the facing wall.

"The Romans did one good thing," said Hector. He was a great shaggy bear of a man, with shoulder-length red hair and a full beard. "They knocked the fight out of most of the hostiles."

Everyone nodded in agreement.

"All the troubles began again when they left these shores."

"When was that?" asked AP, figuring that someone who lived north of Hadrian's Wall wouldn't be expected to know when the Romans left Britain.

"About the time my grandfather was born," replied Arthur, adding, "he died last spring. He'd seen seventy-eight summers."

"So the Romans left around the year 400," AP concluded.

"400?" Arthur looked confused. "What is the year 400?"

AP had forgotten that it was only after Christianity came to Britain, over a century later, that people started numbering the years.

Kate came to her brother's rescue. "What AP—um—*Arthur* meant to say was that the Romans invaded England about 400 years ago."

"Yes, that's it," agreed AP, surprised his sister knew the date of the Roman Conquest.

"You must be getting tired," Arthur told AP. "Time for sleep."

One side of the longhouse was partitioned into several open cubicles that served as bedrooms. There was little privacy, but the open planning made sure sleepers stayed warm in their beds on winter nights. Arthur and Gwendolyn's cubicle was opposite one of the fireplaces, with Medoc's next door. AP and Kate were given a cubicle close by, used only for special guests.

"AP—are you awake?" Kate whispered into the darkness. No reply came from the bed beside her. She nudged his shoulder and tried again.

"Huh? What?"

"I just wondered if you were awake."

"Well, I am now! Why?"

"What do you make of Medoc?" she asked.

"He's alright—a bit weird, but that's probably because he's so old."

"Do you think he's the wizard Merlin?" she continued. "Medoc and Merlin sound alike, don't they? Like Gwendolyn and Guinevere."

"Yes. Like Hector and Ector. Or Gavin and Gawain—they were both Knights of the Round Table."

"So that old guy could be Merlin?"

"Maybe. Dad says the whole story of King Arthur and his knights could be based on truth. Some people think there was a real Arthur, but that he was a local chief rather than a full-blown king. This Arthur's no king, but he seems important around here."

"He certainly does," agreed Kate.

"You seemed to be getting along well with Gwendolyn."

"She's nice. We're going down to the river tomorrow to bathe. My hair feels gross—I'd give anything for a hot shower."

"A comfortable bed would be nice too," said her brother. "A sheepskin rug's too thin for these hard wooden boards." Yawning, he was about to nod off, when suddenly he remembered something. "How did you know when the Romans invaded Britain?"

"One of the guys on my baseball team," she began casually. "He was doing a project and I helped with the Web search."

"Sounds like a *special* friend."

"I'm tired. Go to sleep."

❀ ❀ ❀

The villagers who had traveled to the lake to meet Arthur were spending their second night around a campfire, on their way back home. Just before stopping for the day, they'd come upon a tall, thin stranger. He was thirsty, hungry and lost.

"I'm not from these parts," he'd explained between gulps of water. "I was—uh—traveling with a friend who knows his way around here, but we got separated." The cloaked stranger spoke their language without any accent.

The others nodded. Getting lost in the forest was easy.

"Where were you going?" asked one of the men.

"To his village in the south, near the sea." The words came easily—he'd had two days to work out a cover story.

"That's a long way," said the villager. "You'd never find it alone. Come back with us. Perhaps a guide can take you there."

"Thank you," said the stranger gratefully. Although anxious to secure the abacus, he was more concerned for his survival.

The villagers' conversation turned to yesterday's excitement.

"That boy's enchanted," said one of the men. "The way he took to the water—I've never seen anything like it."

There was a chorus of agreement.

"Imagine a person being able to *swim*, like a fish." said another. "Who would have thought such a thing possible?"

"Do you think his sister can swim too?" asked one woman.

"Two sorcerers in the same family? That'd be too much to expect!"

The thin man was now listening intently. "Who are these children?" he asked.

"Strangers. We met them yesterday. They were hungry and thirsty, like you."

"Where are they now?"

"They went with Arthur," the villager replied, thinking no further explanation was necessary. "They'll be there by now."

The stranger looked bewildered. He'd been surprised enough to discover that the abacus had been used to visit medieval England. But why was the organization allowing *children* to time travel?

4

The Young Warrior

T ip up!" roared Arthur. "Never let your sword dip. Come on, try again!"

AP tightened both hands on the hilt and focused his energy on keeping the blade vertical. The heavy sword, almost as long as he was tall, made his arms and shoulders ache. He lunged at Arthur's sword with all his might.

"That's good!" encouraged his instructor as the two blades clashed. Kate could hear the clang all the way down at the river.

AP and Kate had been in Arthur's Camelot for almost a week, and swordplay was now part of the daily routine.

"Keep going! You must maintain the pressure."

When AP swung again, the two swords met in a bone-jarring crash. Then, summoning all his strength, he got in one more lunge.

"Well done, young Arthur! We'll make a swordsman out of you yet. Practice is all that's needed."

Many boys of AP's age were already skilled with the sword and bow—some had been in battle—so he had lots of catching up to do. His fighting spirit compensated for his small size. Indeed, AP's stubborn determination was one of the reasons Arthur had so taken to him—that and the fact that Arthur had no children of his own.

"Are you ready?" asked Arthur, holding up his sword again.

AP nodded, gripped the sword firmly, and lunged into action. This time Arthur returned AP's swings to see how well his pupil could defend himself. He was delighted with the result. After half an hour of thrusting and clashing, Arthur called a halt.

"Come, my fine warrior," said Arthur, laying down his sword. "We'll take a rod down to the river and catch some fish."

AP was panting to catch his breath.

As they strode downhill, Arthur pointed out the defensive features of his fortress.

"See how it's built on the highest point, young Arthur? That way nobody can approach without being seen. Even more important is the steep gradient."

"So it's harder to climb?"

"Yes. And harder to bring things up to the top," Arthur explained.

"Like the giant catapults the Romans used for knocking down walls?" AP suggested.

"Exactly!"

When they reached the river, Gwendolyn and Kate were getting ready to return to the fort. The two had become good friends, which pleased Arthur.

The river was knee-deep, with a stony bottom that made the water gurgle and churn. "We'll walk downstream—the water's deeper there. That's where we hook the biggest fish."

The two Arthurs spent a lazy afternoon lying on the riverbank, under the dappled shade of a willow. Fish were plentiful, and while some were big, none reached AP's heightened expectations.

"How far does the river go?" asked AP.

"A long way. A three-day march brings you to the sea."

"Have you been there?"

"A few times. Raiders from other lands come that way." Arthur explained how the river widened and became deeper toward the sea. "So boats can sail far up the river, bringing marauders with them."

"Ever seen any?"

"I've seen many—and what they can do. But enemies are all the same. They'll stop at nothing to get what they want. That's why a warrior must always be at his best. You get no second chances in battle."

When AP asked him what battles were like, Arthur replied they were the most horrific and terrifying things you could possibly imagine.

"But *you* don't get scared," marveled AP. "Your men say you're fearless in battle."

"Ah, young man, you have much to learn." He absent-mindedly picked a leaf from an overhanging branch. "Being scared is normal. The trick is not letting your fear control you. Men follow others into battle because the leader shows no fear."

AP sat in silence, thinking about what Arthur had just said.

"Enough talk." Arthur leaped to his feet. "Let's get back and do some work with your bow. You've got the makings of a good marksman."

AP and Kate were adjusting to life in ancient Britain, but Kate, missing home more than her brother did, was increasingly anxious about their chances of returning. Every day they'd tried activating the abacus, to no avail.

"It's no use," she said in despair. "We'll never see anyone again."

"Yes we will." AP wanted to comfort Kate, but he was beginning to wonder whether the device was broken.

Kate became quarrelsome. "Don't you miss Mum and Dad?" she cried.

"Yeah—I just don't show it." He paused, wondering what to say. "Maybe I'm being *scientific* about things. We can't *make* the abacus work. So while we're waiting, we might as well get involved in the past. That's what I've been doing."

Kate was quiet.

"The abacus might need more time to recharge. We could be draining the battery by trying to activate it every day. Let's give it a rest for a while."

❊ ❊ ❊

One morning Kate caught her brother kneeling beside the cold fire pit, scooping ashes into an iron pot that was half-filled with muddy water. He was working on a secret project to help Kate cope with the discomforts of medieval England. "What are you doing down there?" she asked as she stepped into the longhouse. "I thought you'd grown out of making mud pies!"

When AP carried on in silence, Kate eventually left to find Gwendolyn.

After boiling the pot for over an hour on the other fireplace, AP lifted it off to cool. Then he went outside to practice his swordsmanship with Arthur.

When he returned, the liquid in the pot was only luke-warm, so he could test it with his fingers. "Success!" he exclaimed. "It's nice and oily! This stuff's as strong as the liquid Mum uses to unblock drains."

He rinsed off his fingers. Then, taking care not to disturb the thick sludge at the bottom, he poured off the clear liquid into another pot.

Suddenly, a man started shouting outside. He was obviously excited about something. Soon other voices joined in, and people began running. AP peered around the door to see what was happening.

He was surprised to see the gate had been opened, and a dozen villagers had crowded inside. They were all talking at once. Some had terrible sword wounds. Two of them were wailing uncontrollably. Then he saw Kate, hurrying toward him.

"One of the villages was attacked during the night," she burst. "The raiders were well armed and surprised everyone. Arthur is organizing a troop to track them down."

Arthur chose his men carefully. Meanwhile, Medoc prepared a special healing potion of herbs and tree bark. Some of the women dressed the injured villagers' wounds.

"Well, my young warrior," Arthur said to AP as he was about to leave with his men. "Are you ready for your first battle?"

AP was speechless.

"Um…yes."

"Let's go then."

"W—what about a sword?" stammered AP.

"Not yet, my young friend. It's too soon for you to carry a blade. You'd be cut down in no time."

"Then what am I going to do?"

"You're going to watch, young Arthur—and learn."

❋ ❋ ❋

First-aid courses had not adequately prepared Kate for dealing with sword wounds. She could feel herself becoming faint. However, the sight of the other women working calmly steadied her, and she put her first-aid training into practice.

They had no disinfectants to clean the wounds, not even soap. Kate, knowing salt killed germs, wondered how she might persuade these women to use it. If she could convince Gwendolyn, the others would likely follow.

"Where I come from, we clean wounds with salt water," she began casually.

"With water from the sea?" Gwendolyn asked in disbelief.

"Sometimes," said Kate, recalling how her parents never worried when she or AP cut themselves on rocks when playing on the coast. "If we're far from the sea, we just use salt dissolved in water."

"You northern people have strange ways," said Gwendolyn, shaking her head. "You were never conquered by the Romans though, so you must have something to teach us." Then, turning to the other women, she said, "We will clean the wounds with salt water."

Kate had been so absorbed in helping the injured that she was unaware her brother was missing. When she discovered where he'd gone, she was distraught.

"Have no fear," reassured Gwendolyn, "Arthur will take good care of him. He'll be safe."

Gwendolyn was shorter than Kate and more slightly built, yet like her husband, she had a strong presence.

When the warriors failed to return that evening, Kate became frantic. Gwendolyn spent the night with her, recollecting all the times she'd lain awake in the dark waiting for Arthur's safe return. "Chances are the raiders escaped and there was no fighting," Gwendolyn reasoned. "They'll be back tomorrow, you'll see."

"I suppose you're right," said Kate hopefully. "The raiders had time to get away before the villagers reported the attack."

"Exactly," Gwendolyn echoed. "And now we should get some sleep."

Kate nodded and closed her eyes.

When morning came, there was still no sign of Arthur and his men. Afternoon slipped into night without any news.

By the end of the third day, Kate was convinced something terrible had happened, and Gwendolyn's fading confidence only reinforced her fears. How could she face her parents without her brother? But AP had the abacus, so there was no going back without him anyway. She was alone and marooned in the fifth century.

Just before midnight on day four, a lookout shouted, "Warriors approaching!"

"Friend or foe?" bellowed the watch commander.

"Too dark and too far away to see!"

The standing order was to assume everyone was a foe until proven otherwise, and the alarm was sounded. Men burst into the compound, carrying weapons and donning their clothes. The bowmen took their positions at the fence top, while the swordsmen lined up before the gate.

Within minutes, everyone in the fortress was awake and desperate for news.

"This could be dangerous," Gwendolyn warned Kate. "Most raiders attack at night."

Burning torches cast long, dancing shadows across the compound. All the men, except those too old to fight, took up their positions. Meanwhile, the women, children and elderly were ushered into the longhouse. Kate, hoping her brother might be among the approaching men, pleaded with the warriors to let her stay outside. Regardless, they herded her inside with the others, and the door was bolted. Medoc, whose life was considered too important to risk, had been one of the first inside.

Gwendolyn tried to comfort Kate, unsuccessfully. Medoc was no help either, as far as Kate was concerned. He was standing in the middle of the longhouse performing an ancient ritual to ward off enemies. Waving a hawthorn branch above his head, he began chanting:

"Galoo ban tithero!

Dag bunn venero

Speen tull fron

Havud! Havud! Havud!"

Medoc's warbling seemed to go on forever. Then there was a loud banging on the door.

"Open up!" shouted a voice. "It's Arthur and his men."

Kate pushed her way to the front of the crowd. Where was AP? Then she saw him, standing behind Hector.

"You're safe!" she screamed above all the noise. "I thought I'd lost you." She grabbed him in a rib-cracking hug. "I was *so* scared."

Everyone was anxious to know what had happened. The returning warriors were exhausted and ravenous. So the longhouse fire was stoked, food was prepared and someone opened a cask of wine.

Once the small band had eaten their fill, Arthur began recounting the events of the last few days. Over one hundred people sat in silence, listening.

After attacking the village, the raiders had escaped. There were ten of them, to Arthur's dozen men.

"They had half a day's start," Arthur continued, "but I thought they were hiding somewhere, biding their time to make a night raid on another village. So we began hunting for them." He took another swig from his goblet.

Gwendolyn stayed by her husband's side throughout, one hand resting on his arm. A wizened old man—the scribe—sat on Arthur's other side, scratching notes on parchment with a quill pen. AP, feeling grown-up after his adventure, sat among the warriors.

"We searched in vain for two days. We thought we might never avenge the death and destruction at the village." Arthur paused for effect. "And then we found them! A small band, skulking in a thicket of trees. We skirted around to the other side, using the trees for cover. They never knew we were there—until they felt the thrust of our swords. Their time had come."

Cheers erupted, and Arthur's face betrayed the hint of a smile. He raised his hand for silence.

"We cut them down where they stood. The ground turned red with their blood."

Another thunderous roar.

"Who were they?" asked a voice from the back.

"Dogs!" yelled Arthur. "Now they are no more. We killed all those we saw, but there could be more, so stay close to the fortress." He stood up. "And now get some sleep, everyone."

Before anyone got up to leave, he added, "I want my council to stay behind. You too Medoc. Not for long."

As AP made his way through the crowd toward Kate, Arthur called out to him.

"Stay, young Arthur. It is time for you to see how battles are planned." Noticing some concern among his council members, he quickly explained his actions. "I trust this lad and so can you. He will sit at this table because he has special powers. Believe me, he is destined to go far." Arthur's words were met with nods of approval. AP felt embarrassed by all the attention, but Arthur laid a reassuring hand on his shoulder.

When she reached their cubicle, Kate intended to stay awake to talk with her brother. But minutes after pulling up the sheepskin rug, she was asleep.

Council began. Hector, the only member besides Arthur who had gone on the expedition, spoke first. "Look," he said, unwrapping a bundle of swords and daggers taken from the slain invaders. "You won't find weapons like these on our shores." The raiders were from across the sea, and there had to be more of them.

Everyone leaned closer for a better view—everyone except Medoc. Rising slowly, he closed his eyes and spread his hands so they hovered above the weapons, as if he were warming them over a fire. Then he began whispering in a strange language. The onlookers watched in wonder. Medoc, falling silent, opened his eyes, blinking as if he'd just awoken from a deep sleep.

"What do you see, old friend?" murmured Arthur.

"Warriors. Fierce warriors, from another land."

"How many?"

"That is for you to discover."

"How did they get here?"

"Again, that is yours to determine."

"So be it," said Arthur, and Medoc sat down. The men gazed at the white-haired oracle in silence: he truly was a great prophet.

AP believed otherwise. "Arthur already knows everything Medoc told him," he thought to himself. "All that mumbo jumbo with the spreading hands was nothing more than acting. Medoc's a fraud."

"We must find out how many there are and where they're camped," Arthur concluded.

During the discussion that followed, it was decided to send out three-man scouting parties.

"The mouth of the river is the likeliest place. We must also search the forest. Any other thoughts?"

"How about Benedict's Cave?" suggested Gavin, a willowy man with blond hair, seated beside Hector. "You could hide fifty men in there."

"Fifty men like you, maybe!" exclaimed Hector. "But not if they're my size."

The laughter ended when Arthur reminded them that people were sleeping nearby.

Next, they discussed who should go. The men chosen were all renowned for their ability to move swiftly and quietly across the land. They would be sent at first light.

Before the meeting ended, Arthur emphasized the need for secrecy. "Keep this to yourselves," he warned. "We must not cause alarm."

As the group broke up to leave, Arthur took AP to one side. "So what did you think of your first council meeting?"

"It was interesting," AP offered.

"Any questions?"

AP might have asked why Arthur bothered with Medoc. Instead, he asked about the scouts, and why three should go rather than one or two.

"The most important battle preparation is knowing your enemy," replied Arthur. "Who is he? Where is he? How does he work? What are his movements?" He spoke with calm authority. "I must learn his weaknesses and his strengths, so I can predict his actions and plan his defeat."

AP listened intently.

"So I send three good men. If the enemy is sighted, one man stays to watch while the others return with the information. Those facts are vital and must get back to me at all costs—having two messengers is a safeguard against misadventure."

5

Floating Phantoms

A P awoke the following morning to the sounds of snoring. He turned over to check on Kate. She was deep in sleep and unlikely to wake before noon. Now was the perfect time to complete his experiment.

Afraid of disturbing anyone, AP tiptoed to the other end of the longhouse and found his iron pot. Nobody had touched it while he'd been away. He tested the clear liquid between his fingers and decided to boil off more water, just to make sure it was strong enough. While the liquid was simmering, he went outside to see who else was up.

When the lookouts at the top of the fence saw him strolling across the compound, they waved. Some children were playing quietly outside one of the huts while their parents slept inside. The rest of the compound was deserted. As soon as the youngsters saw him, they ran across.

"Come and play Slay the Dragon with us!" they pleaded. "You can be Kroner."

"I'm busy right now," AP explained. "Maybe later."

"*Please*," implored a little girl with huge, round eyes. "Just for a while."

"Alright," he agreed reluctantly, "only for a short game, though."

Joyfully, they led him away.

When AP returned to the longhouse, the liquid was as thick as syrup. "Perfect!" he thought, and unwrapped a bundle of cold fat he'd been saving from his meals. Dropping a greasy dollop into the boiling liquid and stirring all the time, he watched as it melted. AP continued adding more fat, a little at a time, until it all disappeared. The result was a sandy-brown paste, like porridge. When he tried cooling some on the end of a stick, it formed a ball.

Now he just had to wait for Kate to wake up.

❀   ❀   ❀

"So, what happened at your big powwow last night?" Kate asked her brother as he wandered over after archery practice. It was early afternoon, and she'd only just got up. She was sitting outside the longhouse, removing tangles from her hair with a wooden comb.

"Not much. Battle tactics—that sort of thing." He was purposefully vague. "You were fast asleep when I got back."

"Like, *totally unconscious*. I had a lot of sleep to catch up on—I hardly got any while you were away. I was worried sick about you." She stopped combing. "You could have told me you were going. How do you think I would've felt if something had happened?"

AP apologized, admitting he should have talked to her before leaving. But it all happened so quickly.

"I've got a surprise for you," he announced, changing the subject.

"The abacus is working?" she asked. "We can go home and have showers again?"

"No—nothing to do with the abacus. But it does have something to do with showers. I'll go get it."

He returned a few moments later with the iron pot and a small bowl of water.

"Look at this," he said, picking up one of the muddy brown lumps he'd rolled into a ball.

"That looks *disgusting*," she said indignantly "What is it?"

"Soap," he said proudly. "Try it. Just rub it between your hands while you dip them in water and you'll get a lather."

"*Soap*? Where did you get it from?"

"I made it."

"Yeah, right. You just get that stuff away from me, Arthur Percival," she threatened. "I'm not falling for one of your dumb jokes."

"Okay, watch this." He dipped the ball into the water and worked up a lather with his hands. "See? And look at this." Making a ring with his hands, he blew a soap bubble.

Kate looked on—astonished.

"That's amazing!" she marveled. Before long, her hands were full of bubbles too. "How did you do it?"

"Simple." Surprisingly, when he started explaining about potassium hydroxide and fatty acids, she didn't cut him off. She just sat there, listening and thinking.

"I guess science *is* useful," said Kate, looking at her brother with new regard. "Now I can see why you find it so interesting."

AP grinned. Picking a blade of grass, he twisted it into a loop and started blowing bubbles. They floated up into the air, reflecting all the colors of the rainbow.

One of the children playing in the compound spotted the bubbles and ran over for a closer look. After watching a few more float away, she shrieked for her friends to come and see the magic orbs. Within seconds, a crowd of squealing children were gazing at the sky and pointing. Soon some adults joined them. No one had seen anything like this before, and the whole place was thrown into a frenzy. Someone sent for Medoc.

Medoc, robes flowing and arms raised to the heavens, came sweeping through the crowd that was now gathered in a spellbound circle around AP and his sister.

AP, who was normally shy, was beginning to warm to his audience. Dipping the grass loop into the bowl, he swept it quickly through the air, forming a long string of bubbles. The crowd cheered enthusiastically. He made a larger loop and dipped in again, but this time blew with his lips. Slowly, a big bubble grew. And it kept on growing until it was almost as long as his arm. Then, reluctantly, it separated, moving off like a giant caterpillar, wobbling as if it were alive. The audience gasped.

An excited toddler made a grab for the big bubble, only to see it disappear, right in front of his eyes. Those standing close enough to witness what had happened were every bit as amazed.

"Magic!" murmured one woman.

Kate noticed the bewildered expression that flickered across Medoc's face, but it disappeared in an instant.

"He hasn't the faintest idea what's going on," Kate thought, "but he's not going to let anyone know that."

Medoc turned toward the crowd, bobbing and smiling as if none of this were new to him. Yet when his attention returned to AP, there was an entirely different expression on his face.

"That's probably enough," said Kate, leaning across to AP, whose back was toward Medoc. She'd seen venom in the old man's eyes.

❀ ❀ ❀

Arthur's revenge on the attacking raiders had occupied everybody's attention that day. But by late afternoon, everyone was talking about floating phantoms instead. A few people had tried dipping their own grass loops into water. Their lack of success only intensified their belief in the young visitor's magical powers.

"You've got a rival here, Medoc!" Arthur declared at supper that night. "Word of his rainbow phantoms is spreading throughout the land."

Kate grimaced—she'd seen the look of sheer hatred on Medoc's face that afternoon. But the white-haired old man was being as warm and friendly as a favorite uncle.

"That was indeed an impressive piece of sorcery," Medoc complimented, "especially in one so young. You clearly have the sight—such a shame if it is not developed." He turned to Arthur, then back to AP. "How would you like to learn from me? I have much to teach you."

"Well?" beamed Arthur. "You could be Medoc's apprentice."

AP had to think carefully before replying. He was wise enough not to undermine the high regard Arthur had for Medoc. But he had no desire to study under the bumbling old fraud.

Then he thought of a way out. "I would be honored to be your apprentice," he began respectfully. "But I should concentrate on improving my skills with the sword."

Medoc nodded sagely. Arthur smiled, glad they'd still be spending time together. Kate breathed a sigh of relief.

Instead of sitting around the table chatting after supper as usual, Kate told her brother they must talk. Once they were alone, Kate explained what was on her mind. "It's

Medoc," she began, making no attempt to hide her loathing for him. "I used to think he was just an old weirdo, but he's worse than that." She paused. "He's evil."

"Why do you say that?"

"You should have seen the look on his face while you were doing your magician's act."

"What look?"

"Listen. You saw the reaction the soap bubbles were having on the crowd. Along comes Medoc to find out what all the fuss is about, and he sees magic that's way beyond his pathetic little tricks. He's as mystified as everyone else, but pretends it's nothing new to him. Worse, this powerful new magic is being performed by a kid."

AP looked skeptical.

"His eyes were filled with hatred, as if he'd do anything to stop you."

"If that's true, why did he ask me to be his apprentice? Why would he want me hanging around him all day?"

"AP, you amaze me at times. You're good at science and stuff, but when it comes to street smarts, you haven't a clue."

"I saw Medoc was a fraud," he protested.

"Yes, and he's dead jealous of you, so you can't take any chances with him."

"Look at all those stars," said AP, glancing skyward. "See the moon? It's in its last quarter."

"Stop trying to change the subject. I'm serious about Medoc."

"I'm impressed by all the attention," he said, smiling. "It takes a bit of getting used to, though!"

"And so do you!" she said, landing a punch on his shoulder. "That was nice of you to make the soap."

"Did you know you can use the moon as a calendar?" said AP with a wry smile.

Kate groaned.

"See how the moon's crescent, the white bit, is on the left side? That means the moon's in its last quarter. Just remember, LEFT and LAST."

"So it's going to keep getting thinner—it was a full moon when we arrived." Then she had a thought. "Hey, *l* also stands for *less*—LEFT, LAST, *LESS*."

"Lunar linking logic," said AP.

They both laughed.

"And how thin is it now?

Kate squinted up at the moon again. "It's skinny."

"That shows it's getting close to a new moon. When the crescent disappears altogether, all we see is a black disk in a blacker sky. The new moon's the halfway point in the monthly cycle between one full moon and the next. So that shows we've been here for almost two weeks."

"Brilliant! Who needs a watch when you've got the moon to tell the time? Speaking of which, I'm ready for bed. End of lecture."

AP smiled. "Good to see you're feeling better."

Kate gave him a blank look.

"For a moment back there, I thought you'd gone mushy on me. But I'm glad the effects of the soap were only temporary."

6

Battle Plans

A week after their secret departure, the last pair of scouts slipped back to the fortress. They had important news to report.

"We followed the river almost to the sea without seeing anything," said one. "Then we rounded a bend and spotted over one hundred armed men!" he paused. "Young Wilf stayed behind to watch them."

"What weapons?" asked Arthur. Once again, the longhouse had been cleared of everyone except council members. AP, now a revered mystic, was also present.

"Swords, axes and spears. But no bows."

"Where are they?"

"Two leagues beyond Benedict's Cave, the river takes a wide bend. The left bank opens onto a lush meadow—that's where they've set up camp."

"We have a nest of vipers on our soil!" exclaimed Arthur. "We must stamp them out!"

The council roared its approval.

Arthur looked at AP. "You're silent," he said, above the cheers. "What are you thinking?"

AP was surprised to be asked his opinion on a military matter. "I'm—um—only a boy," he mustered.

"Maybe so, young Arthur, but you have mystical powers. Medoc has them too, yet he is a frail old man. Neither age nor stature has meaning here. All that matters is the special gift you possess."

AP wanted to tell everyone that he had no supernatural abilities—the soap bubbles they saw were science, not magic. There was no such thing as sorcery. But he knew they wouldn't listen.

"Well, young Arthur, should we act now or delay?"

AP thought it best to agree with the others. Striking the raiders before they had a chance to attack *them* made good sense. So, straightening his shoulders and pushing out his chest, he answered, "Act now," using his most grown-up voice.

Council discussed how many warriors they could raise. Even if they recruited every man and boy from the nearby villages, the invaders still outnumbered them. Provided Arthur acted quickly, he had the advantage of surprise. They would leave before dawn the following day.

After the meeting ended, AP headed for the door at the far end of the longhouse, along with the warriors. Medoc remained behind—he had something urgent to discuss with Arthur.

Just as AP was about to step into the afternoon sunshine, Arthur called out to him, "Wait for me. I'll be with you soon."

Rumors flew around the fortress that evening. A huge dragon was roaming the land, burning villages and eating children. Some said the fearsome Iceni tribe was about to attack. Others warned the Romans had returned to reconquer the country.

AP and Kate went for a walk before bed—he had something important to tell her.

"Arthur wants me to go on the mission with him."

"What?" croaked Kate. "You *can't* go. No way. You're a kid—they'd *slaughter* you."

"What could I say?" asked AP, aware of the seriousness of his plight. "I had no choice."

"If Arthur wants a sorcerer, he can take Medoc. He's been at every other battle."

"Medoc's getting too frail."

"The old devil was fit enough the other night—leaping about the longhouse waving a chunk of tree around!"

"There's a big difference between that and having guys hacking at you with swords! Besides," he continued, "Arthur obviously thinks my powers are greater than Medoc's."

Kate scowled. "I bet Medoc was all for your going."

AP nodded sheepishly.

"See? That proves my point. I *knew* he was out to get you."

"Medoc's a fake for sure, and my soap bubbles must have bugged him. But I can't believe he wants to harm me. He's been nice to me, especially at today's council meeting."

"Of *course* he has—he wants to make sure you go off into battle. He's trying to get *rid* of you! Can't you see that?"

"What's the difference?" AP sighed. "Without a miracle, I'm leaving before dawn. End of story."

"The abacus!" exclaimed Kate. "Let's try activating it."

"I doubt it's had enough time to recharge," he said dismissively, wanting to avoid another disappointment. "Let's just go to bed."

"No way. Let's have another go—it might work this time."

AP turned on the screen and double-checked the settings. Kate then grabbed his arm, squeezing so tightly it hurt. "Okay, press the button. We've got to get you out of here."

"What's Plan B?" AP quipped as the abacus failed yet again.

"How about a sudden illness? One that keeps you in bed for a couple of weeks."

"Come on. My mystical powers could cure any illness."

"Let's just disappear! We can make it on our own out there."

"And how do we get past the gatekeeper?"

Kate had overlooked that detail. "So what *do* we do?"

"You stay here and look after this." He slipped the abacus over her head. "And I go off with Arthur."

"I'm not taking this thing," she said, grabbing the pendant. "I know why you're giving it to me and I refuse."

"I'll be back—for sure. It's just for safekeeping."

If there had been any moonlight, she may have noticed his fingers were crossed. And he may have seen tears in her eyes.

7

The Vipers' Nest

The black sky was studded with stars, and the chill in the air hinted of fall. Warriors stamped their feet and blew into their hands as they waited in the compound. Names were called, groups formed, and weapons checked. The bowmen, outnumbered by the swordsmen, took up their positions in the middle of the column. Each man carried a day's food rations—the rest were loaded onto packhorses.

Some wives and sweethearts had left their warm beds to see their men off. AP was glad he and Kate had faced their farewells hours before. Gwendolyn comforted the women with her strength. Medoc was there too, his robes flapping like a giant crow's wings. Passing among the men, he touched each one with a bundle of herbs, chanting mysteriously. When he got to AP, he put on an extra show, drawing wide circles in the air with his hands.

The great gate swung open. It was time to leave. Arthur, striding over to AP with sword in hand, laid an arm across his shoulder. "Walk beside me, young Arthur. You shall be my second sight."

AP smiled pensively, wondering how he'd measure up in the days ahead.

As the column was about to move, Medoc swooped down and whispered something into AP's ear. Then they were off.

❋ ❋ ❋

For several hours they'd been marching at the same brisk pace. AP, anxious to know what was expected of him, asked Arthur what Medoc did during battles.

"He's a powerful sorcerer," Arthur began. "He sticks to my side like a shadow, reading signs and interpreting omens. And when we sight the enemy, he turns into a falcon, flying overhead to read their minds."

"He doesn't stay by your side during the actual fighting?" queried AP.

"No—not in human form—though I've sometimes seen him flying over the battlefield."

AP let this new information sink in slowly. Then, after a long pause, he asked when Medoc transformed back into a man.

"Usually when the battle's over," replied Arthur. "Yet there have been times—during long campaigns—when he appeared as a man before the fighting was done." Arthur stroked his beard. "One such battle occurred several years ago. We were laying siege to a fortress that took many days to win. Although the fighting was fierce during the day, we could rest in peace at night. Every evening, Medoc returned as a man, to share his secrets and to eat."

AP weighed his next question carefully. "Have you ever seen Medoc turn into a falcon?"

"Yes. Many times."

AP looked Arthur straight in the eye.

"Rather," said Arthur, after a pause, "I've seen him slip into the bushes many times, but have not actually witnessed his transformation. As you know, he must focus all his energies on this. That requires seclusion."

AP, feeling more relaxed than when he'd left the fortress, had been walking on his own for the last two hours—Arthur had dropped back to talk with his commanders. Flanked by rolling hills and woods, they were following the river's course. Suddenly, a falcon swooped on a flock of sparrows, and AP was reminded of Medoc. Just hours ago he was only a fraud. Now AP realized Kate was right—he *did* mean him harm. Why else would the sorcerer have whispered that warning in his ear as they were leaving? "Stay beside Arthur throughout the battle and you will be safe." Now AP knew how to avoid danger—he'd follow Medoc's example and disappear into the bushes!

AP pondered his new role as Arthur's "second sight." The leader obviously valued Medoc's guidance, even though he could tell him nothing new. Medoc's sole usefulness was to confirm Arthur's own conclusions. Arthur didn't need him—he merely *thought* he did. "Well, I can do the job as well as Medoc," AP thought. And if that involved playacting, he was up to the challenge.

As time was of the essence, there was no stopping along the way, and each man ate his rations on the march. They maintained the same tough pace until darkness. Most of the men then fell fast asleep, but Arthur, full of nervous energy, seemed ready to talk all night.

"I must tell you about my omen," he began. "A large crow flew down from a tree and landed only two spans from where I was walking."

AP stared into the distance, frowning in fake concentration. "Which way did it face?"

"Downstream," affirmed Arthur.

"Toward the enemy?"

"Yes."

"And what do we know of crows?"

"They are omens of death."

"Exactly," agreed AP. "So this can only mean one thing."

"Death of the enemy."

"Yes," said AP, nodding wisely. "You will succeed in your quest."

Arthur was elated. His young namesake had truly outstanding mystical powers. He'd been right to bring him on this dangerous mission.

❋   ❋   ❋

Arthur's forces reached the bend in the river on the third day. Anxious to see the enemy camp, Arthur summoned the scouts who had located it. The other commanders wanted to go too.

"No!" said Arthur. "There is too much risk of being seen. Hector, you shall come. And Thomas," he nodded toward one of the scouts, "you will lead the way." Then, turning to AP, "Young Arthur will come also—to read the omens. There will be a battle council immediately upon our return."

The left bank was dappled with color—purple vetch, buttercups and pink knapweed. The broad expanse of grasses and bulrushes was a haven for butterflies and birds. A high ridge backed the opposite bank. Densely wooded, it provided the perfect vantage point for the third scout, the one still spying on the enemy. Thomas pointed up to his hiding place.

"What are we waiting for?" exclaimed Arthur. "Let's get up there and see for ourselves."

Hector, for all his large size, moved through the woods like a cat and maintained a brisk pace all the way to the top. AP had to jog to keep up.

"They're still there," said young Wilf, who was the same age as AP. He pointed down at the enemy camp. "About forty of them raided another village today, but they didn't leave until midday—these warriors like their beds! They returned loaded with goods. Barrels of wine too. They've been drinking ever since."

Loud singing carried across the river.

"They'll feel bad in the morning!" declared Arthur jubilantly. "Well done, Wilf. Keep a close watch on them tonight."

Arthur described what they had seen to his battle council. He favored a dawn attack, and everyone agreed. Then they devised a battle plan. Arthur would lead his swordsmen into the sleeping camp before dawn. Meanwhile, the archers would form an encircling ring. At first light, the swordsmen would attack the sleeping invaders. The bowmen's job was to stop anyone escaping.

"I want everyone to eat his fill," Arthur told his men, "but no fires—they might see the smoke—and no noise." His men listened intently. "Then we sleep. We have a battle to win tomorrow."

AP was in a deep sleep when suddenly everything started shaking. "Wake up!" Arthur whispered. "I've just had another omen."

"What did you see?" AP murmured.

Arthur leaned forward, eyes blazing. "A shooting star. Is that a good omen? Did I make the right decision?"

AP was no military strategist, but Arthur's plan made perfect sense. More importantly, his commanders—all seasoned warriors—endorsed it.

"Which way did the shooting star point?" AP was now enjoying his role as wise oracle.

"To the east."

"What direction is first light?"

"To the east—" Arthur paused. "So my plan for a dawn attack is the right one?"

"Yes," said AP solemnly.

Arthur slumped back as if a great burden had been lifted.

"It is strange," Arthur began. "Despite your youth I can confide in you." He then spoke of his concerns regarding the battle. AP was shocked to hear such uncertainty from someone whose actions were so decisive.

Still playing his role, AP reminded Arthur that his most experienced warriors had all agreed on the plan. "Trust your judgment, as do your men."

They sat in silence watching the stars, feeling remote from their world and what lay ahead.

"We have a big day tomorrow," said Arthur at last. "Both of us must rest."

AP lay down, but it took ages to get back to sleep.

Arthur always addressed his warriors before battle. Raucous yelling and the clashing of swords then followed. On this day, though, he had to rely on the force of his words to raise fighting spirits. As AP listened to his rousing speech, he could scarcely believe their conversation beneath the stars. When Arthur was finished, everyone believed victory was inevitable.

The warriors set off before daybreak, snaking through the dark countryside in an orderly column. Hector strode on Arthur's left, with AP symbolically on his right. Wet grass soaked their legs and feet, but nobody seemed to notice. Everyone heard the singing of the birds, though. AP wondered if the dawn chorus had ever sounded so loud.

"I wonder what they're saying," whispered Arthur.

"Time for breakfast!" suggested Hector, patting his big belly.

"Tell me what you hear, young Arthur."

AP cocked his head to one side. "A good omen," he declared. "They thank you in advance for ridding their home of intruders."

Arthur gazed at the birds. Then, turning to AP, he asked whether he was going to do what Medoc did and turn into a bird.

"No, not yet. I'll stay longer."

When they reached the top of the ridge, young Wilf appeared, rubbing his eyes. "Nothing changed during the night," he reported. "The invaders are asleep."

Suddenly, Hector's stomach gave an enormous rumble.

"Hush that belly!" whispered Gavin. "You'll wake the entire camp."

Arthur gave the order, and the warriors set off, moving like stalking lions.

Soon Arthur's men were in position, waiting for dawn. The invaders slept on, oblivious to the peril surrounding them.

AP could have stayed behind on the ridge and "disappeared" like Medoc. Instead, he was now standing beside the camp, beneath the fading stars. Time seemed to stand still. But as he stood there, staring at the heavens, the eastern skyline was turning gold. It was time.

Swords raised high, the warriors moved forward, each picking his own man. Then, on a signal from their leader, the battle began. AP, horrified by the scene, was riveted to the spot. Sights and sounds assaulted his brain—swords slicing flesh, agonized screams, blades chopping bone, spurting blood. Then the odor of carnage wafted his way—a revolting blend of butcher shop and farmyard. Sour bile bit the back of his throat, and he could feel the world beginning to spin.

AP could have blamed the warriors for the bloodshed, but that would have been unfair. The invaders had slaughtered defenseless villagers—now they were paying the price. Maybe what disturbed him most was the euphoric way the swordsmen went about their grisly business.

Eventually, it was over. Arthur's men, although heavily outnumbered, had killed every invader and suffered few casualties themselves. All was deathly still. AP could hear the sound of the sea, being carried on the wind. He thought the warriors would be shouting with joy, but most of them just stood there, surveying the scene as if shocked by their deeds.

Arthur strode up and laid an arm across AP's shoulder. "You never changed into a falcon." He sounded surprised

"No." AP's voice was flat and lifeless.

"You have helped me win a great victory. I am again in your debt, young Arthur. First my grandfather's dagger, and now—this."

AP remained silent.

"Medoc was right. After our council meeting, when he suggested I take you with me, I thought he'd lost his mind. 'How can I take a boy who cannot even handle a sword into battle?' I asked him. Then Medoc reminded me of your great powers as a sorcerer, and it began to make sense."

Suddenly the horror of the battle, and the thought that somebody hated him enough to want him killed, was too much for AP. He needed to be alone.

"The time has come for me to become a falcon. I must fly over the land to restore my powers."

Arthur smiled. "As you wish, my gifted young friend."

AP headed for a lone tree, off in the distance. Walking around to the other side, he crouched down and vomited.

8

Marooned

News of the victory reached the hill fort before the warriors returned, giving everyone time to plan a rousing welcome.

People waved and cheered from the top of the fence. They lined the path leading up to the gate. Some ran down the hill to greet the returning heroes. There was shouting and clapping, laughter and tears.

Kate grabbed her brother before he reached the gate, lifting him off the ground.

"I thought you were dead!" she cried, forcing the air from his lungs.

"Keep this up and I will be," he croaked. "I can't breathe."

Medoc waited inside the gate to hail the returning heroes, alongside Gwendolyn. After greeting Arthur and his commanders, he turned to AP.

"Welcome home, young Arthur!" he cried aloud for all to hear. "I see my protective spell kept you safe."

"More like a curse," AP thought to himself. Kate shot Medoc a look that said exactly what she thought of him.

AP planned to keep well out of Medoc's way, but the old man disappeared from the fort soon after their arrival.

Arthur explained this was normal—the sorcerer needed solitude to meditate.

When the excitement had died down, Kate and AP walked down to the river so they could talk.

"Here," she said, slipping the abacus over his head, "back where it belongs." Then she asked, "So, how was the battle?"

"Bad."

The long trek home had given AP time to think, and now he was ready to talk. His account of the fighting shocked her into silence. Then he told her that his going with Arthur had been all Medoc's idea. Kate was enraged.

"That evil, scheming, lying old goat needs a lesson. I'd like to—"

"Save your breath, Kate, he's not worth it. We'll just stay out of his way and keep an eye out for him."

"I'll tell you one thing, AP, I'm not letting you out of my sight. Nothing's going to happen while I'm around."

AP told her how Medoc "turned" into a bird just before battles began.

"Typical!" she scoffed. "Just what I'd expect from a fraud like him."

"But get this," AP continued. "He turns into a falcon! One of the English falcons is called a merlin—I read about it in that field guide."

"Medoc—Merlin," murmured Kate.

"Exactly. This must be the way the Merlin legend started."

The final straw was when AP told Kate what Medoc had whispered before he left the fort.

"WHAT?" she exploded. "He told you to go into battle, knowing you were unable to defend yourself?" She was yelling so loudly that AP wondered whether she'd be heard all the way back at the fort. "I'd like to string that hateful old devil up by his beard and let the crows peck him to pieces!"

AP had never seen his sister so mad. Thinking it best to change the subject, he asked what she'd been doing while he was away.

"Mostly thinking of what I'd say to Mum and Dad if I returned without you."

"That won't happen. We'll go home together, or not at all."

"*Not at all?*" Kate shot back. "Are we stuck here?"

"Maybe," he admitted. "We've tried activating the abacus so many times, with no luck. Something must be wrong."

"The thing's broken?"

"It *seems* okay," he said, pressing the white button. "See? The map and the displays still light up."

"Could it need a new battery?"

"Well, if it does we're out of luck."

"So what do we do?"

"We try the abacus, every so often. But we…" He left the sentence unfinished.

"But we *what*?"

"We might…have to stay here."

"Never go home again?" she gasped. "Never see Mum and Dad again? Or any of our friends?"

"I—don't know."

Kate was distraught.

"If it comes to that," he began, hesitantly, "the people are nice…"

"It's okay for you!" she snapped. "You can be the big sorcerer. And play sword fighting and bows and arrows with the grown-ups. What's here for *me*?"

"You like Gwendolyn and her friends. I thought you were having a good enough time."

"Gwendolyn's cool. Some of the others are okay too. But I want more from life than sitting around talking with the girls and playing with children."

"Maybe you'll meet Sir Galahad—you know, get married," he joked, but she wasn't amused.

"Look, the last few weeks have been better than I expected. But I want to get back to our own world. I want to take a shower, text my friends, watch TV—"

"Let's try it again." AP checked the settings. "Are you ready?" he asked, finger poised.

Kate, dreading disappointment, nodded and grabbed his arm. AP pressed the button. Nothing. He tried again. Still nothing.

AP tucked away the abacus and they continued walking. A dove sang a mournful song to the sky.

"Guess what Arthur said on the way home?" AP began, after a long silence. "Medoc is getting frail and has only a few years left. Arthur asked if I'd take his place—he trusts me."

"Laying that on a twelve-year-old is a bit unfair."

"So what will he do when Medoc's gone?"

"He'll manage. You said he makes the right decisions by himself."

"But he *thinks* he needs help. Before the battle, he was so unsure. What if I hadn't been there?"

Kate snorted. "You're really sold on this mystic thing! Do you want to be the power behind the throne?"

"No!" AP protested. "I just...feel sorry for him."

As they headed for the fort, Kate told him about the planned victory feast. She was bursting to share something else too. AP recognized the signs—Kate was hopeless at keeping secrets.

"Okay," he said. "What's the big news?"

"I can't tell you. It's private."

"So what's Gwendolyn's secret?"

"Who said anything about Gwendolyn?"

"Come on—I know it's about her!"

Kate hesitated. "Promise not to tell anyone."

AP gave his word.

Kate looked around furtively, even though nobody was in sight. "Gwendolyn's expecting a baby!"

"That's nice," he said with a shrug.

"Is that all you can say? I've just given you *the* most amazing news."

"Well, she *is* married."

"Oh, why did I even bother?" Kate groaned. "I can see my secret's safe with you."

❀　❀　❀

On the day of the feast, people were in a festive mood. Those not involved in the preparation—most of the men—relaxed and enjoyed themselves. Arthur spent the morning with AP, working on his swordsmanship.

"I see an improvement," said Arthur. "You're sidestepping well and parrying my sword. Let's work on your attack." Holding his own weapon upright to fend off AP's blade, Arthur instructed him on lunging.

AP swung the sword toward Arthur's right shoulder. The two weapons met with a deafening clang. AP immediately raised the blade and aimed in the opposite direction.

"Good!" shouted Arthur.

They continued for several minutes, until Arthur noticed AP was tiring.

"Let's take a rest."

"No!" AP defied, and continued lunging with renewed determination.

"Enough!" bellowed Arthur. "You'll injure yourself. We will rest."

Slumping to the ground beside his mentor, AP panted to catch his breath.

"If I had a son, I'd want him to be like you," Arthur declared, patting him on the shoulder. "You've got courage. You refuse to let your small size stop you." He paused, "So, will you be Medoc's successor?"

AP thought long and hard before answering. "Kate and I may be going away," he began uncertainly. This caught Arthur off guard. "If we stay though, I'd be honored to do so."

Arthur smiled wistfully. "I can't ask more than that." A comfortable silence followed.

"I may be having a son of my own soon. Gwendolyn is with child."

AP blushed. Nobody had ever talked to him that way before. Arthur's words made him feel special.

Shortly before noon, someone started a bonfire in a shallow pit. Once the fire died down to burning embers, some men erected wooden spits and began roasting pig carcasses. AP watched, fascinated.

"I wonder whether one of them is *our* pig?" asked Kate.

"Maybe."

"That's it for me," she said, making a snap decision. "From now on I'm a vegetarian."

Early that afternoon, AP learned that the old scribe wanted to talk with him about the battle. "I won't be long," he told Kate.

"I'm going with you," she said firmly.

"But it's the scribe who wants to see me, not Medoc."

"Suppose he's in league with him? They're both odd-balls."

"You don't even *know* the scribe!"

"All the more reason to suspect him!"

❀   ❀   ❀

The scribe lived in a tiny shack close to the gate. AP knocked on the door, wrinkling his nose against the stench from the nearby garbage.

"Is he home?" asked Kate when there was no reply.

"Somebody is—I can hear noises."

Several moments later the door opened a crack, and the scribe's wizened old face appeared. He had pale, watery eyes, shoulder-length hair and a long, straggly beard. His hair, once snow white, had discolored to a pale shade of straw. Seeing Kate confused him at first. Then AP made the introductions, and the scribe invited them indoors.

"I'm afraid it's cluttered," he apologized as they squeezed inside his one-room home. His faded brown robe reached the floor. Both elbows were threadbare from long hours spent leaning over his work.

A large table occupied most of the space, piled high with parchment scrolls. Each cream-colored roll was tied with a red ribbon. More scrolls were stacked on the shelves along the walls. A bed was crunched into one corner. The only other furniture was a pair of rickety chairs.

"Please, sit down," he told AP, pointing a bony hand toward one of the chairs. He turned to Kate. "I fear there's nowhere else to sit but my bed."

"That's fine," she replied, stepping over a pile of rumpled clothes.

"Now, my young sir," he said, lowering himself into the chair opposite AP. "I would like to hear everything you remember of the battle."

AP's account lasted almost an hour. The old man scratched notes on a piece of parchment, using a quill pen. He kept stopping and squinting, holding the parchment at arm's length to read it.

"What are all those other scrolls?" asked AP.

"Records of our great leader's exploits," he replied reverently. "I'll show you."

Arms outstretched, the scribe read from the most recent one. "…young Arthur streaked through the water like an arrow to rescue the precious dagger. He moved so quickly that the water boiled, sending up great clouds of steam that could be seen far across the land…"

Kate and AP were astonished at how exaggerated the story had become. So this was how legends began!

The records dated back to Arthur's birth. Unfortunately, the scribe could no longer read them. "In those days my eyes were bright and my writing small."

AP had an idea. "Have you got a scrap of parchment and a pin?"

AP pricked a hole through its center and held the parchment up to his eye. Then he handed it to the scribe.

"Try reading one of your scrolls through the hole."

The old man tried, with no luck.

"Hold the scroll closer," said AP, raising the frail hand. "Can you see anything now?"

The scribe peered intently for several seconds. Then with a whoop he cried, "I can read! This is *miraculous*!"

He wept for joy, proclaiming AP to be the greatest sorcerer.

"I'm confused," said Kate as they left the shack. "Why did the hole in the parchment help him read?"

"The lens in your eye, like the lens in a camera, is curved, back and front." AP cupped his hands together to make the point. "The two surfaces must be perfectly rounded, otherwise the image at the back of the eye—on the retina—will be out of focus."

"That makes sense."

"As people get older, the lens changes shape, making the image fuzzy. This distortion get worse toward the edge of the lens."

"So it's better in the middle," said Kate.

"Exactly. Holding a pinhole in front of your eye blocks out the distorted part."

Kate was impressed by the simplicity of the solution.

"It's still early," said AP. "What do we do with the rest of the afternoon?"

"I haven't swung a bat in ages," said Kate. "How about doing some pitching for me?"

"Sure, I can work up an appetite for that delicious pork and crackling."

Kate groaned.

The longhouse was barely big enough to house all the merrymakers at the feast. People had to sit shoulder to shoulder along the makeshift table running along its length, but this only added to the festive mood. After eating, drinking and enjoying themselves, the speeches began. Hector was first on his feet and gave a stirring account of the battle.

"When the deed was done, we counted their dead," he concluded. "Our small force of fifty-three men had slain more than twice that number of raiders!"

The burst of applause carried all the way to the river.

Several other commanders described the fighting. The men listened intently, cheering in all the right places, but the women were less interested in warfare. When Arthur's turn came, though, everyone wanted to hear.

Arthur began by honoring their fallen comrades. Then, after praising each of his commanders, he paid tribute to his warriors. "No leader has ever been so proud of his men," he roared, raising his goblet.

"But there is one among you who is not a warrior, though he tries so hard to become one. His miraculous powers helped secure our victory."

AP began to blush. Kate nudged him beneath the table and grinned.

"Young Arthur has been with us such a short time, yet has astounded us all with his powers. He can swim like a fish, fly like a hawk, and summon phantoms from the air. And, as our learned scribe discovered this afternoon, he can restore sight to aging eyes."

The longhouse buzzed with excitement at this latest news.

AP was mortally embarrassed.

Kate turned around to check Medoc's reaction. He was beaming. And when Arthur announced that her brother could become the greatest sorcerer of all time, Medoc nodded enthusiastically. "That slippery snake's up to something," she said to herself.

"Nobody knows how long young Arthur and his sister will be with us," Arthur continued. "But if they *do* stay, our young sorcerer has pledged to become Medoc's successor."

A thunderous roar of approval followed, and Arthur had to raise his hand for silence.

"To that end, Medoc has graciously agreed to help young Arthur complete his studies. Our oracle is journeying to Fordon Forest to replenish his stock of herbs. He has invited young Arthur to accompany him, so he may benefit from his vast knowledge of plants."

AP was stunned. Kate was livid. Medoc was elated.

Then Arthur, changing the subject, announced that Gwendolyn was expecting a child. At this, the audience exploded into a cheering, table-banging display of jubilation.

"How can I get out of the trip?" AP asked Kate later that night.

"You can't," his sister conceded. "Not when it's been announced to the whole world. That was Medoc's intention. He wants you all alone, so he can take care of you—once and for all. But I'm going to upset his plans. I'm going with you."

9

A Poisonous Plot

For all his powers, Medoc was unable to stop Kate from accompanying her brother. Her last-minute inclusion disrupted his planning, but he never let it show. Indeed, the old sorcerer went out of his way to be kind and considerate to them both.

Medoc spent the day following the feast preparing for the week-long journey. He harnessed a packhorse to carry their supplies, declining Kate and AP's offer to help with the food. "That is most generous," he beamed, "but I know *exactly* what we need. I'll take care of *everything*."

Kate and AP exchanged suspicious looks. "He's going to poison us," she whispered, when Medoc was out of earshot. AP agreed this was likely, especially given his knowledge of potions. They must be vigilant—they would refuse anything Medoc didn't try first. As an added precaution, they packed a secret supply of food and water. They even devised a way of pretending to drink without swallowing—just in case he slipped them something. If Medoc thought he was dealing with gullible kids, he was in for a surprise!

The trio departed the following morning, as the sun peeked over the hills. "I'll take care of them!" assured Medoc as Arthur and Gwendolyn waved goodbye.

✳ ✳ ✳

Hours later, a tall, thin man arrived at the fortress. After enduring weeks of strife, he had finally reached his destination. During that time he'd been tricked by a guide, chased by a bear, hunted by raiders and lost more times than he cared to remember. But none of that mattered anymore. Soon he would have his hands on those children, whoever they were. They had no right to be time-traveling, and he would make sure they never did so again.

✳ ✳ ✳

The first day of the journey was uneventful. Medoc was the perfect guide, pointing out interesting things along the way and showing AP and Kate every consideration.

Before they went to bed that night, he stressed the importance of rising early. "We'll leave before dawn," he told them. Noticing their puzzled looks, he explained how they must reach the forest before dark.

"Look," said AP pointing skyward, "a full moon."

"Right now I'm more interested in sleep," said Kate. "I'll never get up tomorrow."

"He's in a big hurry," whispered AP the following morning. The sky was just getting light, and Medoc was striding along as if late for an appointment.

They were traveling in chalk country, with rolling hills of short, tough grass and few trees in sight. The sun had yet to show its face, but the sky was already bright. Soon they began climbing, following a footpath worn into the chalk by generations of travelers. Because of its narrowness, they had to walk single file.

Medoc glanced up at the eastern sky expectantly. Kate noticed this, and the route they were taking. If necessary, her navigational skills would get them back to the fortress without his help.

Suddenly, Medoc came to a halt and began adjusting the horse's harness.

"What *is* he up to?" whispered Kate.

"Haven't a clue."

"It's no good," called Medoc, fiddling some more and checking the sky. "The mare keeps slipping her bit—she doesn't like being followed. You'll have to take the lead, young Arthur. I'll take the rear."

They set off again, with Kate close on her brother's heels. Medoc let them get well ahead before he started, explaining the horse was better behaved that way.

The hill had become steeper, and they began rounding a long bend. Glancing to her left, Kate noticed the sheer drop. The near-vertical hillside, with large boulders at the bottom, made her nervous. Moving as far from the edge as possible, she focused her attention on the way ahead. "Good job Medoc's a long way back," she muttered.

Without warning, the sun exploded in their faces. AP lost his footing and disappeared over the top.

Kate screamed, convinced her brother had fallen to his death. Heart racing, she peered over the edge, expecting to see him lying at the bottom. Instead, she saw him sprawled against the hillside just beneath the precipice, clinging to a clump of grass.

Kate had the presence of mind to throw herself flat on the ground. Then, legs splayed for stability, she grabbed both of AP's arms. Her fingers dug into his flesh like fishhooks, anchoring his arms to the spot. Feet scrabbling, hands grappling, AP clawed his way to the top. Medoc, meanwhile, was still out of sight.

"I thought that was *it*," stammered AP. "And it would have been if not for you."

"No big deal," she said, smiling, her heart still pounding, "that's what big sisters are for."

When AP went to see where he'd slipped, he found that part of the footpath was broken away. Looking more closely, he saw marks on the chalk, as if someone had been digging with a pick. Then Medoc came hurrying around the bend, asking what had happened.

"How *terrible*," he gasped when they told him. "You could have been killed!"

"I bet *he* sabotaged the footpath, during his disappearing act from the fortress after the battle," said Kate when they were underway again.

"That's a bit far-fetched."

"Okay—why else would he make *you* take the lead just before we came to the dangerous part? And why did he keep looking up at the sky? Is it just coincidence that the sun happened to blind us as we reached the break in the path?"

AP admitted she had a good point.

The rest of the day was uneventful, and they reached the forest late in the afternoon. Kate took a fix on their position by checking the direction of the sun and noting landmarks.

Delighted with their progress, Medoc suggested they continue for another two hours, "Then I'll cook us a splendid supper."

"Look at the *size* of those trees," murmured Kate. "Even if we joined hands, we'd still be unable to hug one of them."

"They're beeches," said AP. "See how they spread out at the top." Both peered up at the dense forest canopy, high above their heads. "No wonder it's so dark."

"Quiet too," added Kate. Aside from the rustle of dead leaves underfoot, everything was as silent as the grave. Not even birds sang.

"See over here, young Arthur," called Medoc, crouching beside a knee-high clump of vegetation. "This is enchanter's nightshade. I use it to treat wounds, so we must collect some."

AP, kneeling beside the sorcerer, examined the large-leafed plant with its small white flowers.

Kate watched uneasily. She couldn't say why, but there was something ominous about Fordon Forest.

Medoc called a halt before sundown, and they began setting up camp. Their tents were simply rectangles of goat hide sewn together. Without backs or fronts, all they provided was a roof over their heads. AP built a fire while Medoc, under Kate's watchful eye, prepared a leg of pork for roasting. This seemed too much meat for three people, but Medoc explained they would finish the leftovers the following day.

"Your vegetarian phase didn't last long," AP commented to Kate as they feasted in the firelight.

"After what we've been through," she said between mouthfuls, "I'm ready for anything."

After supper, Medoc announced he would make them something special. "It's been a hard day," he declared, wiping greasy hands down his front. "And you've both had such a *terrible* ordeal."

"Thanks to you," thought Kate.

"I've got the very thing to help," he continued, "one of my elixirs."

"Poison for sure," whispered Kate when he left to prepare the potion.

Medoc returned with three goblets. After handing over theirs, he took a long draft from his own. "A little bitter," he said, pursing his lips, "but it'll do us the power of good." Then, gesturing with his free hand, he encouraged them to drink up.

Each took a swig, making loud swallowing sounds, but no liquid passed their lips. Lowering their goblets, they commented on the unusual taste.

"It's a mixture of rosehip, camomile and burdock, with a pinch of yarrow."

"And a generous slug of rat poison," Kate said to herself.

Medoc, closing his eyes in ecstasy, drained his goblet. Seizing the opportunity, AP and Kate tipped their drinks away.

Kate noticed how Medoc's eyes kept flitting between her and AP like a snake's. "He's watching for the potion to take effect," she thought. "Let's give him something to think about."

"I feel so tired," she yawned, rubbing her eyes.

"Me too," agreed AP, taking the hint. "I'm almost asleep."

Excusing themselves, they staggered from the fire and collapsed onto the fern mattress inside their tent.

"I can't see him," said Kate, staring toward the glow of the fire. "Can you?"

"No," said AP, focusing on the other tent.

"So where's he gone and what's he up to?"

"Maybe he's getting ready for bed," AP replied hopefully.

Soon they were fighting real tiredness.

"Stay awake!" Kate whispered into the dark, but AP had already drifted off.

Alone in the dark, Kate was determined to fight sleep. She failed.

AP awoke with a start. Something large was moving through the forest. "Wake up!" he hissed into Kate's ear.

Peering cautiously through the front of the tent, AP was surprised at how light it was. Then he realized the moon had risen. The rustling of leaves was growing louder, but all he saw was the silhouettes of trees.

Kate, now crouching beside him, could see nothing either. "Maybe it's Medo—"

They both froze. Lumbering toward them was an enormous bear.

"What shall we do?" squealed Kate.

"Out the back," whispered AP. "But move *slowly* and *quietly.*"

The bear, now dangerously close, kept stopping to sniff the air. Kate was convinced it had picked up their scent and would charge any second. Regardless, she kept backing out. Then they were clear of the tent.

The temptation to run was irresistible, though both knew this could trigger an attack. So they crept away, disappearing behind the nearest tree.

AP peeked around the trunk.

"What's it doing now?" whispered Kate.

"Going into the tent."

Grunting and snorting like a pig, the bear poked its nose into the fern mattress. Moments later AP saw it had something in its mouth: the remains of their pork roast. Medoc must have tucked it under their mattress while they were asleep.

After eating the meat and crunching the bone, the bear rooted around for more. Finding nothing, it lost interest and ambled away.

"Let's get back to the fort and tell Arthur *everything*," said AP. "He should know the truth about Medoc."

"You think Arthur will take your word against Medoc's? He's known him all his life, and you've been here only a month!"

Still believing he might persuade Arthur, AP asked Kate if she could find the way—to get a head start on Medoc.

"We've been traveling east since noon, so we just have to head west. Simple enough in daylight, but at night…"

"Look," said AP, pointing to the sky. "That's Polaris, the North Star. We can use that as our compass."

Kate stared at the small star intently. "Okay," she said after a long pause, "we can try."

"I'll grab our stuff," he said, heading for their tent.

Minutes later, they were underway.

The eerie shadows cast by the moon added to their fear of meeting another bear. But as they continued walking, they began to relax. AP even cracked a few jokes.

"My feet hurt," complained Kate after a couple of hours. "Let's take a rest."

Slumping to the forest floor, they leaned their backs against a tree. Neither of them noticed the black shape flitting between the trees.

"It's like when we first arrived in medieval times," said AP, staring up at the heavens, "a full moon and we're in a forest. We've been here exactly one month."

"Maybe the abacus will work." She slipped her arm through his. "Let's give it a try."

"Ready?" asked AP, his face glowing in the light from the map.

Instead of replying, Kate let out a piercing scream. "There's Medoc!"

A dark shape, wearing a hooded cloak, slipped into view. "You have something that belongs to me," he said ominously. He started moving toward them, hand out-stretched.

"That's not Medoc!" shouted AP, staring at the tall, thin stranger. Then AP pressed the button, and the forest lit up in a blaze of blue light.

The next instant they were sitting on the floor in the antique shop. "High Water" was still blaring from the radio. They'd been gone for precisely one second.

10

Counting the Seconds

This is your captain again," announced the pilot. "We're now number two in line and will be pushing back shortly. Please turn off all electronic equipment. Once again, I apologize for the delay. Our flying time to Boston today will be seven hours, twenty minutes, so we'll be setting you down at the gate shortly after 3 p.m. local time. Sit back, relax and enjoy your flight. Cabin crew, prepare for takeoff."

Uncle Miles's affairs had been settled, and the Littletons were on their way home.

"Going through security was scary," whispered AP once they were airborne. "I was sure they'd check my knapsack after it'd gone through the x-ray scanner."

"So the abacus didn't show on their screen?" asked Kate.

"I guess not, but it must be full of electronics. I wonder who *built* it?"

"Maybe the hooded guy," suggested Kate. "He said we had something that belonged to him."

"But that doesn't mean he built the thing."

They had gone over their medieval journey many times, but found no answers. One thing was certain—their recollections were identical, so everything really did happen.

Kate popped in her ear buds. And while she listened to music, AP took another look at the device.

When he turned on the map, it showed the British Isles and the eastern part of North America. The blinking red dot was moving toward the Atlantic.

"Look at this," he said, nudging Kate's arm. "You can see the position of our aircraft."

"Cool. How does it do that?"

"How does it do any of it?" AP marveled.

Just then, Kate remembered the pilot's warning. "Quick, turn it off!" she gasped. "It'll mess with the airplane's equipment."

"I'll only be a second—I just want to copy down that equation."

AP stared at the numbers: $s = 2,551,442.9s$. What did it mean? Then he had an idea.

"Maybe s is the usual abbreviation for *second*," he thought. "We were away from one full moon to the next—how many seconds in a month?"

Pulling out his calculator, he found that twenty-eight days was 2,419,200 seconds.

"Close," he said, writing down the number. Then he remembered that February was the only month with twenty-eight days. How long was a lunar month?

"Okay," he said to himself, "I'll divide three hundred and sixty-five days by twelve. That's 30.41666 days."

This time, a month worked out to be 2,627,999.4 seconds.

"Closer, but still not right. Maybe that's not a lunar month. I'll have to check online when we get back."

AP turned the computer on as soon as he had dropped his suitcase in his room. When he Googled *lunar month*, he got 29.53059 days. Working this out in seconds gave 2,551,442.9.

"Yes!" he yelled, punching the air.

He ran into Kate's room without bothering to knock, waving his piece of paper. "Look at this!" he sang out, not noticing that she was on the phone. "One month in the past takes exactly one second in the present! We could live a whole year in the past and be away for only twelve seconds!"

Kate tried waving him away.

"Our first solid fact!" he continued, ignoring the hint. "Hopefully this is just—"

"Get lost!" she screamed. "I'm busy?" Then, speaking into the phone, "Sorry Whitney, just my brother being a pain."

AP spun on his heels and left. "Welcome home," he said to himself.

11

The Old Routine

R esolving the lunar month gave AP such a boost that he was determined to discover more about the abacus. However, after two days of experimenting, his enthusiasm was fading. Then, on the third day, he got a lucky break. He had been rearranging the beads—checking that the number on the screen changed to match the one he'd just "beaded-in"—when the phone rang downstairs.

"It's Michael," called his mother. "He wants to know if you're going to judo tonight."

AP went downstairs, forgetting to turn off the abacus.

Returning minutes later, he beaded-in a new number—12231826—and watched an unfamiliar number flash up on the screen—*12/23/1826*. AP was baffled at first. Then he realized that instead of showing a certain number of years, the numerals appeared as a date—December the twenty-third, eighteen-twenty-six. The screen button must have a double function! When the screen's *off*, the beads count for *years*. But when the screen's *on*, they stand for months, days and years, letting you travel to a particular date.

Feeling pleased with himself, he went downstairs to raid the fridge.

❊ ❊ ❊

Kate was spending a lot of time with her best friend Whitney. Her sister owned a car, so they often went to the mall. Between shopping for back-to-school clothes and seeing friends, Kate hung out at the ball diamond with her team. A few months ago, a new addition, Mitch Bailey, had joined the team. Mitch had recently moved from Montana with his family. He and Kate got along really well.

Although Mitch loved baseball, he hadn't shown up to play since Kate's return.

"Where's Mitch?" Kate asked Whitney one day.

"Oh, he had to fly home for a wedding—he'll be back next week. Why do you ask?"

"No reason," she fibbed.

❊ ❊ ❊

AP was happy about returning to school and slipping back into the old routine, but not Kate.

"Everything's so *boring*," she complained one night at supper. "I can't see the point of school. Who needs all that useless stuff they teach us?"

Her parents exchanged glances—it was going to be another of *those* meals.

"No knowledge is useless," reasoned her father. "Some things are just more interesting than others."

Mrs. Littleton shot him a warning glance.

"So what's interesting about the French Revolution or the U.S. Bill of Rights?" challenged Kate.

"Well..." began Mr. Littleton.

The discussion lasted most of suppertime, with her father doing all the reasoning and Kate all the grumbling.

Things ended when Kate stormed upstairs and slammed her door. Kate lay on her bed staring at the ceiling. Then she got a phone call from one of her teammates.

"Hey, Kristen...Nothing much...Yeah that sucks...No, what?...Christie Ford? No way. But she's *so* evil. How could *anyone* want to take her? No I don't...I have zero interest in him. Listen, Mitch can take Christie Ford or anyone else to the dance...That's *so* not true. You can think that if you like...Seriously, I *have* to go now. Bye." She tossed her cell phone aside and buried her head in the pillow.

While Kate skulked in her room, AP was in the basement helping his father shelve some old *National Geographic* magazines. A cover picture of the *Titanic* caught his eye. He flicked through the article, looking at photos of the rusting hull. Then he came to another, titled "Ghosts on the Little Bighorn." He started reading every word.

When Mr. and Mrs. Littleton went to bed that night, Kate's light was still on. Samantha Littleton thought of checking to see if her daughter was okay, but her husband persuaded her not to. When Kate was in one of her moods, it was best to leave her alone.

"Tread with care," AP's father warned him the following evening. "Your sister's having a bad day!"

"What's wrong?"

"I have no idea. She's hardly spoken a word, not even on her cell phone. No text messaging either!"

"Where is she now?"

"Two guesses."

AP nodded. "I'll go upstairs and see what I can do."

"You're a braver man than me!"

"Kate?" AP called, knocking gently on her door.

No reply.

"Kate?"

Plucking up his courage, he turned the handle and opened the door.

Kate was lying on her bed listening to her iPod. She barely reacted when she saw him.

"Can I come in?" he asked, loudly enough to be heard over the music in her ears.

"Suit yourself." She shrugged.

"What's bugging you?"

"Nothing's bugging me. Everything's fine."

"*Sure.*"

"Just go away and leave me alone."

"I want to help."

"Well you can't, so forget it."

"Remember Camelot? We looked out for each other then, didn't we?"

He thought he saw the slightest nod.

"How about another trip? I've got a great idea."

Seconds passed.

"Where to?"

AP knew he'd got her attention. "Montana."

Kate sat up and pulled off her ear buds. "Montana?"

"It's a cool place. And an amazing time period—June, 1876."

"What's so special about that?"

"The Little Bighorn."

"Is that some sort of cattle?"

"It's a river."

She stared at him blankly.

"Custer?" he said, expecting her to clue in. "General Custer and the Battle of the Little Bighorn."

That got a reaction.

"There's no way we're getting involved in any battles. I had enough of them in medieval England."

"We'd be nowhere near the battleground. We can find out about it by talking with the locals."

Kate sat in silence—pondering. Things could hardly be any worse for her.

"When should we go?" asked AP, pushing his luck.

"Right away," Kate replied.

"Like, *now*?" AP was stunned.

"Don't you want to go, then?"

"Sure I do. I'll get the abacus and we're out of here."

12

Buffalo!

K ate lay on her back staring up at a vast blue sky. How could it be so big? She closed her eyes, breathing in the fragrance of flowers and fresh grass. It was like the first days of summer.

"Are you ever going to move?" AP's voice rang through her head like an alarm bell, ending the daydream.

She stood up beside him and gazed around in wonder. The grassy plain, with its gently rolling hills, went on forever, with barely a tree in sight.

"This is *so* beautiful," sighed Kate. "Look at all the colors. And I've never seen such tall grass—it's above our knees."

"It's taller farther east. Way over my head."

"Grass doesn't grow *that* tall."

"Not in the twenty-first century, but it does in *these* times."

Kate looked doubtful.

"This was one huge grassland before the settlers turned the prairies into farmland. Speaking of prairies—" He smirked. "Did you ever see *Little House on the Prairie*?"

"Yeah, why?"

"You'd fit right in," he said, looking her up and down.

Kate was wearing a long gray dress that almost reached her ankles, with a button-up collar, long sleeves with cuffs, and big pockets. Her laced-up boots looked scuffed and worn. The only splash of color was a blue bonnet, tied beneath her chin with a white bow.

"What about you then, Mr. Smarty-pants? You've got a scruffy old shirt, *suspenders*, and your pants are *way* too short. As for the battered cowboy hat—"

"I think I look good," AP grinned, and spun around on the spot.

Kate immediately burst out laughing.

"What's so funny?" he asked, as if she'd hurt his feelings.

"It's your—*butt!*" she blurted between howls. "The seat of your pants has a *huge* patch!"

"So?"

"Well, your pants are black, and the patch is blue. You look like Bozo the Clown!" She howled again.

"Are we discussing my clothes all morning, or are we going exploring?"

"Lead on," she said, wiping her eyes. "Though how do we know which way to go?"

"We don't. That's why we're going climbing." He nodded toward a hill. "We'll get a good view from up there."

After checking to see that the abacus was safe, he shoved both hands into his pockets. "Hey, what's this?" he said. "A pencil and paper. That'll come in handy."

They'd been walking for ten minutes and the hill was still a way off. Distances could be deceiving in this terrain.

"Anyone for rabbit pie?" AP joked as a rabbit hopped away. "This place is teeming with them."

"I'm not hungry right now," said Kate, "but what *are* we going to eat?"

"Well?" He nodded toward another rabbit.

"You wouldn't."

"What's the choice? We have to live off the land—there are no stores!"

"Look," she whispered, pointing off to the right.

A small herd of deer was grazing in the sun, unaware of their presence. As they watched, a buck raised his antlered head and stared at them. Others followed until they were under the gaze of the entire herd. Eventually, the deer returned to feeding.

"I've never been so close to deer before," said Kate. "This place is *wild*."

"The whole country was like this before 'development' took over."

A hummingbird appeared from nowhere. After hovering for a few seconds, it shot off to a bright red flower.

"I hope there are no snakes," Kate groaned, remembering a camping trip out west. Their father had constantly reminded them to watch where they stepped.

"Just remember what Dad always says," offered AP.

"Stay alert!" they sang in unison, and burst out laughing. Nevertheless, they kept focused on where they were walking.

Kate and AP were unaware they were being followed. Their stalker—a tall, thin man—had been trailing them since their arrival. At first, they were small specks in the distance. Now he was close enough to hear their laughter. He must be especially careful. If they spotted him and ran, they'd likely get away—he was not athletic, and they were young. He had to get close enough to rush at them. Locking onto his target like a predator to its prey, he was determined to catch them.

Unlike the youngsters, he had little experience with the outdoors. Although aware of rattlesnakes, they held no significance, so he was not looking out for them.

When the rattlesnake struck, he thought a stick had hit him on the foot. Then the most excruciating, burning pain followed, and he fell to the ground writhing. The snake had already slithered away. He wanted to scream, but they would hear him, so he clenched his teeth in silence. Tears ran down his cheeks, and his forehead glistened with sweat.

Tearing off his boot and sock, he lay in agony, watching his foot swell like a balloon. His heart was racing, and his tongue began tingling. Was he going to die? Would he ever walk again? Those kids were getting away, but survival was all that mattered now.

❀　❀　❀

AP and Kate had been traveling almost an hour and still not reached the top of the hill.

"It's a lot higher than I thought," AP admitted.

"And farther away," Kate complained. "Let's take a break."

Nothing could have prepared them for what they saw on cresting the hill and looking down on the other side.

"What's *that*?" gasped Kate.

A large valley stretched before them, shimmering in a heat haze. And there, dancing in the distance, was a huge brown mat. It was as if a shaggy carpet had come to life, throwing dust clouds from the valley floor.

"Buffalo," said AP, though he knew the proper name was bison.

"No way!" said Kate. "If that *was* a herd of buffalo, there would be *hundreds* of them."

"Thousands," corrected AP.

"Buffalo are *massive*—I've seen them at the zoo—there can't be *that* many!"

"I read that fifty million buffalo roamed North America before the settlers arrived. And do you see that green line on the other side of the herd?"

She nodded.

"It's trees, growing along a riverbank."

Soon Kate and AP were walking across a wide-open plain, with stark badlands in the distance.

"It's so hot and dry down here," said Kate. "That grass looks as parched as my throat feels."

"I know what you mean," rasped AP. "All I can taste is dust."

"This is serious. Are you sure there's a river over there?"

"Positive. You saw it too."

"I saw something green, that's all. I'm still not convinced we were seeing buffalo either." Kate scanned the skyline as they walked. "You can't even make out that brown swirly thing anymore."

"That's because we're down much lower, so the horizon's closer. But you *can* see the dust cloud, and I bet thousands of hooves are throwing that up."

According to AP, they'd been walking in the valley for under an hour. Kate disagreed.

"Two hours at least. And—"

Without warning Kate stopped dead, body rigid, eyes fixed, mouth agape. Finally, she uttered, "Hundreds of buffalo—coming straight for us. What are we going to do?"

"Stay still," stammered AP. "Try not to scare them."

Kate, petrified with fear, wondered how she could possibly frighten the enormous beasts heading their way. If the herd took fright and stampeded, their hooves would trample them to death. But there was nowhere to hide, so they had to stay where they were. Seeing the look of terror on his sister's face steadied AP.

"It'll be alright," he said, trying to convince himself too.

Some of the buffalo brushed against them as they walked by—AP and Kate could smell their musty odor. Terrified, Kate stared at their sharp horns, imagining the damage they could inflict.

The buffalo, for their part, seemed uninterested in humans. Apart from a few grunts and some stares, most walked past staring dolefully ahead with huge brown eyes, like commuters on a train. Kate and AP, realizing nothing terrible was going to happen, began to relax.

Aside from their sheer size, their unusual shape impressed Kate most. Their massive shoulders—as high as she was tall—overshadowed the rest of their bodies, even the huge, low-slung heads. Remarkably, their tongues were black, as if they'd been chewing licorice.

"Wow!" exclaimed Kate, when the last of the stragglers had passed. "That was unbelievable."

For once, AP was speechless.

❋   ❋   ❋

Kate peered at the sun. "I figure it's late afternoon—we've got about five hours before dark."

"We've got to do a lot in that time."

"And finding water is the first thing." Kate slumped down to the dusty ground. "I've never been so thirsty in my life."

"Me neither. Let's take a rest. Then we'll find that river."

They sat in silence, each thinking the same thing—if they didn't get something to drink, they would die. After several long minutes, AP stood up and scanned the horizon.

"That's more like it. Now the dust has settled, we can see again."

Kate, still sitting, squinted up at him. From the grin on his face, she knew he'd found what he was looking for.

"Trees," he announced triumphantly. "Look for yourself."

"Okay, Smarty-pants," she agreed. "So there *are* trees over there. The big question is, will there be any water?"

"Guaranteed."

"How can you say that?"

"When the pioneers crossed the Great Plains, they were always looking for one tree—the cottonwood."

"So?"

"So those trees are cottonwoods. And cottonwoods are usually found beside water."

"Usually!" she blurted. "What happened to your *guarantee*?"

"Just look at the way they're lined up. They have to be growing along a riverbank."

"I hope you're right, AP. Otherwise we're in trouble."

"I know," he said grimly.

All the time the trees were a long way off, they could travel in hope of spotting a river. But as they drew closer, they dreaded seeing nothing but dust. Neither one spoke. Kate's heart began to race. Then she saw it. Letting out a great whoop, she started running. AP was right behind her.

"That feels *so* good," said Kate, closing her eyes in ecstasy. She was sitting with her back against a steep riverbank, long dress hoisted up to her knees. She had used her bonnet as a facecloth, and water was still trickling down her neck. AP, crouched like a dog at the river's edge, had his face in the water. All she could see was his backside and the enormous blue patch on his pants.

"Hey, Bozo, have you had enough yet?"

AP stood up, dripping water and smiling. "Did water ever taste that good?"

"Never!" Then a thought struck her. "What if it's unsafe to drink?"

"No problem—pollution hasn't been invented yet!"

"Any idea what river this is? It's huge."

"Maybe the Powder. That's one of the large rivers around here. They all flow north, into the Yellowstone. Here, I'll show you." Picking up a stick, he drew a line in the gravel. "The Yellowstone River runs east to west." Drawing four vertical lines beneath it, he pointed to the one on the right. "The one in the east is the Powder River."

Kate pretended to be listening.

"The Bighorn is in the west, and its side branch is the Little Bighorn."

"The Little Bighorn!" yelled Kate. "That's where the battle took place."

AP nodded.

"But you said we'd be nowhere near the battleground."

"And we're not. If this *is* the Powder River, we're a hundred miles to the east."

"Sounds close to me."

"That's because you're thinking in modern times, with cars and highways. A trip like that would take days on horseback.

"I'm starving," he said, changing the subject.

"Me too." Kate's stomach rumbled, perfectly on cue. "What are we going to eat?"

"Suppose I catch a rabbit?"

"How do you plan to do that, oh brave hunter?"

"I could build a trap," he said hopefully.

"What's Plan B?"

"Okay, check this out," he said, clambering up the bank. Cottonwood trees lined the river on both sides, and a tangle of plants grew in the shade. Their greens contrasted with the browns beyond. AP pointed to an ankle-high plant that spread everywhere and was dotted with small red berries.

"Here, try these," he said, picking a handful and popping some in his mouth.

"You can't eat those!" she shrieked. "They could be poisonous."

"Don't you recognize them?" He held out his hand. "They're wild strawberries."

After picking strawberries, they set to work building a shelter for the night—when the sun set in a couple of hours, it would get cold. All they did was lay branches against a fallen tree, filling the gaps with twigs and piling on dried grass and leaves for insulation. They topped this off with more branches to hold it all in place. By leaving both ends open, they each had their own entrance.

AP used armfuls of leaves to build his mattress, but Kate, who seldom felt the cold, was less fussy with hers.

Before crawling into bed, AP spent a few minutes scanning the night sky. Kate, already comfortable, was dozing off.

"Did you notice the moon?" he called out.

"No," she said, yawning.

"It's really neat—the thinnest crescent. And it's on the *left* side. Does that mean it's going to get thicker or thinner?"

Kate groaned. "Left means less so it's going to get thinner! Now let me *sleep*."

AP scribbled a note on his piece of paper.

13

Talking Cloud

"Y ou fidgeted all night," Kate complained the next morning. "I hardly slept."

"Sorry. I was dreaming about buffalo eating ice cream. Probably all those strawberries we ate."

"And guess what's for breakfast?"

"I'll pass," said AP.

"You have to eat."

"Not right now. We'll find something later—there must be plenty of fish in the river."

"So what's the plan?" asked Kate. "Hang out here for a while?"

"Better to keep moving. If we follow the river down-stream, we'll reach the Yellowstone. There'll be steamboats —lots of people—so we can find out what's happening."

"Sounds good to me," said Kate. "Let's go."

In contrast to the parched terrain of the previous after-noon, they were now traveling along a lush green corridor beside the river, which was on their right. The water was deep in parts, but there were many places where they could have waded across.

AP nodded toward the sandstone hills, banded like a layer cake, on their left. "How far away are those badlands?"

"At least a mile," guessed Kate. "They look so desolate. I'd rather have this." As she gazed around, something caught her eye down by the river.

"See over there," she said, pointing. "A huge dog. What's *that* doing out here?"

Shading his eyes against the glare, AP stared long and hard.

"That's no dog," he said finally. "It's a grizzly bear."

As they watched, the grizzly plunged into the water and came up with a large trout wriggling in its mouth.

Soon they discovered that the river was teeming with fishes—there were turtles too.

A blue heron swooped low across the water. "I can't believe it," Kate marveled. "It's like we're in some exotic land. We never saw *this* much wildlife on that camping trip with Mum and Dad."

"Goes to show how people have changed things," said AP thoughtfully.

Both walked on in silence, captivated by the unspoiled beauty.

Later that day, AP became aware of an unfamiliar sound. "Do you hear that?" he asked.

"What?"

"Like the rumbling of thunder."

They stood still, listening.

"Okay," said Kate, "I hear it now. Sort of a drumming in the distance, and it's getting louder. You can almost feel it through the ground. Is it an earthquake?"

"No," said AP, "it's coming from over there." He pointed away from the river. "Let's check it out."

Before going far they both saw what was making the noise—buffalo! Hundreds of them, charging across the plain toward the river.

"Quick!" AP shouted, grabbing Kate's arm. "Run for the trees!"

They threw themselves behind the nearest tree, wishing it was bigger. Peering around it, they saw the stampede was heading straight for them. The sound of pounding hooves and snapping branches was unbelievable. AP looked around nervously. He wondered if their tree would withstand the onslaught.

AP watched in grim fascination as the lead buffalo closed the gap. Soon it was so close he could see the terror in its eyes. Then, at the last moment, it swerved away and the rest followed.

Kate gasped. "That was *so* close. I thought we'd be killed."

"Me too. I wonder what spooked—"

The next instant they saw the cause of the stampede—Sioux horsemen were chasing the herd.

"What do we do?" shrieked Kate. "Those warriors will attack us!"

"Keep calm," said AP, sounding more composed than he felt. "They're too busy hunting to bother with us. And they can't see through solid wood." He banged the trunk to emphasize his point. "Besides, maybe they're friendly.

"Look at those guys go!" cried AP. "How do they stay on their horses like that?"

Kate peeked cautiously.

"They're riding without saddles," said AP, "using their knees to guide their horses. That leaves both hands free to fire their bows."

The riders seemed to flow with the motion of the horses. They were bare to the waist, their pigtails streaming out behind them.

"See that?" yelled AP. "A buffalo tried to butt that guy's horse, and he just swerved away—the horns barely missed him."

As he spoke, the hunter swung his horse back again. Then, with horse and buffalo charging neck and neck, he pulled back the bowstring and fired. The arrow streaked across the narrow gap, burying itself into the buffalo's chest. In a flash, the hunter drew a second arrow from the quiver and shot again. The buffalo kept running, but was slowing down. A third arrow followed, and the buffalo crashed to the ground, dead.

"Wow," exclaimed AP. "That was *awesome*."

"That was *horrible*," rebuked Kate. "The poor buffalo. How could anyone kill an animal like that?"

"They're hunting for food, Kate. Without buffalo the people would starve."

"They should find other things to eat."

"Like wild strawberries?"

Kate had more important things on her mind to bother replying. "We ought to plan our escape route while they're still busy," she said.

"Good idea," agreed AP. "If we can make it down to the riverbed, we'll be out of sight."

"That's just what I was thinking."

"The tricky part is getting there without being spotted," said AP. "We'll have to crawl on our stomachs. Ready?"

Using their elbows and knees, they wriggled through the grass like lizards. Kate, more athletic than her brother, was well in front. Minutes later they arrived at the river and slithered down the bank.

"Do you think they saw us?" asked Kate anxiously.

"There's only one way to find out. Stay here while I peek over the top."

AP returned, looking grim-faced.

"What's wrong?" she gasped.

"I saw over a dozen warriors. Heavily armed."

"What can we do?"

"Just keep going," he said with a grin. "They're still busy chasing buffalo!"

"Arthur Percival!" she said, grabbing his collar. "I could STRANGLE YOU!"

They started walking, enjoying the sights and sounds of the river again. One unexpected occurrence was a flock of white pelicans, flying overhead. "I thought they were seabirds," said AP, chewing on a stalk of grass.

The babbling of the river was gently soothing. A brilliant gold butterfly flitted into view and landed on Kate's shoulder.

"That's a good omen," said an unfamiliar voice from above.

Glancing up, they saw an old man sitting comfortably on an overhanging bough. He wore a knee-length deerskin shirt fringed with tassels. His tight-fitting leggings were a darker shade of tan, as were his moccasins. The weatherbeaten face was lined with age, the wrinkles revealing a man accustomed to smiling. His black hair was braided into two waist-length pigtails.

He seemed friendly and AP thought it only polite to reply.

"I didn't know that—about butterflies," he began awkwardly. "We're not from here."

"Where are you from?" There was nothing intimidating in his question.

"We're from the east," explained AP, pointing in that direction.

The old man smiled and nodded. Then, glancing down at Kate, he asked, "Is she your woman?"

"Who, Kate?" blurted AP, surprised at the question. "No! She's my *sister*."

"Huh," the man grunted, throwing back his head. "She's dressed wrong."

Then turning back to AP, "And your clothes are not those of a young blood." There was no hint of suspicion—he was simply curious. He sat pondering for several moments. "You people puzzle me," he began again. "You dress like white folk. You look like white folk. Yet you speak with our tongue. How is that so?"

AP's mind was racing to come up with a likely story, but the old man resolved the problem for him. "You were taken by the Sioux when you were young. Your parents died, and my people raised you like their own. Is this so?"

"Yes," agreed AP, "that's exactly what happened."

Kate smiled and nodded too.

"We stayed with our Sioux family for three summers and three winters," AP said, slipping into this new role. "Then we were taken back east." He emphasized the word "taken" to suggest it was against their will.

"We have been away from this land too long," continued AP, noticing Kate's astonished expression. "Now we've returned."

"So much has changed in our world," said the old man sadly. Then he asked, "What name do they call you out east?"

"Arthur Percival," AP replied after a moment's hesitation.

"That is a bad name." Then, with a twinkle in his eye, he said, "I will call you Young Man Who Sits Too Much."

Turning to Kate, he said, "You shall be Gold Butterfly Woman. It is a lucky name—you will have a good life."

Kate smiled at the old man. And for reasons she couldn't explain, she felt a closeness, like the bond she had shared with her grandfather.

"What is *your* name?" asked AP.

The old man smiled. "I am Talking Cloud." Grasping an overhead branch, he stood up from his comfortable perch. "Come. We will go to the village now. You have chosen a good day to return—the hunting goes well, and there will be feasting tonight."

What Talking Cloud meant by a "village" is what Kate and AP would have called a campsite—a scattering of tents in an idyllic spot where campers could be at one with nature. But this was like no campsite they knew. The towering tipis would have dwarfed their tiny pup tent, and there was so much activity. Children and dogs ran wild, while adults attended to chores or relaxed in the shade.

Two small boys sneaked up on a rack of buffalo meat drying in the sun. Using a tipi for cover, they waited until the woman preparing the meat turned her back. Then they each made a grab for a tasty treat. When she spotted them, all they got was a mock scolding. Dashing off, they joined a band of hunters who were running and whooping between tipis, aiming make-believe bows at imaginary buffalo. Several dogs joined in the chase. When the woman returned to her work, she noticed that Talking Cloud had returned.

Talking Cloud made several stops along the way to greet people, giving Kate and AP an opportunity to talk alone.

"How come everyone's so friendly?" asked Kate. "We've just walked into their village, a pair of total strangers— *white* strangers—and nobody minds."

"I guess it's because we're with Talking Cloud. Things might be different if we came here on our own."

"I think he's the chief," said Kate.

"He could be," agreed AP. "Everyone listens to him. When he comes back, ask him."

Kate's question amused Talking Cloud. "You've been living with the Wasichus—the white folk—too long! We don't have chiefs like they do, each reporting to the one above. Our people do what they want."

"But they listen to you," Kate reasoned.

"People listen to me and to other old men." He smiled. "With wrinkles comes wisdom, they say."

"Do the people ask elders for guidance?" Kate continued.

"They seek our advice, and we give it. Nobody tells anyone what to do, though. We have some great leaders, but they don't rule."

AP pointed to the tipis. "Do the same people live here all the time?"

"We come together for spring and summer to hunt game. Some also spend winter together, while others go their own way.

"Are you all from the same tribe?"

"Yes. We are Oglala Sioux. Part of the Sioux Nation." He stared at the village, as if searching for something. Then he closed his eyes. "Young Man Who Sits Too Much, how many tipis do you see?"

AP counted them quickly. "Twenty-two."

"Is that all?"

AP counted again. "Yes."

"Do you know how many I see?" asked Talking Cloud, eyes still closed. "More tipis than stars in the heavens.

"Once, we were many people from different Sioux tribes—Lakota, Nakota, Santee, Hunkpapa—together with our Cheyenne and Arapaho brothers. They were good times."

He stood for a moment, and then opened his eyes. "Enough talk. Come, you must meet Sings To Her Children."

Arriving outside his own tipi, Talking Cloud gestured for Kate and AP to enter. After the hot sun, it was cooler and dark inside. Compared with the tents they knew, the tipi was a mansion. The walls tapered high above their heads, with a smoke hole at the top for the fireplace below. "This is my wife, Sings To Her Children," he announced, introducing an elderly woman the same height as AP. "My dear, this is Gold Butterfly Woman and her brother, Young Man Who Sits Too Much."

His wife grinned, revealing more gaps than teeth. She was happy to meet them and, with typical Sioux hospitality, invited them to use her tipi as their own.

Talking Cloud made more introductions. "This is my second wife, Running Deer. She is my wife's youngest sister. I married Running Deer after her husband was killed during a raid on the Crow tribe."

His second wife was equally friendly, and just as old.

"And this is my older brother, Sleeps A Lot, and his wife, Buffalo Woman."

His brother shuffled forward, yawning and stretching.

"So many names," thought AP. "But I'll remember *his*!"

While AP talked with Talking Cloud and his brother, the women led Kate away.

"We've so much room," Sings To Her Children told Kate. "Most families sleep eight and more." Then, pointing to a pile of buffalo-hide blankets, "I'll put you and your brother here. I hope you'll be comfortable."

Kate thanked her and said they'd be fine.

"We usually cook the evening meal at this time," she continued, "but tonight there's a feast and—"

Suddenly a loud commotion erupted outside. Shouting and screaming heralded the thunder of hooves as riders charged through the village. Then the shooting began.

"We're being attacked!" yelled AP.

Talking Cloud was first out of the tipi, followed by his family. AP and Kate were last. They just stood there, terrified, not knowing what to do or where to run.

"They're back!" shouted Talking Cloud. "Let's give them a good welcome."

Kate and AP exchanged bewildered stares.

"The buffalo hunters have returned!" cried their host. "Be prepared for some brave talk!"

"I am the greatest hunter in the land," yelled one young brave, waving his bow. "My arrows flew fast and true. I took two buffalo!"

"Only two?" shouted a second. "I got twice that number!"

"I killed more buffalo than either of you!" shouted a third. "My bow hand was flying so fast it was invisible."

"See this?" yelled another, holding up a rifle. "I shot more buffalo with my fire-stick than all you bow-pullers together!" He was one of the few with a firearm.

The boasts and taunts continued, until the aroma of roasting meat proved too much for them.

"Their bellies are bigger than their tongues!" scoffed Talking Cloud. "But first, they must cleanse themselves." Kate thought he meant the usual washing of hands before dinner, but she was wrong.

"Buffalo, like birds in the air or humans on the land, have spirits. Everything has a spirit, even the smallest pebble. And everything is connected by Wakan Tanka, the supreme power of the universe."

Kate and AP wondered where all this was leading.

"When an animal has been killed, the taker of that life must make peace with its spirit. This clears the record, restoring balance to the universe. By appealing to the spirits of the buffalo they have killed, hunters ensure that others will be willing to die in future."

The fire pit reminded AP and Kate of the one in medieval England, except it was larger and the spits longer. And these were skewered with big buffalo roasts instead of sizzling pigs. The feast itself bore little resemblance to the Arthurian one. Held outdoors, without tables or chairs, it was more like a picnic than a banquet. Everyone sat on the ground wherever they pleased, with no special places for elders. Although it seemed casual, people dressed up for the occasion, and most of the men wore a single eagle feather in their hair. Without speeches or wine, there was no raucous cheering, and everyone was content to chat among themselves and focus on the serious business of eating.

"I can't believe people's appetites!" whispered Kate, nodding toward one lady. She was tearing bites from a piece of meat bigger than what the Littletons usually had for Sunday dinner.

"But it was *so* good," said AP. "Even you ate a lot!"

Kate nodded, smiling.

The feasting continued late into the night, with people returning to the fire pit time and again to hack off more meat.

"Would it be okay if we went to bed before Talking Cloud?" asked AP, stifling a yawn.

She glanced across at the old man, engrossed in a lively discussion about hunting.

"I think so. Let's go."

❈ ❈ ❈

Kate and AP's adventures in the West had been enjoyable so far—aside from their water shortage and the stampede scare. But for the man who was stalking them, things had gone disastrously wrong from the start.

14

Robert Drew

When Robert Drew opened his eyes and saw the sky, he knew he was still alive. His swollen foot was turning purple, and he barely recognized the sausages that used to be toes. He gulped from his water bottle, stopping himself in case he drank it dry. Without help, death was certain.

Keeping the weight on the good leg, he struggled to his feet.

The grass, blowing in the breeze like an ocean, seemed to go on forever. Then he spotted a lone tree, off in the distance. Although stunted, it would be visible for miles in this terrain. If he could tie his shirt to a branch, someone might notice and come to investigate. This was his only hope.

Hopping to the tree was exhausting—the pain unbearable—but he made it. After a short rest, he pulled off his shirt, reached as high as possible and tied it on. Slumping to the ground, he took a short drink—the bottle was half empty.

The rest of the day was spent drifting in and out of sleep. As he lay there, trying to ignore his raging thirst, he heard an unfamiliar jangling. He struggled to his feet, but his good leg buckled and he tumbled to the ground.

"Lucky I saw your shirt," said his rescuer. "You wouldn't have lasted another day the shape you're in."

The injured man nodded without taking the bottle from his lips. Like his own water canister, this one was flat and round and made of tin—but it was full.

"Now you can drink all you want, I've plenty more, but it does no good filling your belly like that."

"You're right," he replied, lowering the bottle. "I'm so thirsty, though."

"My name's Sam Carter, though the Indians call me One Tooth." He grinned, leaving no doubt how he got his name. "What's yours?"

"Robert Drew. And I'm *so* thankful to meet you." He struggled to shake hands, but Sam stopped him.

"You just stay put—you're too weak to move—and let me see that foot.

"It looks *real* nasty," he said after a brief examination. "What happened?"

"A rattlesnake bit me."

Sam Carter let out a low whistle. "You should've been more careful where you was walking, boy. Nobody gets bit by a rattler!" He shook his head. "You ain't from these parts, right?"

"No. I'm from out east. Philadelphia."

"You sure look like a city dweller."

Robert Drew frowned—he thought he looked the part with his cowboy hat and boots.

Sam shook his head, smiling. "Apart from getting yourself bit," he began to explain, "your hands are as smooth as a baby's. Your bones have no meat on them either!"

Robert Drew was painfully thin, and without a shirt, he was a living skeleton. Every rib showed, and his spine stuck out like a row of knucklebones. Even his face was bony, with its sharply-pointed nose and high cheekbones. He was in his early forties, though his blond hair and sharp features made him look younger.

"You're real lucky, boy!" said Sam after a closer inspection of his foot. "That ol' rattler missed you with one of his fangs, so you only got half the poison. Mind you, if you'd done your boots up right, he'd have missed you altogether."

"My foot will be alright then?"

"It'll hurt for a few days, but you'll be back to normal in a week or so."

Drew was so relieved at this that he managed a smile.

"Just sit tight," said Sam, making toward his mules. "I've got something that'll help the swelling."

Sam had six mules, one for riding and the others for hauling. They were piled high with packs of all shapes and sizes containing kettles, pans, mugs, jugs, brushes, choppers and knives.

Like his mules, Sam was short and stocky. He wore a tall, battered hat with a long feather, an old army jacket with unmatched pants and worn-out boots. His ruddy face always looked happy.

"I'm a trader," Sam told his guest over supper before a campfire. "I also mend pots, grind axes, sharpen blades, make brooms and fix things. A jack-of-all-trades!"

"And an excellent cook!"

Sam nodded at the compliment.

"Who do you trade with?"

"Anyone and everyone. Indians, settlers, the Army— they're all good customers."

"What do you get from the Indians?"

"Mostly buffalo hides. Dried meat and pemmican too— that comes in handy during winter."

"Are the Indians friendly?"

"Sure. I get along with them fine. I've been trading with the Indians all my life. Be fair with them, and they'll treat you right." He tossed more wood on the fire and started brewing a pot of coffee.

"So, Robert Drew, what brings you to Montana? You're obviously not here to trade with the Sioux!"

"Family business," he replied vaguely.

Sam looked puzzled.

"My brother's kids." He paused, scratching an imaginary itch while he thought about his story. "They—ran away from home. The family's worried sick. I've got to find them."

"How old are they?"

"The boy's about twelve, his sister's a few years older."

"Where are they from?"

"Well, they *were* from the east—originally. Born and raised in Philadelphia. But my brother decided to move out west and start farming."

"How long ago?"

"Three years."

"And how long have the kids been gone?"

"A few days."

Sam pulled an old rag from his pocket to lift the hot coffee from the fire.

"Maybe they'll meet up with some homesteaders." Sam paused to pour the coffee. "More likely, Indians will pick them up. You can tag along with me when you're feeling better—I'm visiting all the hunting camps. If anyone's seen or heard of those kids, I'll be the first to know." Sam smiled. "Indians *love* to talk."

Robert Drew's sudden alertness had nothing to do with the strong coffee.

15

Counting Coup

K ate awoke to the sound of snoring. She could see blue sky through the top of the tipi, and AP was already awake.

"I've been lying here for ages," he whispered. "I couldn't sleep with all this noise. Let's get dressed and sneak outside."

The village didn't stir until late morning. Even then— with meat to dry, hides to clean, and all the other chores— nobody was in a hurry to do anything.

"You got up early," said Talking Cloud, sitting cross-legged outside his tipi. "You don't like sleep?"

"Yes I do!" said Kate, who seldom awoke before 10 on weekends. "I just saw the sun and felt like getting up."

"The sun's still there." He glanced up at the sky. "No need to leave bed so early to see it."

The hunters were riding out for buffalo again that afternoon, and Talking Cloud invited Kate and AP to go along. He asked the question in such a way that refusal would have been impolite. So they accepted.

"Good," said Talking Cloud. "Now we must find you proper clothes. I'll talk with Sings To Her Children."

"Awesome!" exclaimed AP later, astonished at the transformation in his sister. Kate wore a simple deerskin dress that hung straight down from her neck to below her calves. Fringed with long tassels, it shimmered when she moved. She also wore deerskin leggings and moccasins. Her hair was parted at the center and braided.

"Gold Butterfly Woman," thought her brother—the name was perfect.

"Okay, it's your turn," said Kate, smiling.

Minutes later AP emerged from the tipi wearing a long-sleeved shirt and leggings, both made from deerskin edged with tassels, like Kate's dress. In front he wore what appeared to be a cloth apron, with a second one behind.

"Young Man Who Sits Too Much," said Kate, "you look good!"

"Well, these leggings feel weird. They're just the leg part, held up by straps attached to my belt." AP looked uneasy.

"There's no backside?" Kate asked with a smirk.

"Exactly. I'm wearing this diaper thing instead." He pointed to the apron flaps, back and front.

She began to giggle.

"What's so funny?"

This made her laugh even more.

Talking Cloud had planned to keep up with the hunters, but when he saw Kate and AP trying to mount their horses, he changed his mind.

"You have done little riding," he observed.

"We've ridden a *bit*," Kate admitted, remembering an hour spent one summer holiday.

Finally, they got into their saddles and the trio departed.

The young braves trotted past, each with a second horse in tow.

"Once buffalo are sighted," Talking Cloud explained, "each hunter will swap the saddled mount that he's riding for his running horse."

With Talking Cloud's guidance, the novice riders grew more confident. And as they trotted along at their leisurely pace, he pointed out animals they would otherwise have missed. A clump of bushes appeared, some way off. When he asked if they could see the deer feeding there, they thought he was joking. Only after they stopped and stared for a while did they see the large buck with its rack of antlers.

Talking Cloud explained how animal signs could be read. He pointed to a distant flock of black birds that had suddenly swooped down behind a rise. "They're after insects, disturbed by horses' hooves." To prove his point, the trio headed that way and sighted a herd of wild ponies over the hill.

He spoke of the old days. "Once, the whole land teemed with game—herds of buffalo, elk, deer, pronghorn..." Talking Cloud sighed wistfully. "Now the Powder River country is the last place we can find enough game."

"We white people," said AP gloomily. "We messed everything up."

"Not at first. When I was a boy, things were good between us and the settlers. They traveled freely across our land. We were happy to help them. When they were lost, we guided them. When they were hungry, we fed them. We traded buffalo hides and deerskins for things like knives and pots. All are one in Wakan Tanka's universe.

"The settlers were few at first. Then their numbers grew, like flies in summer. Soon, they were not content just to travel our land—they wanted to *own* it." He spread his arms wide.

"How can anyone own the land, or the sky or the air?"

He paused.

"They made us promises—their treaties. 'Let us have this piece of land,' they would say. 'You shall have the rest, and live there in peace.' But they always broke their promises and took more land. They built forts, and the soldiers attacked us, just for being here.

"The Wasichus had no use for certain land. They said we should go and live there, on reservations. We would be safe. Instead of following the buffalo across the plains, they wanted us to become farmers, like them. Pah!"

Talking Cloud pointed out a herd of pronghorns, which had stopped feeding to watch them go by.

"They bribed us and threatened us, and many bands went to live on the reservations. The Wasichus said Indians could have white-man's things, like coffee and sugar. Food would always be plentiful, they said, but the agents who run the reservations make mistakes and Agency Indians go hungry.

"How many Indians live on reservations?" asked AP.

"Most of them."

"Have you tried it?"

"Never. I will live my life on the open plains, free like the buffalo."

"And there are still lots of *them*," said Kate.

"Yes. But when the iron horse pushes farther west, all the buffalo will be gone."

"Why's that?" she asked. "Do the trains frighten them away?"

Talking Cloud shook his head and smiled a sad smile. "White hunters ride the iron horse. They shoot buffalo by the thousands. Some don't even bother taking the hides to send back east—they just kill for pleasure, leaving the carcasses to rot in the sun." He looked down at the ground. "The Wasichus know that when the buffalo are finished, so are we."

AP and Kate exchanged dismayed looks.

By late afternoon they had caught up with the hunters, who were busy butchering the kill. Kate didn't want to watch, but AP was interested in the process, so Talking Cloud took him closer while Kate stayed back.

Working in small groups, the hunters began by skinning the carcass with sharp knives. Once the hide was free, they folded it into a bundle, tying it with strips cut from the pelt.

"Good thing Kate isn't watching," said AP as they slit open a carcass, spilling intestines onto the ground. Then, plunging their hands deep inside the body, the hunters cut off wedges of warm liver to eat.

"Try some," said Talking Cloud, offering AP a slice. "It's good!"

"No thanks."

After carving large slabs of meat from the carcass, they tied them onto the sides of a waiting horse.

Talking Cloud explained how little was wasted. "We carve the bones and horns into tools and ornaments. We boil some of the hooves to make glue, and others become ceremonial rattles." He pointed to one of the hunters who was cutting something large from the pile of intestines—he was covered in green glop. "That's the stomach. We use them to make cooking pots."

When they returned to the village, Sings To Her Children was busy inside the tipi preparing the meal. A low fire burned in the middle of the floor, and something smelled good. Kate asked if she could help.

"That's a first," thought AP. "She never volunteers at home."

"You can keep this hot," said Sings To Her Children. She was squatting beside a large, round pot hanging beside the fireplace on a tripod.

"Here," she said, handing Kate a pair of sticks. "Use these to pick up the stone from the bottom of the pot."

Kate, looking confused, gave it a try.

Picking up a large stone with a pair of sticks is difficult, especially when it's sitting in a bubbling pot of stew. After several attempts, she succeeded.

"Good," said Sings To Her Children, "now swap it for one of those in the fire."

Plopping the wet stone into the fire, Kate picked up a hot one, lowering it into the stew with a loud sizzling.

They ate outside, sitting in the shade of the tipi.

"That was delicious," said Kate after the meal.

"The best stew ever," added AP.

Horse riding had given them large appetites, and both had returned for seconds.

"What was in it?" asked Kate.

Sings To Her Children smiled proudly and explained it was one of her special recipes. She then listed the ingredients. "Fresh turnips, dried corn, and a mixture of meats— buffalo, rabbit, turtle, crow, porcupine and dog."

Kate became quiet, but AP, recalling the cheese incident in medieval England, kept talking about it.

They sat outside until late evening, enjoying tales from the past—the Sioux were wonderful storytellers. Surprisingly, Sleeps A Lot stayed awake to the end, entertaining them with stories of the Sioux's favorite pastime: raiding the Crow, their traditional enemy.

"I was the bravest warrior in the band," he declared, and there was a chorus of agreement. "We had many battles with the Crow, and I counted more coup than any other warrior."

"What's counting coup?" asked AP.

"Hmm," pondered Sleeps A Lot, wondering where to begin. He was big on battles but small on explanations, so his brother stepped in.

"A man wins respect by his deeds," Talking Cloud explained. "For a warrior, bravery counts highest. The man with the highest number of brave acts is the greatest warrior."

Kate and AP nodded.

"The highest award for bravery is to count coup upon an enemy. This is done by touching him."

"Touching him?" queried AP. "So if Kate, um, Gold Butterfly Woman, was my enemy and I touched her on the shoulder, I'd score a bravery point?"

Talking Cloud shook his head. "No, that would be worthless because you're not fighting. Most coup counting is in battle—you approach your enemy and touch him." He paused. "But if you rode into his camp, burst into his tipi and touched him, that would count."

AP looked puzzled. "So, if a warrior *touches* another warrior during battle, but does nothing else to him, he wins a bravery point?"

"Yes. That is counting coup."

"What if the warrior kills his enemy instead of just touching him?"

"That is bravery too, though it doesn't score so highly."

This made no sense to AP—surely the idea of battle was to kill enemies. However, he didn't want to offend his host, so he tried another approach. "The warrior who's touched is lucky because he's unhurt and gets to fight again."

Talking Cloud and his brother were both horrified at this.

"To have coup counted against you is the greatest shame. Better to die in battle than suffer such disgrace."

"So the Sioux battle the Crow so they can count coup against them?"

Talking Cloud shrugged—the *reason* for waging war was unimportant. The Sioux fought the Crow because it was the proper thing to do.

"We take their horses too. Taking a horse from your enemy is honorable. And it is good for a man to have many horses."

"Me and my brother have *lots* of horses," offered Sleeps A Lot.

"Why do you want so many?" asked AP.

"Why do Wasichus want so much yellow metal?"

"So horses are like gold?"

The old men nodded.

"If a young man wants to marry a man's daughter," Talking Cloud began again, "he's expected to give a gift. A horse is a good gift." He smiled. "If she is pretty and many men want to marry her, a warrior may have to give her father many horses!"

Kate and AP went to bed that night knowing more about Sioux culture, yet understanding less.

16

The Sacred Hills

A P kept a daily calendar on his piece of paper. Talking Cloud would have been amused had he known because his people measured time in seasons, not days. The Sioux led a simple life, and having been with them for almost a week, Kate and AP had slipped into their familiar routine. Then one morning, without warning, everything changed.

"What's going on?" asked Kate as one after another tipi was dismantled.

"I've no idea," replied AP. "It looks like the whole village is packing up."

Taking down tipis involved only the women, and the men had little to do. Most of them just stood around chatting. Talking Cloud was sharpening a knife on a stone, so AP went over to ask what was happening.

"Time to pack up and go. Buffalo move, so we must follow."

Kate and AP asked Sings To Her Children if they could help. The old woman smiled, shaking her head. She and her sister could manage—they were used to it.

"The tipi belongs to the wife," Sings To Her Children explained, "so she does everything."

They'd already removed the buffalo-hide cover, leaving the framework of wooden poles still standing.

"See the ring of stones that were used to hold down the cover?" said AP, pointing at the ground.

Kate nodded absentmindedly.

"It's called a tipi ring and shows where a tipi once stood."

After spreading the semicircular tipi cover out on the ground, the two sisters started folding it up. The result was a heavy bundle the size of a refrigerator.

"That's made of twelve buffalo hides, sewn together with sinews," said AP.

"They only last about two years. No wonder they need so many buffalo."

Kate stared blankly.

Now the old women worked their way around the poles, lifting them off one by one. Three poles were left standing, firmly roped together at the crossover point.

"How are they going to handle *them*?" asked Kate. "We should help." But the women lowered them to the ground with ease.

Using strips of buffalo hide, they tied the poles into two bundles. Then they lashed the end of each bundle to the side of a horse, leaving the other end free to drag along the ground.

"That's pretty basic," commented AP.

"And how would *you* do it?"

"I'd load them onto a wagon."

"That's okay if you've got wheels," she said, "but they *don't*."

AP nodded sheepishly.

Two more horses were needed to carry the tipi cover and all their other belongings. Each had a V-shaped trailer for the job.

"That's called a travois," said AP. "It's a pair of poles tied together at the front and joined together halfway down by that narrow platform. See how it's attached to one side of the horse?"

"Yeah," she replied dutifully.

When everyone was ready, the band moved off. Many rode on horseback or hitched rides on the travois, but others walked. Mothers transported their babies in a carrier strapped to their backs or secured to a travois. Most toddlers rode piggyback, but others preferred bouncing along on a travois or sitting wedged in the saddle with an adult. Dogs—some pulling tiny travois—trotted everywhere.

Kate and AP rode horses. "You both need more practice," Talking Cloud told them as he showed them how to harness the horses and saddle up.

The band moved at the speed of the slowest walkers, so progress was modest. "That suits me fine," AP confided to Kate. "I'm still sore from yesterday's ride."

After trotting alone together for an hour, Kate and AP were joined by Talking Cloud and his brother. AP thought this an ideal opportunity to inquire about Custer. As soon as he mentioned the name, he got a reaction.

"Long Hair," said Talking Cloud in a flat voice. "Long Hair Custer."

His brother repeated the name and spat on the ground.

They rode on in silence, and AP wished he'd never said anything.

After some time, Talking Cloud began to speak.

"Young Man Who Sits Too Much, I must tell you about Paha Sapa and what has happened these last two summers and winters. This story is long, but we have far to go. Talking helps pass the time."

He began by explaining how Paha Sapa—the Black Hills of South Dakota—was the Indians' most sacred land. "It is a place of ghosts and sprits. A place where we can speak with Wakan Tanka. Few Wasichus have ever been there. They are not welcome."

He paused.

"White men went there, looking for yellow metal. Some found it and told others."

"And some never lived long enough to tell," added his brother gleefully.

"The Great Father in Washington was short of yellow metal. So, two summers ago, he sent Long Hair and his cavalry to Paha Sapa, to see if the stories were true.

"Long Hair found what he was looking for and told every Wasichu. They swarmed there like ants, tearing up our cherished land."

"But weren't white people supposed to stay away from that area?" asked AP.

"They made a treaty with us eight summers ago. Paha Sapa was ours—until the end of time."

"Another one of their broken treaties!" snorted Sleeps A Lot.

"Didn't anyone complain?" asked Kate.

"Some important Wasichus protested," said Talking Cloud.

"So what did the government do about it?" she continued.

"What it always does: it sent a commission—a gang of politicians and soldiers—to make a deal. The commission knew they had to include free Indians as well as Agency Indians in the talks—otherwise the deal wouldn't work. So they sent word to Sitting Bull and Crazy Horse."

Kate repeated the two names.

"Sitting Bull is leader of the Hunkpapa Sioux. Crazy Horse leads our tribe, the Oglala Sioux. Both refused to attend."

"So what happened?" asked AP.

"Most of their people still went along, together with our friends the Cheyenne and Arapaho. We have never seen such a gathering of the Sioux Nation."

"Did they make a deal?" asked Kate.

"They argued a lot. Not only did the Wasichus want to buy our sacred hills, they also wanted to buy *this* land, our last hunting ground." He swept his arm across the horizon. "Tempers flared. Some of the warriors started jostling the soldiers."

"A great battle was about to begin!" yelled Sleeps A Lot.

"But calmer heads won the day," continued his brother.

"More meetings took place, but no agreement was reached. So the government decided how much we should be paid, even though we refused to sell our land, and they let the Wasichus flood into Paha Sapa."

"Tell them about last winter," said Sleeps A Lot.

"The Great Father blamed the free Indians for the commission's failure. He met with his army general, and they decided that every free Indian must move to a reservation by the end of January. If they didn't, the Army would attack. But the order wasn't sent out until the Wasichus feast of Christmas. By then the snow was deep, and it took many weeks for messengers just to reach our people. How could they possibly break up their winter camps and get to the reservations in time?"

"They *knew* it was impossible," snorted his brother. "They just wanted an excuse for war."

"Agency Indians are allowed to leave the reservation to go hunting, and one such band set off into the snow, led by

Two Moons. They found plenty of game. With meat in their bellies, they slept soundly. Then, one night, soldiers charged into the camp, firing into tipis and killing people in their beds. Women, clutching infants, ran barefoot through the snow."

"That's *terrible*," cried Kate. "Those poor people."

"Then soldiers burned the tipis and drove away the horses."

"Did *anyone* survive?" asked AP.

"Many did. Two Moons led them to Crazy Horse's winter camp on the Powder River."

"Imagine attacking people when they're asleep," protested Kate.

"They've done it many times before."

"Sand Creek," hissed Sleeps A Lot.

Talking Cloud let out an anguished cry. "Sand Creek!"

Kate and AP expected another terrible story, but he remained silent. After several minutes AP asked him what had happened.

"Some things are better left unspoken." The only thing he would say was that Sand Creek made the Two Moons massacre seem insignificant.

The open plain provided an opportune diversion from the long silence that followed.

"Look over there, Young Man Who Sits Too Much." Talking Cloud stopped his horse and pointed into the distance. "What do you see?"

"Nothing really—a few bushes, a lone tree."

"How about you, Gold Butterfly Woman?"

Kate stared hard, but saw nothing either.

"You see no hawk sitting near the top of that tree?"

They both shook their heads.

"Keep watching," said Talking Cloud.

Suddenly, a hawk swooped down from one of the branches and disappeared into the long grass. Seconds later it flapped into the air, carrying a lifeless rabbit in its talons.

"That's incredible!" cried Kate. "How could you possibly have seen that hawk? It was *totally* invisible."

Talking Cloud smiled. "When you live on the plains, you have to use your eyes and all your other senses. You must be part of the living world."

Just after sunset, the band came to a halt. People had been snacking on dried food throughout the day, so few bothered with an evening meal. Most were content to spread out their rugs and settle down for the night.

"Are you asleep?" whispered AP.

"No. I'm dead tired, but I can't take my eyes off the sky. Did you ever see so many stars?"

AP pointed out several constellations, including the W-shaped Cassiopeia.

When he glanced across at Kate again, she was fast asleep.

Just a few miles away, Robert Drew was staring up at the same constellations. The pain in his foot had gone, along with most of the swelling, but the skin was still discolored. He was walking again, but Sam Carter insisted he take things easy. They had only visited one camp so far—a small band of Crow—without any news of the youngsters he hunted. No matter, he would find them eventually—of that, he was certain.

The Sioux's next campsite was an ideal spot in a meadow beside a river they called the Laughing River. Tall cottonwoods provided shade, and huckleberries—which AP and Kate mistook for blueberries—grew everywhere. Bears and Sioux alike loved the berries, and when the time travelers tasted them, they understood why. But for Kate, the best part of their new location was that it had a perfect place for bathing.

The Sioux, especially the children, loved swimming, and Kate spent much time splashing in the shallows with them. Most of the mothers were Kate's age, and she enjoyed their company.

AP tried fishing, with great success, proudly presenting his catches for everyone to eat. One afternoon, Talking Cloud invited him to shoot some arrows. The old man, surprised at how quickly AP learned, asked him if he had ever used a bow before. "Yes," he replied with a smile, "*many* years ago."

Talking Cloud enjoyed talking with AP and his sister. One afternoon, while Kate and AP were skipping stones across the river, he stopped by for a chat.

"When we broke camp to follow the buffalo, how did you know where to find them?" asked AP.

The old man smiled at the simplicity of his question.

"Finding buffalo is easy. You just have to read the signs—trampled grass, hoofprints, droppings—like following footprints in the snow."

"It looks hard to me," said AP.

"That's because you look but do not see. You must sharpen your eyes."

"Like the hawk Kate and I missed?" AP sounded discouraged.

"It takes time. I've lived here all my life. If you train your eyes, they *will* see."

AP nodded determinedly.

"The buffalo is a creature of habit too. Every year he makes the same journey, visits the same places. I knew he was headed for this area. Every hunter knows that."

"But how do you know which way to go?" asked Kate. "I'd never find my way, and I'm good at navigating."

"She's fantastic!" echoed AP.

"I need landmarks," Kate continued. "We were traveling through flat grasslands. I saw *no* features! How did you know the way?"

Talking Cloud chuckled. The idea of a Sioux getting lost was as absurd as that of a fish drowning. "Hold up your right hand," he told her. "Gold Butterfly Woman, have you ever misplaced that hand?"

She shook her head, smiling.

"I know the plains as well as you know that hand. For me to lose my way would be like you losing that hand."

The Sioux elder bent down and picked up a flat stone. Then, taking careful aim, he let it fly. The stone glanced off the water several times before hitting the opposite bank. Chuckling to himself, he carried on with his walk.

❊ ❊ ❊

One morning, Kate and AP were watching a sunrise. "I feel connected to everything—the animals, the plants, even the sky!" she said.

"I know exactly what you mean."

"It's been fun too—lazing under the trees, swimming, listening to stories under the stars."

"My favorite part has been galloping across the plains on a horse," said AP. "It feels like flying!"

They both knew their summer with the Sioux could not last forever—no holiday ever did—but they never expected it to end so abruptly.

17

Ho-Ka Hey!

The day began like any other. Kate and AP woke before the others and went for a walk. Then they made plans for the rest of the day over breakfast with Talking Cloud and his family. The hunters were riding out, so there would be feasting that night. Talking Cloud was staying in camp. Kate would play *Tawinkapsice*—the Sioux equivalent of hockey—with some of the young women. She had played before and was getting good. Afterwards, she would go swimming. AP wanted to practice his observational skills and then go fishing.

AP wandered off alone, reading the signs the way Talking Cloud had shown him. When a patch of grass caught his eye, he bent down for a closer look. As he focused his attention on the spot, a pair of unseen eyes fixed upon him. Someone, slinking through the grass like a phantom, had been following him since he left camp.

Suddenly, two hands grabbed AP's shoulders, and he leaped into the air.

"Your reactions are quick, but not your senses," said a voice.

"Talking Cloud!" gasped AP. "I thought I was being attacked!"

"And what if I had been an enemy?"

"I suppose I'd be dead."

"Yes. So why didn't you hear me coming?"

AP looked blank.

"You were not *hearing* because you were too busy *seeing*. You must use *all* your senses, *all* the time." Talking Cloud let his words sink in.

"Now, tell me what your eyes see."

"I see where a deer was lying," AP began, heart still pounding. He pointed to a hollow in the grass.

"How do you know it was a deer?"

AP pointed to some small round pellets.

The old man's gaze then shifted to a distant bush.

"What do your eyes see now?"

"Nothing in the bush…but there's a small lizard sunning itself on the boulder by the side."

Talking Cloud smiled. "Good. You have made much progress since your eyes were blind to the hawk. But you must remember to stay alert."

AP told Kate about Talking Cloud's lesson when they were alone together, just before the feast.

"I got a quizzing too!" She smiled. "We went for a hike after lunch. I thought Talking Cloud was testing me, so I paid great attention to the terrain. Just before we headed back, he made me close my eyes and spin around. Then he told me to open them and lead the way home."

"How did you do?"

"I got back without any problem. He was impressed." She paused and her grin became a sad smile. "He reminds me so much of Granddad."

"You miss him, don't you?"

"Yes. He was—" She was too upset to finish.

They sat in silence for a while. Then the smell of roasting meat wafted their way.

"Come on," said Kate, standing up. "Let's get over there before all the buffalo's gone!"

After carving off some thick slices from the roast, they sat down on the grass beside Talking Cloud. AP was about to take his first bite when two riders charged into the camp. They were wearing war bonnets. This was the first time Kate and AP had seen Sioux warriors in headdresses. Seconds later the entire camp was in an uproar, wondering what had happened.

After speaking with the riders for several minutes, Talking Cloud held up his hand for silence.

"Bad news," he announced so all could hear. "Large numbers of troops are moving across the land. From the west, along the Yellowstone River, rides Colonel Gibbon, with over four hundred men.

"From the south comes Three Stars Crook."

Everyone howled angrily at the mention of his name because General Crook had led the Two Moons massacre.

"Crook leads one thousand soldiers," Talking Cloud continued, "with two hundred Crow."

Their outrage at this last piece of news was as much because their sworn enemy fought alongside the Army as it was because they were Crow.

Talking Cloud signaled for quiet, and the yelling stopped. "And from the east rides One Star Terry, with three thousand cavalry." He paused. "He rides with Long Hair Custer."

The mention of Custer's name was like throwing a switch, and the screaming reached new heights. Talking Cloud waited to continue. "One of the warriors who brought this news wishes to speak. He is Black Hawk."

"We rode straight from the valley of the Little Bighorn," Black Hawk began.

"His name suits him," AP thought, focusing on the great hooked nose and icy black stare.

"We bring word from Sitting Bull and Crazy Horse." There was a hushed murmur at the mention of the revered names. "Since early spring, our people have been flocking to their camps. Our allies, the Cheyenne and Blackfoot, have joined us too. So have our Assiniboine and Arapaho friends. People have left the reservations to join us. We are three thousand warriors and growing stronger every day. The time has come to deliver a crushing blow to the Army."

The explosive outburst at this remark lasted for some time. Black Hawk remained silent. Then he said, "This is the message we bring you. Come and join us for the greatest gathering of the Sioux Nation. Come and join us for the greatest battle of all time. Come and join us for a great victory over the Wasichus!"

Everyone started screaming the Sioux war cry, *Ho-ka hey*—Let's go now.

"Now what?" Kate shouted into AP's ear.

Soon the women began packing away the uneaten meat and taking down their tipis. Meanwhile, the men checked their weapons and attended to their horses.

Anxious to keep out of everyone's way, Kate and AP stood back, wondering what to do. Talking Cloud, who had just finished a conversation with Black Hawk, hurried across to talk with them.

"The young bloods speak of beating the Wasichus, of driving them from our land," he began. "This will not be. We may win a great battle. We may win another summer to live our lives. But that is all we can hope for." He shook his head. "The Wasichus are unstoppable. We cannot halt the iron horse. We cannot fight the Army's big guns. The flood of settlers will not cease."

AP tried to find something to say. There was nothing.

"You must return to your people. We have no future."

"I *hate* the Wasichus," Kate blurted, "and I hate myself for being one."

He smiled at her. "You may be Wasichu on the outside, but you have Wakan Tanka in your heart. So does your brother."

"Do we have to leave now?" asked Kate.

"Soon. Sings To Her Children is packing food and blankets for you. You should go and change into your other clothes."

"Which way should we go?"

"I'll show you when it's time."

Kate and her brother felt wretched as they made their hurried farewells. Sings To Her Children fussed over them as if they were her own. Then Talking Cloud appeared and led the way down to the river. The sun was low, with only two more hours of daylight.

He stood beside the Laughing River, pointing against the flow. "Keep traveling upstream, to the south. That will take you to the Bozeman Trail. You'll find settlers driving their wagons." He paused. "Make sure you head *south* along the Trail—the other way leads to the Little Bighorn."

"Well," said AP, "we'd better go."

Talking Cloud placed both hands firmly on his shoulders. "Look after yourself, Young Man Who Sits Too Much. You are wise beyond your years. Use that sharp mind of yours. And remember, keep those senses keen."

AP shook his hand, even though this was not the Indian way. "Goodbye, Talking Cloud. I wish you could come back home with us. Our world needs people who care about it the way you do. You've taught me so much—" He wanted to say "thank you," but that seemed inadequate.

The old man knew exactly what AP meant. "Just pass it on, my friend. That is thanks enough."

Turning to Kate, he said, "Go well, Gold Butterfly Woman. You have a good heart and a good life before you. Be happy."

"I—I'll miss you so much," she stammered, fighting back tears. Then, throwing her arms around him, she buried her face in his chest and wept.

❀　❀　❀

Two days later, while AP and Kate continued walking along the river to the Bozeman Trail, Sam Carter and Robert Drew caught up with Talking Cloud and his band. The wily old trader had heard they were headed for Sitting Bull's camp, and wanted to do some last-minute trading. He'd also heard they'd picked up two young Wasichus.

"Fetch me another box of knives," Sam said to Robert, who was acting as his assistant. A circle of young braves surrounded him, eager to trade their buffalo hides. "The big ones, with the curved blades," he added.

"They're all gone."

"The whole lot?" queried Sam.

"Every last one. The straight ones too."

"What about the smaller ones with black handles?"

"We might have a few of those left. I'll go and check."

When the last knife had been traded and the warriors had left, Sam approached Talking Cloud.

"I hear two young Wasichus are staying with you," Sam began casually.

"No longer," said Talking Cloud. "I sent them back to their own people."

Robert Drew, busy packing up buffalo hides, listened intently.

"That's good you sent them back to their parents," said Sam.

Talking Cloud shook his head. "Their parents died when they were young. They were raised by our people—they speak our language. But it was time for them to return to the Wasichus."

Sam gave his assistant a puzzled look.

"Which way did they go?"

"I told them to follow the Laughing River to the Bozeman Trail. Then they were to keep traveling south and join up with a wagon train."

Robert tried explaining the discrepancy over the children's parents as he helped Sam load the mules.

"Of *course* they'd say their parents were dead. They'd hardly tell Talking Cloud they were running away from home, would they?"

"Maybe not," said Sam, "but how can two kids from Philadelphia speak Sioux?"

"My brother married a woman who was half-Sioux."

"In *Philadelphia*?"

"Well, no, not exactly, he was on this trip and—"

"Listen," Sam interrupted, "I don't know what's between you and those kids—that's your business, not mine."

There was an uncomfortable silence.

"Talking of business, I'm heading north to meet up with the Army."

Robert looked puzzled.

"We're out of knives, but we still have pots and pans. With a big battle looming, the Army will want supplies.

You've been a good assistant these last two weeks—I'd be glad to have you along."

"I can't. I must catch up with those kids. It's urgent."

"Suit yourself. But it's a long walk to the Bozeman. You'll need a horse."

"How can I get one?"

"I'll have a word with Talking Cloud. I'm sure we can work out something."

18

Wagons Roll

Kate and AP had been traveling through hilly country for the last few hours and were at the bottom of a deep dip, with a huge hill in front of them like the one they had just walked down.

"I wonder why it's called the Bozeman *Trail*? All they've done is clear some rocks and bushes so wagons can pass."

"It's not exactly busy either," added Kate. "No sign of anyone all day."

"I'm hot."

"And thirsty," said Kate. "There's nothing here but dust."

"What time is it?"

She squinted up at the bright sun. "I'd guess late afternoon."

"Let's keep going until dark."

"I'd *love* to jump into that river again," said Kate.

"We might find another one when we—"

"What was that noise?" Kate interrupted.

They both stood still, listening.

"I hear it," said AP. "A creaking sound, coming from behind us."

"I think it's a wagon!" said Kate eagerly.

Shading their eyes against the bright sky, they could see a dust cloud at the top of the hill.

As they watched, a covered wagon came into view. Several more followed, until there were six of them.

Minutes later Kate and AP were bouncing along on the front seat of a wagon, wedged between the driver and his wife.

"Where'd you young people say you're from?"

"We're from out east," AP replied. "Boston."

Kate and AP had worked out their cover story during their long trek. They decided AP should do most of the talking, as he sounded more convincing.

"You say your folks took sick an' had to get back home?" continued the driver.

"Yep," said AP.

"My, that's a real shame," said his wife. "'Specially with you an' your sister being so young an' all."

"Seeing as how sis an' me weren't planning on giving up the West," said AP, feeling his way into the role of settler, "we decided to stay behind and make a go of it on our own."

"Good on ya, boy!" said the driver, slapping AP on the back so hard he nearly fell off the seat. "That's the spirit we need!"

"Now you're Kate, an' your brother's name's Aiy Peey," said his wife.

"Yes, Ma'am," said Kate.

"You can call us by our first names, you being kinda grown up an' all. This here's Zach and I'm Libby. Ma's in the back with our two little boys, Jacob and Luke. Real good kids, they are."

The screaming coming from behind made Kate doubt the last point.

"Where are you heading?" asked Zach.

"Nowhere in particular," AP replied. "Just some place to get a good start. We plan on making a fortune, right sis?"

"Yep," said Kate, wondering how much further he would push his acting role.

"Well they sure picked the right wagon train, eh Libby?"

His wife nodded and smiled.

"We're *all* planning on making a fortune," said Zach. "That's why this here wagon train's heading straight for the Black Hills."

"Black Hills?" Kate and AP gasped in unison, recalling how settlers had plundered the Indian's sacred place. But they bit their tongues and said nothing.

"There's gold in those hills from the grass roots down!" said Zach. "You just dig in your shovel an' out it comes."

"We're going to be so rich!" sang Libby. "We'll buy a big swanky house, and a fancy new rig to drive around town."

"How far away is it?" asked Kate, mostly to stop Libby's jabber.

"Maybe a hundred miles," said Zach. "Should take us about a week."

They called a halt well before sundown and drew the wagons into a circle. "Just in case any of them murdering injuns attack us in the night," Zach explained. Then the horses were unhitched and left to graze.

"What can I do to help?" asked Kate as Libby began preparing supper.

"You can play with the boys. Ma's had 'em all day."

Once everyone had finished supper and put their children to bed, they gathered around a campfire. Someone started playing a mouth organ.

They welcomed Kate and AP like family. When Zach explained their situation, they cheered in support.

"They're all so *friendly*," Kate said to AP—everyone was too busy chatting to overhear their conversation. "When I heard they were going to the Black Hills, I thought they must be the most hateful people on earth. And there was the nasty comment about Indians. But they're nice people."

"I know what you mean," agreed AP.

"So why would they want to take things that belong to the Indians?"

"They don't see it that way, Kate. As Zach said at supper, the Indians have no interest in gold, so why not take it?"

"What are *we* going to do? They think we want to join in the gold rush."

"I don't know. But it would be good to see Paha Sapa."

❄ ❄ ❄

Robert Drew had been furtively trailing the wagon train since the previous night. He could hardly believe his luck when it stopped to pick up the two children. But the odds had been in his favor—it was the only wagon train on the Bozeman Trial.

He could hear someone playing "Oh! Susannah" on the mouth organ. The sounds of conversation had died down and people were settling in for the night. "Not long now," he said to himself, "and I'll get my device back."

Most folks took their blankets and slept inside the circle of wagons. Kate and AP preferred to sleep on the outside, where they could talk in private. Choosing a spot beside a sage bush, they unrolled their blankets and got comfortable. Too tired to talk for long, they drifted off to sleep.

AP stirred, vaguely aware of something brushing against his chest. The next instant, a skeletal hand tore the abacus from his neck. He was awake instantly.

"Kate, wake up!" he cried, shaking her hard.

"What do you want? I'm asleep!"

"Somebody just took the abacus!"

Kate, now wide awake, was on her feet.

"Look, there he goes," said AP, pointing. The retreating figure was silhouetted against the eastern sky, which was growing light. "Let's follow him."

The intruder was limping, and they were gaining on him. Then he disappeared into some bushes. Seconds later he charged out on a horse, heading toward the dawn. Slipping and sliding in the saddle, he was desperately clutching the reins.

"What are we going to *do*?" croaked AP in a panic. "We can't get home without the abacus."

"There's only one thing," snapped Kate, taking control. "Let's grab a horse and go after him."

19

Tracking Trouble

Daylight, and they had been riding for two hours without seeing a trace of the phantom rider. "Talking Cloud would have no problem tracking him," said AP, desperately searching the ground for clues. "We lost so much time having to find a horse and saddle up. All we can do is keep heading east and hope he's doing the same."

By noon the situation had become serious. In their dash to get away, AP and Kate had grabbed only one water container. That was already half empty.

"We won't find water out here," said Kate, looking around at the parched landscape. "Just cactus and sagebrush." They were now walking, to give the horse a rest.

"Look," said Kate, pointing into the distance. "Is that a horse between the tree and those bushes?"

"Yes!"

Even with the heat haze, Kate was convinced the horse was tethered, and that somebody was lying under the tree.

"Is it our guy?" AP sounded optimistic.

"Who else would be out here in the middle of nowhere?" She smiled. "I think he's taking a nap!"

"Let's circle way over there, to the other side of the bushes, so we can sneak up without him seeing us."

"We'd better leave the horse here," said Kate. "Otherwise the two might start whinnying."

AP and Kate crept silently through the scrub, toward a gap in the bushes. Sure enough, they had found the thief, fast asleep in the shade, with a hat covering his face. His horse stood nearby.

Kate pointed at his outstretched hand. "There's the abacus!" she whispered. "We could take it without even waking him."

"I'll go," whispered AP, and he slipped through the gap.

Tiptoeing forward as silently as a Sioux, he stopped beside the sleeping man. He was about to reach down for the abacus when he noticed that the cord was wrapped around the man's fingers. Picking up the abacus in one hand, AP unraveled the cord with the other. Then, just as it came free, the man stirred.

AP froze. As he crouched there, wondering if his pounding heart could be heard, the stranger settled down again.

Kate saw AP slowly stand and slip the abacus over his head. Then he crept toward the man's tethered horse.

"What is he doing?" Kate wondered. "If that horse starts whinnying, we're done!"

Seconds later AP was back, carrying two extra water bottles.

"You took his water!" she gasped.

"Yep." Her brother grinned. "His horse was loaded with it."

"Let's go," said Kate as they climbed back into the saddle. "I want to get as far away from that guy as possible."

"Where to?" asked AP, taking up the reins.

"Back to the wagon train," said Kate. "We can tell them how we were robbed, which is why we borrowed the horse."

"Do you know the way?"

Kate smiled. "After our training with Talking Cloud, it's easy."

The cactuses were in flower, brightening the barren browns with their brilliant yellows. Kate felt a little threatened in the arid land of thornbush and tumbleweed, but AP thrilled to the challenge of surviving in such a desolate place.

They failed to reach the wagon train before sundown and had to camp where they were. With nothing to eat and no blankets for warmth, it was a long, cold night.

When AP awoke, Kate was already up. Rubbing his eyes, he stood beside her and watched the sun peek over the horizon.

"I've never been so pleased to see morning!" said Kate, stamping her feet to get warm. "Things will get better now."

"The abacus is safe too," said AP, patting his chest. "And we'll soon be back with the wagon train."

As they stood there, AP suddenly realized somebody was behind them. Next thing they knew, they were thrown to the ground.

"Let me go," Kate screamed, kicking and struggling.

AP grappled to grab an arm, hoping to apply a judo hold, but their attacker was far too strong.

Turning his head, AP came face to face with the largest and most terrifying Indian he had ever seen.

They expected to be scalped and were therefore surprised when their attacker—realizing they were harmless kids—let them go. They were even more astonished to hear him speak English.

He told them that his English name was Laughing Jack and that he worked as a scout for the Army. He was a

Crow, and was on his way to the Yellowstone River to join up with the cavalry.

"So, what are two young settlers doing in the middle of nowhere?"

"It's a long story," said AP, and he explained how they were robbed.

"This thin man of yours," said Laughing Jack, "was he a bad rider?"

"Terrible. Why?"

Laughing Jack smiled. "Just before dark, a tall, thin rider came crashing into my camp. I didn't like that."

"What happened?" asked Kate.

"I took his horse." He nodded toward the bushes, and they saw he had two.

"Where do you think he is now?" asked Kate.

"Probably with the wagon train—I camped close to them last night." He paused. "So what are you going to do now?"

"We're not going back to the wagon train." Kate was adamant. "We don't want to run into *him* again."

"We'll have to avoid the Black Hills too," reasoned AP. "With only one road, we'd be sure to run into him."

"This is difficult country," said Laughing Jack, glancing around. "There's no water unless you know where to find it, and you've no rifle for hunting. You'd both be dead in days." He shook his head. "You'd better come with me."

20

Joining the Army

Kate and AP spent most of the next week in the saddle. Sometimes Laughing Jack rode alongside them, talking. More often he trotted ahead, which gave them ample time to discuss the mysterious, thin man.

"That hooded man at the end of our medieval trip was tall and thin," said AP. "This could be the same person."

"But this guy walks with a limp."

"He could have just injured himself."

Kate nodded.

"The first one said we had something that belonged to him," AP continued, "and the second guy grabbed the abacus from me. I think they *are* the same person."

"If he owns the abacus, where did he get it?"

"Maybe he made it himself," AP suggested.

"How come it turned up in a crate of things from Africa?"

"Who knows. The whole thing's a mystery."

Kate and AP had done so much riding that they could enjoy the journey without becoming exhausted. Laughing Jack was a good hunter, and they lived off the land. Despite his fearsome appearance, he was friendly and cheerful and true to his name. Feeling so much at ease, they decided to ask him about some things that had been puzzling them.

"Why are the Crow and Sioux such deadly enemies?" asked Kate one night after supper.

"Why not? The Cheyenne are enemies of the Pawnee. The Pawnee are enemies of the Arapaho. The Arapaho are enemies of the Shoshone… The white man's the same. When I was young, the North went to war with the South." He smiled. "What would we do without enemies to fight?"

Kate wondered how to raise the next question. "You work for the Army that's helping white settlers move onto Indian land."

Laughing Jack nodded.

"And you help the Army fight other Indians. Is that hard for you?"

"Why should it be? The Army's fighting the Sioux, and they're our enemy."

"But the white people are the enemy of the Indians. We are destroying the old way of life."

"I knew a long time ago that the old ways were over. Too many people want to live on the plains. I can't stop them." He shrugged. "So what should I do? Live on a reservation and sometimes go hungry? Or work for the white man and always eat?"

Ever since their first night in Montana, AP had made a daily note on his piece of paper, so he always knew the date. "Guess what day it is tomorrow?" he asked Kate one night.

"Who cares?" she said, yawning. "I'm only interested in sleep."

"Tomorrow is June 21, the longest day of the year."

"So what?"

"Well, I think it's interesting. Especially since Laughing Jack says we'll be meeting up with the Army tomorrow."

"*He* might be meeting up with the Army," she whispered. "*We're* meeting up with a riverboat that'll take us east—well away from the action. Right?"

"Yeah, whatever," he said, turning over.

"AP, don't do this. We had a deal to go nowhere near the battleground. Remember?"

"Let's decide in the morning."

"You can be *such* a pain," she grumbled, and fell off to sleep.

❀　❀　❀

They had been riding along a ridge most of the morning, giving them a broad vista of green valleys and tree-covered hills—Kate's kind of country. Laughing Jack had warned them of the spectacular view to come, but they were still unprepared when they rounded the next bend and caught their first glimpse of the Yellowstone River. Reining in their horses, they gazed down at a majestic river, lazily winding its way through a fertile valley dappled with trees.

"What's that over there?" asked Kate, pointing to what appeared to be a giant mushroom patch nestled in the widest bend of the river.

"That," said the Crow, shaking his head in disbelief, "is the largest Army campsite I have *ever* seen. Let's get down there."

❊ ❊ ❊

Soldiers in blue uniforms were busy everywhere—moving equipment, erecting storage tents, organizing supplies, and cleaning weapons. Kate and AP didn't stand out because there were other civilians there too. Most of them were wagon drivers, hauling supplies from the riverboats. There were also large numbers of Indian scouts. Some, like Laughing Jack, wore traditional dress, but many wore a mixture of Wasichu clothes.

AP noticed a pile of crates marked AMMUNITION in bold, black letters.

Laughing Jack nodded toward a large tent where two Army sergeants were talking with a group of Crow scouts. "I've got to report in," he said, slipping from the saddle. "I won't be long. Have a look around while you're waiting."

Anyone watching Kate and AP dismount would have thought they were raised in the saddle. Tethering their horses alongside Laughing Jack's, they set off along the track they had been riding on. A group of soldiers passed by, walking in the opposite direction.

"I thought the soldiers would be all polished boots and shiny buttons," said AP. "But they're scruffy—even the officers."

"You can't stay neat and tidy out here. Look at us! I feel *so* gross."

"It's not just their wrinkled uniforms and crumpled hats—they just slouch along. Aren't soldiers supposed to march along with their shoulders back and chins up?

"You mean the way you do?" Kate asked sarcastically.

"I'm not in the Army."

"How long are we going to hang around here before we find that steamboat?"

"What's your rush?"

"I want to avoid the battle. We made a deal."

"We *will* avoid the battle. It takes place on the Little Bighorn, not the Yellowstone River."

"So what's the point of staying here? We could be relaxing on a boat, cruising down the river."

"And how do we pay for the tickets?"

Kate hadn't thought of that.

"Hey, check out this guy." AP nodded toward a sharp-featured man at the center of a small group heading their way. He wore a white cowboy hat and a deerskin shirt fringed with tassels, with a red kerchief tied around his neck. His Army uniform pants were tucked inside knee-high cavalry boots. Young and slimly built, he was striding briskly, just ahead of the others, and talking loudly.

"Think they're part of his fan club?" whispered AP. Then he noticed the three dogs trotting by his side.

Kate and AP overheard him say something about a "wild goose chase" and "that idiot Reno." His followers, including two Indian scouts, were listening to every word.

For a brief moment, his blue eyes met Kate's and he stopped in mid-sentence. Removing his hat with a flourish, he sang out a cheery "Good morning," then hurried on. This happened so quickly that Kate had no time to respond. For reasons she couldn't explain, her cheeks began to burn.

"That *had* to be Custer!" said AP. He was so shocked he didn't notice Kate was blushing. "Imagine seeing him, just like that!"

"Are you sure?" queried Kate. "The Sioux call him Long Hair, but that guy's hair was short."

"Maybe he had it cut for the battle. Did you notice the way everyone was looking at him?"

Kate shrugged.

"We should be getting back to Laughing Jack."

Their friend confirmed they had seen Custer. "Big things happening," he continued. "Let's get something to eat. Then we talk."

He led the way to a cook tent, grabbed a tin plate and fork and motioned for them to do the same. Piling his plate with meat and beans, he took several thick wedges of bread, then strode outside and sat on the ground.

Their full plates looked skimpy compared to his.

"Is that all you're having?" he asked as they joined him.

"Yesterday, Major Reno returned from a long scouting trip to try and find where the hostiles are camped," he told them.

AP had read that Reno led one of the detachments of soldiers in the Battle of the Little Bighorn.

Laughing Jack smiled. "By all accounts there was lots of shouting before he went!"

"Why was that?" asked AP.

"Custer didn't want him to go. He thought it pointless searching for the Sioux along the Powder and Tongue Rivers because he's convinced they're camped on the Little Bighorn."

"Then why did Custer let Reno go?" asked AP.

"Custer's not in charge."

"But Custer's a general, which is higher than Major Reno."

"Right," agreed Laughing Jack, "and Custer commands the Seventh Cavalry, so he can give Reno orders. But General Terry's in charge of the whole thing, and *he* ordered Reno to go."

"Got it."

"Anyway, Reno found tracks heading west off the Tongue River. So he followed them to the Rosebud, but they kept on going. He didn't follow them any farther, though—he just hurried back." Laughing Jack chuckled. "That got him in double trouble! Terry was mad because he disobeyed orders and went beyond the Tongue River. And Custer was mad because Reno didn't carry on and find the camp. If Custer had found the tracks, he would've followed them and *attacked* the Sioux!"

"What happens now?"

"Well, there was a big war council between General Terry, General Custer and Colonel Gibbon."

"Who's Gibbon?" asked AP. The name sounded familiar.

"Gibbon's in charge of the infantry—four hundred and fifty foot soldiers." He then explained the plan. "They're fairly sure the Sioux are camped on the Little Bighorn. So Gibbon and his foot soldiers are going to cut them off from the north."

AP and Kate exchanged glances. Both were thinking of their Oglala friends. "Custer has orders to cut them off from the east. They'll be cut off from the south by old Three Stars Crook. Nobody knows where Crook is right now, except he's heading north with a thousand soldiers. He might find the Sioux before Custer and Gibbon!"

"When does it all start?" asked AP.

"Custer's leading the Seventh Cavalry off tomorrow. I'll be riding out too—I've been assigned to Reno. You two can come if you want—there'll be other civilians going along for the ride."

Kate shot AP a warning glance.

"You can decide tomorrow. I must go. Let's meet at the cook tent for breakfast."

With that, he dashed off.

"We'll just go for the first day or two," suggested AP. "Then turn around and head back here."

"No way," Kate said decisively.

"What can go wrong? We know the battle's on June 25 and tomorrow's only the twenty-second."

"No."

"Laughing Jack's been assigned to Reno. We'd be nowhere near Custer for the last part."

"And what happened to Reno in the battle?"

"He was okay. Besides, we'd be on our way back before the battle began."

"Why am I even *thinking* about this? We're not going. End of story."

21

Cocky Custer

Kate awoke with a start the following day. "What's *that*?" she asked.

"Reveille, the morning bugle call. It's an Army camp, remember?"

"Not for much longer," she muttered to herself.

"Mmm, I smell bacon," he said, folding up his blanket. "I bet breakfast is good here."

As they walked toward the cook tent, soldiers were rushing everywhere, packing up camp. And above all the shouted orders and rumble of wagons was the sound of hammering.

"So what's happening?" asked AP, after meeting up with Laughing Jack.

"The Seventh Cavalry are pulling out first. Custer'll be pleased because General Terry's going with Gibbon."

"Why's that good for Custer?" asked AP.

"Gibbon's foot soldiers won't be traveling as fast as Custer's cavalry, so old Long Hair won't have the General looking over his shoulder. Custer likes doing things *his* way."

"You seem to know a lot about Custer," said Kate.

He grinned. "I hear all sorts of things about him."

"Why?" she continued, surprising AP with her sudden interest.

"Custer's got several Indian scouts, but Bloody Knife's his favorite. They've been together for years, and Long Hair tells him everything. Bloody Knife's my friend."

AP's eyes lit up at this. "Could we *meet* Custer? Just to see what he's like."

"I *could* have a word with Bloody Knife," he said after a long pause. "Don't expect anything today, though."

"I can just see it," said Kate when Laughing Jack left. "Bloody Knife walks into Custer's tent and says, 'Hey, Long Hair, a buddy of mine knows these two kids who want to meet you'."

She landed a playful punch on AP's shoulder. "But wait until Custer hears that one of them is the *famous* AP—he'll drop everything!" She was giggling so much she didn't notice Laughing Jack had returned.

"He'll see you now," announced the Crow, "but just for a minute. Then he has to address his troops. Be quick!"

Custer was sitting at a small table, writing. A pile of finished letters was at his elbow. A young officer was standing to one side, eyes respectfully diverted away from the papers. One of Custer's dogs was lying at his master's feet. Without glancing up from his writing, the General gestured to them to wait.

The scratching of his pen continued for several minutes. Kate and AP exchanged uneasy glances. Then he was done. "Take these down to the riverboat immediately," he ordered, handing over the letters. As the officer hurried away, Custer glanced up.

"I've seen you both before," he said, smiling and standing. "I never forget a face."

AP noticed he was looking only at Kate.

"So you're the two youngsters determined to stay out West?"

They nodded, smiling awkwardly.

"Excellent decision. Would have done *exactly* the same myself."

Custer wore the same outfit as he had yesterday, except he now carried a saber on his belt. As he spoke he struck a pose, one hand on the sword, the other on his hip.

"I love the West," Custer continued. "Wide open spaces, spectacular scenery, excellent hunting—the dogs love it too." As if on cue, the dog started wagging its tail. "When we resolve this little problem with the Sioux, we can go back to enjoying everything again."

Kate nearly snapped at this. "If only you knew what *we* know," she thought to herself.

"Is that going to be a *big* job?" asked AP innocently.

"Not at all!" scoffed Custer.

"Aren't there lots of them, though?" AP continued, using the same oily tone.

"Possibly fifteen hundred."

"Wow!" exclaimed AP, knowing there were over twice that number.

"I declare, you sound like Bloody Knife! He says there are too many Sioux for the Army to handle. And so do the other scouts. But every officer believes we shall win."

Custer moved toward the opening.

"Time's up. I must address my men."

Then Custer turned to Kate and took her right hand. He gazed at her with his penetrating blue eyes. "Charmed to have met you."

As he swept from the tent, he paused and turned, as if suddenly remembering something. "Tag along behind the

Cavalry if you wish." He smiled a superior smile. "Watch history being made."

Kate stood there for several seconds, face flushed, lips pressed tightly together. Then, to AP's disbelief, she said, "We could stay with Reno's group and head back before the battle started."

"We're going?" he gasped.

"We're going!"

"So Custer made an impression on you?"

"Oh yes!" said Kate. "And I'd like to be as close as possible when he falls flat on his conceited face!"

"I guess that's what all the hammering was for," said AP. He nodded toward a small platform where the soldiers of the Seventh Cavalry—over six hundred men—were lined up to hear their commander-in-chief. Bloody Knife, along with Custer's followers, stood in front of the makeshift structure.

Custer leaped onto the stage.

"Men. Fighting men of the Seventh Cavalry. My men. We're about to embark on the hunt of a lifetime. And we're loaded for big game!"

He grabbed his rifle and the troops roared enthusiastically.

"We're after a wily old buffalo named Sitting Bull and his young friend Crazy Horse!"

This time the yelling took longer to subside.

"They're hiding somewhere along the Little Bighorn, with eight hundred, a thousand, maybe even fifteen hundred warriors. Our job is to catch them before they run away." He paused. "And rub them out!" He paced up and down, like a caged animal anxious to be free.

"He's done this before!" AP shouted to be heard above the uproar. "He's good!"

Kate scowled.

Custer pointed to his scout. "Bloody Knife here thinks there are too many Sioux for us to take on. But he's just a worrier!"

Bloody Knife laughed along with the others—he and Custer were always making fun of each other.

"This is what I say: men of the Seventh Cavalry, we can beat the *entire* Sioux Nation!" Then, drawing his saber and waving it above his head, he yelled, "Let's go!"

As the Seventh Cavalry rode out, the band struck up with the tune "Garryowen," one of Custer's favorites.

"Now, Custer," Colonel Gibbon shouted after him, "don't be greedy, but wait for us!"

"No, I will not!" Custer yelled back, waving his hat.

❊ ❊ ❊

Laughing Jack rode at the head of the column with the other scouts, occasionally dropping back to check on Kate and AP.

"We're making good progress," he told them that afternoon. "Come up front for a while."

Kate and AP found themselves just rows behind Custer. Judging from the way the General was laughing and joking, he could have been on a joyride with his friends.

"Who *are* all those people with him?" asked Kate.

The Crow rattled off a list of names that included Custer's two brothers, his brother-in-law, a nephew, some friends and a newspaper reporter. "Then there are his two cooks and his scouts."

"Does he always travel with so many followers?" queried Kate.

"Always. Though he's left his dogs behind! No time for hunting on this trip."

"Does he do much hunting?" asked AP.

"Whenever possible."

"He must be a good shot."

Laughing Jack grinned. "Bloody Knife says he's so bad he couldn't hit a tent if he was standing inside it!"

Kate and AP were surprised at this.

"Make no mistake, though," Laughing Jack continued, now sounding serious, "when it comes to fighting, Custer has no equal. He charges into battle with only one thing in mind—wiping out the enemy. His men would follow him anywhere. He's fearless. Tireless too—he'll ride all day and all night without sleep."

❋ ❋ ❋

After riding a short distance up Rosebud Creek, Custer called a halt for the day. Soon tents were springing up like mushrooms, transforming the meadow into an Army camp.

"Feel like exploring?" Kate asked her brother as dusk fell.

"Sure, anywhere in particular?"

"Let's check on General Custer," she said, lowering her voice.

"Do you mean let's *spy* on Custer?"

She smiled.

The officers' tents were set apart from the others, and Custer's was at the center of the action.

"If you please, gentlemen," Custer called out to his officers. He pointed to a large tent pitched in front of some supply wagons. "War council in ten minutes. I'll have my cook rustle up some coffee."

"Kate, you're not serious," whispered AP as she nodded toward the tent.

"Of course I am. It's getting dark—nobody will notice us tucked between the wagons outside."

The chatter among the officers came to an abrupt end when their commander-in-chief entered the tent.

"I intend to make this campaign both successful and pleasant for everybody," Custer began, saying how much he depended on everyone. "The key to success is the element of surprise," he explained. "So, gentlemen, be as quiet as possible. No bugles, no shouting. And no man must stray from the column."

Custer spoke for several minutes before inviting questions.

"That was boring," whispered AP as they crouched behind the tent while the meeting broke up.

"I thought there'd be at least a *few* war secrets."

Thinking everyone had left, they started creeping around the side of the tent. Suddenly, Kate grabbed AP's arm. "Look!" she whispered, pointing to two officers who were just leaving the tent. "Stragglers."

"I couldn't believe my ears," said one of the officers.

"Nor could I," said the other. "Nobody has *ever* heard Custer sounding so considerate."

"Not his usual abrupt and aggressive self."

"Indeed not. And to say he *needed* us, and to *ask* for our cooperation, well..."

"What d'you make of it?"

"I believe General Custer is going to be killed."

22

Signs in the Sand

"Y ou see more action up front," said AP as they rode along the next day, just two rows behind Custer. Laughing Jack had arranged to make yesterday's temporary switch permanent.

Earlier that morning their friend had galloped off to check the way ahead. Returning less than an hour later, Laughing Jack reported to Custer and the other scouts, then dropped back to update his young friends.

"Signs of hostiles are everywhere," he said uneasily. "Many people have passed this way." He pointed out the way the ground had been churned up by the passage of so many travois. "And see how the grass has been cropped short?"

"A big herd of buffalo?" suggested AP.

"No, Indian ponies. Thousands of them. That means thousands of hostiles."

"And look—burned-out campfires." He chatted with them for a few more minutes before returning to the front of the column.

AP and Kate saw other signs as they rode along. They also noticed how differently the soldiers were acting.

There was no more laughing and joking, and the men spent most of their time scanning the distant hills.

In the early afternoon, two scouts galloped back to the column, looking troubled. After reporting to Custer, they went into a huddle with the other scouts.

"What's *that* about?" murmured Kate.

"Let's ask Laughing Jack," said AP.

But their friend remained with the other scouts. Whatever had upset them was having no effect on Custer.

Soon the entire column came to a halt, and all the scouts, accompanied by Custer and his followers, galloped away from the river. Before going far, they stopped.

"What's going on?" said AP.

Everyone else in the column strained to see what was happening. The officers had their binoculars trained on the spot. They watched as the scouts squatted, looking at marks scratched in the sand. Behind them stood four tall posts that had recently supported some kind of temporary structure.

Custer remained mounted and was the first to ride back, along with his followers. The scouts eventually returned, and the column got underway again.

"Look," said Kate, nodding toward Custer, "Bloody Knife's trying to tell him something, but he's not interested."

"The other scouts are, though," said AP. "Something's stirred them up."

Bursting to know what it was all about, they had to wait a long time before Laughing Jack rejoined them.

"The hostiles held a Sun Dance," he said, pointing back over his shoulder. "That's a really important ceremony."

The Sun Dance was too complicated to explain to Wasichus. However, he told them about the deep trances the dancers fell into, and the importance of their dreams.

"Sitting Bull danced all day and all night without stopping," he said solemnly. "Then he had a special vision."

"How do you know?" asked AP.

"The Sioux left pictures in the sand showing what he saw." He rode on in silence. "It was not good. We are deeply troubled."

They looked at him uneasily.

"Sitting Bull saw soldiers and Indians on horseback. They were falling like grasshoppers. Their heads were hanging down and their hats were falling off."

Kate asked him how Custer had reacted to all this.

"He just shrugged."

The following day was June 24, the day before the battle. AP thought they would soon be heading back to the Yellowstone River. Yet Kate, to her brother's surprise, never mentioned this. The truth was that the thought of leaving the column and traveling back alone worried her. Besides, Kate was now as caught up in events as her brother. So they just continued.

By nightfall, Kate wondered whether she had made the right decision. After a grueling day's ride, Custer, fearing the Sioux might escape, kept them going until 2 a.m. By that time the men were exhausted. Custer consoled them by declaring that the entire next day would be devoted to rest. Meanwhile, he sent scouts ahead to locate the hostiles' camp.

23

The Battle of the Little Bighorn

I don't believe it," growled one soldier as he staggered to his feet. "Why are we getting up?"

"I thought we were having the day off," protested another.

"Stop complaining and jump to it!" shouted the sergeant. "You heard that bugle. We're moving out!"

Custer explained the reason for the sudden change of plan at a briefing for his officers. "The scouts have located the hostiles on the Little Bighorn, just where I said they would be. It's the biggest encampment they've ever seen. We must catch them before they run away!"

"But the men are exhausted," said one of his officers, voicing the concern of all. "They'll be in no shape to fight."

"My men are as ready as I am," snapped Custer.

The meeting ended with no further discussion.

"There are more Sioux than we've got bullets," Bloody Knife protested to Custer as the column moved off. "We should wait until tomorrow when Colonel Gibbon arrives."

"By that time they'll have got completely away!" scoffed Custer. "Besides, the Seventh Cavalry doesn't *need* any help."

The ground looked like a ploughed field, but nobody noticed this anymore. Something else caught everyone's attention, though.

"Look at all those tipi rings!" exclaimed one officer. "Hundreds of them. This must have been a *huge* camp." Every trooper was thinking the same thing.

At midday, Custer called a halt and sent a scout to the top of a nearby hill. The scout galloped back minutes later, riding as fast as he could. "Great clouds of dust!" he screamed. "Way off in the distance."

"That'll be the Sioux, running away!" shouted Custer. "Move out."

The column set off at a gallop.

After a hard ride, they came to a stop on a bushy ridge overlooking The Little Bighorn.

Kate and AP gazed down at the winding river and surrounding hills in disbelief. "Look at all those tipis!" exclaimed AP.

"We've caught them napping!" shouted Custer enthusiastically. Then, turning to his officers, "Major Reno, take your men down into the valley. When you're in place you'll attack the camp from this southern end. I'll take my men north along the right side of the river. When I'm in place, I'll cross the river and hit the far end of their camp." With this, he rode off, leading his column of cavalry.

"That was odd," said Kate as Custer and his men disappeared over the ridge. "I feel as though we should have warned them."

AP nodded, feeling the same way.

"I even felt sorry for *Custer*," she admitted. "But that makes no sense—they're going to attack our friends. And when you think of all the terrible things the Army's done…"

"I guess it's because we've been hanging around with them for the last few days. They're a nice bunch of guys."

Kate nodded thoughtfully. "So, when are *we* going to leave?"

"When the time's right," he said, patting the abacus beneath his shirt, "zap, and we'll be safely back home."

Reno lined up his troops along the ridge, so they could see the terrain below while he addressed them.

"Once we've crossed the river, we'll group up over there, behind those trees," he said, pointing to a clump of cottonwoods. "Then we'll charge the nearest tipis." He walked his horse up and down so all the soldiers—over one hundred men—could hear. "We have the element of surprise— they won't know what's hit them."

Laughing Jack turned to Kate and AP. "You'll be safe up here if you keep out of sight." Then, looking around, he saw a deep gully. "That'll be a good spot. But don't stand up to look around. And keep your horses with you." He paused. "If anything goes wrong, ride as fast as you can."

Before they had a chance to say goodbye, he trotted off to join the others.

❊ ❊ ❊

Across the river, children were playing in the grass while their mothers dug for wild turnips. It was another lazy day after a late night of feasting.

Everyone at the feast knew the soldiers were coming. But they were determined not to let it spoil their last few days of joy. So they had danced, played drums and told stories. Never again would there be such a gathering of the Sioux Nation.

Suddenly someone started shouting, "The chargers are here!"

Chaos broke out. People began running and shouting in confusion. Mothers swept up their children, men ran for their weapons and old people tottered out of the way. Soon warriors were zigzagging their ponies between the tipis as they charged off to fight the soldiers.

They might all have galloped south to stop Reno, leaving the north wide open to attack. But then another cry went up, "Crazy Horse is coming!" and many rode north to join him.

Unlike Custer, Crazy Horse had taken account of the situation. He knew his enemy's strength and location. So when he saw Custer leading his men north, he charged off to meet them.

Custer, still thinking he'd taken the village by surprise, led his two hundred and twenty-five men down a wooded hillside. As they got clear and the ground leveled out, they broke into gallop, feeling invincible.

Then, suddenly, the Sioux warriors came hurtling down from all sides. They converged on Custer and his men like a swarm of angry bees. All too late, the soldiers realized they had ridden into a trap. Warriors, many with hideously painted faces, attacked them with rifles, arrows, clubs and spears.

The firing from both sides was so intense that smoke filled the air. Mixed with the dust from flying hooves, it made visibility almost zero. The roar of gunfire all but drowned out the terrifying screams. Riderless cavalry horses bolted from the gloom, eyes staring from their sockets.

Custer knew the only hope was to make for higher ground. He urged his men to ride up the slope. With soldiers and horses falling all around them, they plunged forward. Just as they thought they might make it, a group of warriors led by Crazy Horse appeared over the top of the hill. They were doomed.

The Sioux wasted little time. Soon Custer and a handful of his men were the sole survivors. Surrounded by howling braves, they were now on foot, guns blazing, determined to take as many Sioux with them as possible. Custer fought like a lion, killing a warrior just as he was cut down himself. He laughed as he fell.

The entire battle took twenty minutes.

Up in the gulley, Kate was tugging on AP's arm, almost shaking the abacus from his hand. "It *has* to work," she was screaming above the noise of shooting and yelling. Try again!"

"I did. Nothing happened."

"So what's *wrong* with the thing?"

"The same as before—it takes time before we can reactivate it."

"So what do we do?"

"We've got no choice. We'll have to stay put."

"We're in the MIDDLE OF THE BATTLE!"

"No we're not. The fighting's way down on the other side of the river."

"Maybe the fighting has spread."

"I'll go and see."

"Don't you dare!" Kate screamed. "You heard what Laughing Jack said about keeping out of sight."

"It's okay, I'm going to crawl on my stomach."

"AP, I'm warning you—"

"We have to know what's happening. I'll be perfectly safe." He fumbled beneath his shirt. "Here, take the abacus so it doesn't get damaged."

Before she could stop him, he was heading for the edge of the ridge.

"Unreal," he whispered, peering over the top. Warriors were swarming everywhere. Reno's men—or what was left of them—had been chased back across the river and were pinned down among the bluffs beneath him. The gunfire was now intermittent.

AP lay there in the grass, unable to tear his eyes away. It was like watching a movie on a giant screen, though he knew the bullets zinging through the air were real. The soldiers were desperate for water. One trooper cautiously picked his way down to the river, carrying a number of containers. By ducking and swerving, he reached the river. He filled the canisters as quickly as possible, and clambered back up the hill. But as he zigzagged his way to safety, one of the bullets found its mark, throwing him to the ground. He never got up.

"You were gone for ages," Kate rebuked. "I thought something terrible had happened."

AP apologized and described what he had seen.

"How's *our* water?" she asked.

"We're fine. But there's nothing to eat."

They lost all sense of time as they crouched in the gully, listening to the sporadic gunfire. By dusk the firing had stopped. Too anxious to sleep, they spent a stressful night awake.

Kate began nodding off just as it got light—AP was already dozing. Then the firing began again, jolting them into wakefulness. An all-out battle raged until midday. Then silence.

With their ears still ringing, the quietness was a welcome relief. But as they hid there, wondering what was happening, the stillness grew ominous.

"Maybe they've run out of am—" Before AP could finish, a terrifying face appeared over the top of their gully.

Kate let out a piercing scream.

Then they both realized it was Laughing Jack.

"It's over," he said. "They've packed up their camp and left. Come and see."

The trio stood on the edge of the ridge, watching in silence. All the tipis were gone. The only sign of the thousands of Indians who had lived there for the last few weeks was an enormous dust cloud.

"The Great Plains will never see anything like that again," said Laughing Jack, as they stared across the valley.

The jubilation among the departing Indians was well deserved. Theirs was the greatest victory ever won over the Army. Two Moons, who had crested the hill with Crazy Horse, felt some justice had been done for the massacre of his village. Custer's defeat also symbolized the righting of many other wrongs.

Talking Cloud looked over the battlefield with mixed emotions. He was proud of their victory, though sad for all the dead soldiers and horses. But most of his grieving was for his own people—their way of life was over.

24

Watch Out!

A P and Kate were looking forward to returning home, but in the meantime they were happy to accompany Laughing Jack to Paha Sapa, the Black Hills. Their second night was particularly special. After eating the best roast meat they'd ever tasted, they lay beneath the stars, listening to Crow legends. And as AP stared up at the moon and the milky way, a thought struck him. When they arrived in medieval England, it was a full moon. After repeated tries to activate the abacus, it finally worked on the next full moon. What if the abacus was linked with the moon's cycles—like the tides? AP mentioned this to Kate just before they went to sleep.

"It only works on full moons?"

"Maybe."

"So when's the next one?"

"In about two and a half weeks."

"We've got to wait *that* long?"

"Maybe not," said AP. "What if it's linked to *lunar months*? We arrived a few days before the new moon, so if that's true, it'll work again a few days before the next new moon."

"When's that?"

"In three or four days."

"I could live with that."

❋   ❋   ❋

They tried the abacus on the next three nights, without any luck. By the fourth night, they were resigned to waiting for the next full moon. But they had other things on their minds that evening. Laughing Jack was restless, which was unusual. At supper, he hardly said a word, and only picked at his food.

"I'm not feeling good," he muttered, tapping his stomach. "I've got to go."

Kate and AP stared after him as he hurried off into the darkness.

"What's wrong with him?" asked Kate. "We've all eaten the same food."

"I've no idea," said AP between mouthfuls. "Maybe he picked up a stomach bug."

Suddenly there was a scuffling sound, followed by a loud bellow. Then silence.

"Laughing Jack, are you okay?" yelled AP.

No reply.

"Laughing Jack!" shouted Kate anxiously. "Where are you?"

Still no reply.

AP had a bad feeling. "We better go find him," he said, trying to sound calm.

Their eyes had become so accustomed to the bright campfire that it was like being blindfolded when they stepped away. Stumbling through the darkness, they headed in the direction of the last sound.

"What's that, on the ground?" Kate whispered, clutching AP's arm.

AP hurried forward and knelt down beside the motion-less body. It was Laughing Jack.

"He's been knocked out!" shouted AP.

"Put your hands on your head and stand up!" shouted a voice from behind. "Slowly. Do as I say, otherwise I'll kill her."

"He means it!" croaked Kate. "He's got a knife."

"Now turn around." The voice was quiet and menacing.

AP pressed his hands against his head and turned around.

It was the hooded man they'd seen in medieval England.

He had one arm wrapped around Kate's waist, pinning her arms to her sides. His other hand held a knife to her throat.

"Have you still got my chronoverser around your neck?"

"The abacus?" In his nervousness, AP had almost patted it.

"Yes. And I suppose you got it from Mordax?"

"Who's Mordax?"

"Mr. *Mordax* of *Multicorp*." Robert Drew pronounced each name with contempt. "The only way you got it is from Mordax—or one of his associates." Then something occurred to him. "You two are Mordax's brats, aren't you? Daddy must have lent it to you as a plaything!"

"Our father's name is *Littleton*, not *Mordax*," protested AP. "I have no idea who you're talking about."

"I have not traveled back 180 years to be bitten by a rat-tlesnake, attacked by an Indian and then lied to by a pair of kids!" he raged. Then he got a grip. "This is what's going to happen. You're going to lower your hands, very slowly, and slip the chronoverser over your head. Do you under-stand?"

AP nodded obediently.

"Then you're going to give it to me. Got it?"

Again, AP nodded.

"If you try anything…" He gestured with the knife.

Kate's mind was racing with the hopelessness of their plight. As soon as AP handed over the abacus, her attacker would take off—or worse. Regardless, she and her brother would be stranded in the nineteenth century, with no hope of ever returning home. Something had to be done.

As AP extended his hand holding the abacus, the thin man reached out for it with his knife-hand. The next instant, Kate stomped on his foot. Hard. Luckily, it was the bad one. He fell to the ground screaming. Snatching the abacus, Kate threw herself at her brother.

"Grab this," she shouted, pushing the abacus into his hand. "Let's get out of here!"

They took off like jack rabbits. By the time Robert Drew had struggled to his feet, they had a good lead.

"Activate the abacus!" shouted Kate, grabbing AP's arm. He was just about to when his boot caught in a gopher hole, sending him and the abacus flying. Kate lost her balance too, though she managed to throw herself forward, as if diving for home base. She slid to a halt beside a sage bush.

"The abacus landed over there, beneath that bush," AP shouted, nursing his badly twisted ankle.

By the time he had hopped over to Kate, she had found it. "Quick!" she said, pushing it into his hand. "He's right behind us!"

AP fumbled with the abacus. Kate grabbed his arm. He pushed the button. With a brilliant blue flash, they crashed to the floor of her bedroom.

25

Future Shock

I 'm worried about Kate," said Samantha Littleton as she and her husband drove to the supermarket. "She has such mood swings. Do you think she's got some sort of... *problem?*"

Ken Littleton smiled. "Sure, it's called growing up."

"Yes, I know all about that, but she flips from one extreme to the other. Look at the way she was yesterday, and again today. After that pointless discussion last night about knowledge, she stormed off to her room for the rest of the evening."

"We got lucky!"

Mrs. Littleton wasn't smiling. "She was unbearable this morning, and even worse when she came home from school."

"But AP braved the lioness in her den!"

"Yes he did, and that's my point. When they came downstairs for supper, she wasn't the same person. She and AP were chatting away like the best of friends, the way they were in England."

"And they're probably still at it."

"So we know the abacus can't be reactivated until after a lunar month," said Kate.

AP nodded. "Let's do this systematically." He reached for a sheet of paper. "I'll write down everything we know about our thin man.

"One. The hooded man in England and the thin man in Montana are the same person."

"Right," said Kate. "But let's give him a name, we can't keep calling him *the thin man*."

They sat pondering. Then Kate yelled, "I've got it! The perfect name—Snakebite!"

"Awesome!" said AP.

"Back to business. What else do we know?"

"He's tall and thin," said AP, and he wrote this down as point number two. "How old is he?"

"About Dad's age," Kate suggested. "Early forties."

"Any accent?"

"Nope. Regular North American."

"Features?"

"Thin face. Sharp pointy nose. Fair hair."

AP scribbled furiously.

"And he's strong—the way he pinned my arms down. He must be fit as well, to recover from a rattlesnake bite."

"Most people survive," said AP, "if they've no medical problems, like a weak heart."

"He's got a strong heart! He kept tracking us even though he'd been bitten—that must have been hard."

"I'll write that down as *tough and determined*."

Kate nodded. "He was a klutz on a horse, though. And he stumbled right into Laughing Jack's camp. I'd put him down as *inexperienced with outdoor life*."

"Anything else?"

"No, aside from disliking us."

"He's smart," said AP. "The way he flattened Laughing Jack—probably slugged him while he was squatting in the bushes!"

"So we've got a tall, thin guy, about Dad's age," said Kate, reading from AP's list, "fair hair, sharp features, from somewhere in North America. He's fit and strong, determined, not the outdoors type, dislikes us and he's smart."

"Now for the really interesting stuff," said AP. "The things he said."

"First, he had a special name for the abacus, a krono-something."

"Chronoverser, I think," said AP.

"What sort of a name is that?"

"Well, the *chrono* part is Greek—it means time."

"Whatever," said Kate. "So where does that get us?"

"Not far!"

"Okay, second, he says he's the real owner. Third, he thinks we got it from some guy named Mordax."

"Not so fast, Kate, I'm trying to write this down, remember."

"Sorry."

"Okay, the next point is that Mordax works for some outfit called Multicorp."

"So all we've got to do is look them up on the Internet," said Kate, turning on her laptop.

"Look at that," she groaned. "*Hundreds* of Multicorps. Everything from computer parts to baby clothes. How do we find the right one? It's impossible!"

"Maybe that's the idea."

"You think Mordax and Multicorp are crooks?" asked Kate.

"They could be."

"Now for the last thing," said Kate. "Snakebite said he'd traveled back 180 years."

"Let's see," said AP, doing a quick calculation.

"That can't be right." He rechecked his figures. "Wow! He traveled back from the year 2056. That means he hasn't even been *born*!"

26

Anyone for the Sun?

February began cold and gray, and everyone in the Littleton family was suffering from the winter blahs. "How about a trip to Florida during March Break?" suggested Mr. Littleton one suppertime. "We haven't done that in a while."

"Sounds good to me," said AP.

"How about you, Kate?" asked her father.

"I'm not sure." She hesitated. "I'll probably be doing stuff with my friends."

"So much for that idea. I just thought it'd be good to have a family holiday, especially since Mum and I are taking that Egyptian trip in the spring."

"The journey down the Nile will be *really* neat," said AP. "Will you visit the Valley of the Kings?"

"Absolutely!" replied his father. "And the Valley of the Queens, aren't we, Sam?"

Samantha Littleton just nodded. She was less enthusiastic about the trip. Her main concern was money. Mr. Littleton was attending a conference in Egypt, and had decided to stay an extra week to take his wife on holiday. "We can afford it," he'd assured her.

"The Valley of the Kings is where the pharaohs' tombs were cut into the cliffs, isn't it?" asked AP.

"Yes. Complete with secret corridors to fool the robbers. Some were huge—as big as a supermarket. Imagine hammering that out with hand tools!" Mr. Littleton had been reading up on Egyptology. "We'll see the statues at Abu Simbel too," he continued. "They're six-stories high!"

Kate sighed. How could *anyone* get excited about a bunch of old ruins? "I've got an assignment due," she said, excusing herself from the table.

When AP went to bed that night, he noticed Kate's light was still on.

"Can I come in?" he said, tapping on the door. "I need to talk."

"Can't it wait until tomorrow?"

"Not really, it's important."

"That's *important*?" said Kate a few minutes later.

"Well *I* think so. It'd be the most mind-boggling time-trip."

"Why would I want to go and look at a lot of boring ruins? It's bad enough listening to you and Dad talking about them."

"They won't *be* ruins, they'll be complete buildings. And they're the most unbelievable ones ever. Look at this." He flipped open the book he'd been reading. "Isn't that amazing?"

The illustration showed a massive temple, with people dwarfed by colossal statues. "And check out these tomb carvings." One depicted a pharaoh wearing the traditional cobra headdress, surrounded by mystical figures with animal faces.

"And if you want gold and jewelry, here are some treasures from Tutankhamun's tomb."

The pictures were impressive, but Kate concealed her curiosity.

"The Egyptians had this fantastic lifestyle because the land around the Nile was so rich," he raced on. "Everything grew like crazy—melons, grapes, dates—"

"You sound like a travel ad."

"Ancient Egypt was big on festivals and parties—your kind of place, Kate!"

"You're making it sound *too* good."

"Well, I guess there were *some* bad thing—like building tombs and hacking up rocks."

"Suppose *we* had to do that?"

"You wouldn't. Only men and boys did stonework."

"That sounds better!"

"When shall we go, then?"

"Hey, not so fast. I didn't say we would."

"But it does sound amazing, doesn't it?"

"Possibly..."

Although Kate decided to go on the trip before he left her room, she didn't tell him for several days—it was fun watching her brother squirm!

AP became preoccupied with planning the trip. Choosing the right time period was the most difficult part.

"What does it matter?" Kate said one night. "Ancient Egypt is ancient Egypt."

"The pharaohs ruled for nearly 3,000 years. Think of all the changes in that time." He started explaining about the Old, Middle and New Kingdoms, but she wasn't listening.

"I've chosen the reign of Ramesses II," AP continued. "He was an important pharaoh from the middle of the New Kingdom."

"Whatever."

"I don't suppose you care why I've chosen the area around Luxor either."

"Not in the least."

AP left her room, shaking his head.

❊ ❊ ❊

"We'll be back soon after 10," Mrs. Littleton called out from the hallway. She was pulling on her heavy coat while her husband warmed up the car. "It's not a long movie."

"Sure, Mum," said Kate. "Have fun."

"See you later," called AP from the dining room. He had books spread all over the table.

"Make sure you clear up all your mess before we get back."

"Will do," he sang out.

As soon as their parents drove off, AP and Kate hurried upstairs to his room.

"All done," he said, moments later. "I've set the time for minus 3290 years. That'll take us back to the year 1280 BC—about the tenth year of Ramesses's reign. And the red dot is set over Luxor." He held out the abacus so she could double-check the settings.

"Ready?"

Kate grabbed his arm and nodded.

❊ ❊ ❊

"Wow," said AP, squinting against the glare, "that sun's so bright. How do you feel?"

"A bit dizzy," said Kate, trying hard to focus her eyes, "but it was much easier this time."

Then she caught sight of her brother. "I don't *believe* it," she gasped. "What's happened to your hair? And what *are* you wearing?"

AP was as bald as an egg and wearing nothing but a short kilt. Made from the coarsest linen, the straw-colored garment reached to just above his knees. Kate, in contrast, wore a white ankle-length dress of the finest pleated linen. High at the neck, with sleeves that stopped at the elbows, it was complemented by a stunning gold necklace. And while AP stood barefoot on the hot sand, she had the luxury of sandals—not the common variety woven from reeds, but leather ones.

"You're tanned, from the tip of your bald head to your toes! I've never seen you looking so brown." Then she glanced down and saw she was the same. "How does the abacus *do* all this?"

AP shook his head in wonder.

Kate's black shoulder-length wig was the height of fashion. But when she explored underneath, she was horrified to find she was as bald as her brother. "And what's this thing I'm carrying?" The unfamiliar object had a handle like a hairbrush, with an oval strip of metal supporting three horizontal rows of buttons on wires.

"Some kind of rattle," suggested AP.

"What am I supposed to do with it?"

"You could shake it." He grinned.

"I'm more inclined to pitch it."

"Not a good idea—there must be some reason for having it."

They found themselves standing opposite a maze of narrow streets, with small houses crammed tightly together. The town was bustling.

"There are *so* many people," said Kate, "and most of them are headed this way. What's going on?"

Before AP could reply, there was a loud explosion immediately behind them. They felt the pressure wave slam into their backs and ring through their chests. More blows followed, in rapid succession. Spinning around, they were astonished to see a band of drummers in flowing robes, frantically beating their instruments. Kate and AP never knew drums could be so loud.

The band's leader was an impish man with a snake-charmer's pipe, which he wielded like a conductor's baton. Prancing before the crowd like the Pied Piper, he led the way across a broad avenue. A massive wall stretched before the crowd, and he was heading for the huge doorway.

"I think that might be a walled city," AP said, nodding toward the wall, which was as high as a house. "Maybe there's an emergency and the townspeople are seeking safety."

"But there's no panic," reasoned Kate. "Everyone's in a party mood. Look at the way they're laughing and singing." Then she noticed how people were beginning to stare. "We shouldn't stand here attracting attention. Let's go over and check it out."

As they mingled with the crowds, AP had the distinct feeling they were being watched. Glancing around, he saw nobody suspicious, but the feeling remained.

"What's wrong?" asked Kate.

"Probably nothing," he said, not wanting to alarm her. "Just the feeling someone's out there—watching."

"Snakebite?" she asked, looking around anxiously.

"The abacus!" AP suddenly realized it was dangling against his bare chest, for everyone to see. In one swift move, he slipped the cord over his head and tucked the device into the waistband of his kilt.

Crossing the avenue, they headed left, following the crowds toward the main entrance. The wall, now on their right, towered high above them.

"Impressive, eh?" said AP, glancing up. "See what it's made of?" He paused to take a closer look. "Mud brick. They mix mud with chopped-up straw, press it into a brick-shaped mould and bake it in the sun."

"The wall's made of *mud*?"

"Yep."

"That's crazy. Wouldn't it become a mud pie when it rains?"

AP smiled knowingly. "But it hardly ever rains."

"No rain. Right!" Now she was convinced he was joking. "So how do you explain all these palm trees? And you said the other day how the land was so rich."

"Palm trees have spreading roots and can find underground water. As for the farmland, all that water comes from the Nile."

"End of lecture?"

AP nodded. "By the way, I never complimented you on your *amazing* makeup." Like almost everyone else, men and women alike, Kate's eyes were highlighted with thick black lines. These extended beyond the outer corners of her eyes, giving them an exaggerated almond shape.

"That's *humongous*," marveled Kate as they stood dwarfed before the entrance. "The opening itself is enormous, but it looks tiny compared to the surrounding stonework."

"It's called a pylon," AP explained, "built from stone blocks. So this entrance leads to a *temple*, not to a walled city."

"Look at those wild carvings!" said Kate. "Who's the guy in the chariot with the bow and arrow?"

"That's the Pharaoh, slaying his enemies. And the one on the other side of the entrance, with the falcon's face, is the god Horus."

Stepping through the opening was like arriving at a small town—there were buildings, a garden, even an artificial lake. But the central feature was the temple, a colossal structure set well back from the wall. Kate and AP stared in disbelief. Its pylon was even grander than the one they'd just passed through, and on either side was a colossal statue of a seated pharaoh.

"Are these like the ones at Abo Sabo that you and Dad were talking about?"

"Abu Simbel," AP corrected. "Yes, they're similar, but way bigger than these."

"*Bigger?* How can statues come any larger than these guys? If I stretched on tiptoe, I could only reach their ankles!"

"The other ones are twice as tall."

"Unreal!"

"So is hacking them out of solid rock. Then the workers had to drag them all the way across the desert from the quarries."

"How about those tall pointed things?" Kate nodded toward a pair of stone columns twice the height of a house flanking the statues. "They're like the thing we saw in London last summer, beside the river Thames."

"Cleopatra's Needle," confirmed AP. "They're called obelisks—they were carved as gifts for the gods."

Walking over for a closer look, they saw that all four sides of the obelisk were carved with hieroglyphs.

"Do they stand for letters of the alphabet or for actual things?" asked Kate.

"Both," said AP. "I don't know much about them, but there's an alphabet of twenty-four letters—*sounds* really—plus lots of other hieroglyphs that stand for certain things." He ran his eye up and down the obelisk. "See that one—the loop sitting on top of the letter T?"

Kate nodded.

"That's the sign for life."

"What about those groups of hieroglyphs inside oval borders?"

"They're called cartouches. Each cartouche represents the name of a particular pharaoh."

Kate reached out and traced one of the hieroglyphs with her fingers.

"You're really getting into this, aren't you?"

"It's *so* cool. All this stuff." She gazed around in wonder. "And everything's so *huge*. I've never seen anything like it."

"Shall we go inside the temple?" asked AP.

They walked through the opening in the middle of the pylon and out into a great courtyard dotted with statues and crowded with people.

"They're not as big as the statues outside," said Kate. "Hey, look at that one over there, the little guy sitting cross-legged. He's as small as you!"

"Thanks!"

"I'm baking," said Kate, glancing up at the noonday sun. "Let's go over there in the shade." She nodded toward the roofed area that ran along either side of the courtyard.

Both were surprised at how much cooler it felt there. "What's with all these stone pillars?" she asked, looking at the close rows of columns.

"They're holding up the roof. Egyptians didn't have steel girders for the horizontal supports, just stone. That's much weaker, so they needed more pillars."

"How do you *know* all this stuff?" asked Kate. "No, don't tell me, you read some book."

They strolled toward the far end of the temple, and as they stopped to admire a carved column, the abacus slipped from AP's kilt. Fortunately, there were few people around, so when he made a grab between his legs, nobody noticed.

"Here," he said, handing it over. "You can take it now."

Quickly slipping the cord over her head, Kate tucked the abacus out of sight.

"Are those gravestones?" asked Kate, looking at some rectangular slabs carved with mystical signs.

"I'm not sure," said AP, who didn't know they were called stelae.

"Check *this* one out," said Kate. The carving, in black stone, showed a baby boy standing on a crocodile's back, holding snakes in his hand.

"That's *weird*."

As they puzzled over its meaning, a man, and a woman carrying a sick little boy, came toward them. Kate and AP moved aside as the couple stopped in front of the stone. The man began reciting a prayer. When he finished, he rubbed his hand over the image of the baby. The boy's mother repeated the ritual. After standing in silence for several minutes, they left.

"That was sad," whispered Kate. "Their little boy's so sick, and they think the stone can cure him."

The far end of the temple was roofed over, like the sides. "I think this is private," whispered AP, noticing they were the only ones there. Kate was unconcerned.

"I wonder where that leads?" She nodded toward a large opening in the far wall. "Let's find out."

As they approached the entrance, an important-looking man in white robes swept past. Hurrying behind him was a bare-chested man, his arms laden with scrolls. Both disappeared through the opening.

"It's an enormous hall," said Kate a few moments later—AP had stood back while she peered through the darkened doorway.

As she pondered whether to go through, several more people hurried past them and disappeared inside.

"Did they just smile at you and glare at me?" asked AP.

"Forget it," said Kate. "Who cares what they think? Come on, let's go and explore."

"We can't go in there!" he blurted, but Kate had already disappeared. Reluctantly, AP followed.

Cool, dim and cavernous, the room was filled with the aroma of burning incense. The only light came from oil lamps on the walls, their flickering flames adding to the mystique.

"Look at those wall paintings," marveled Kate. "They're *amazing*. And check out that door. Do you think it's made of *real* gold?"

"Maybe," said AP, staring at the door's elaborate engravings. One showed a man with a falcon's face, the other a falcon with a sash over its shoulder. "They're both Horus, the falcon god. So this is probably his temple."

"Each god has his own temple?"

"The major ones do—the others share temples. They even go visiting each other."

"You've got to be joking."

"No, honestly. The gods are represented by stone statues, and the priests take them out on wooden stretchers."

"That's *wild!*" she exclaimed.

"Keep your voice down," he whispered. "I'm sure we shouldn't be here. Let's duck behind that column and see what happens."

Kate thought he was overreacting, but didn't argue.

Safely hidden, they watched as a young woman, dressed like Kate, knocked on the golden door. It swung open. As she stepped inside, they caught a tantalizing glimpse of a golden boat. Then the door closed.

"Come on," said Kate, "let's check it out."

"We can't go in *there!*" he protested.

"Why not? They let her in, why not us?"

"Well," said AP, looking down at himself, "I'm a bit underdressed."

"You always are!"

Without a second thought, she strode up to the door and gave two raps. AP stood behind her—anxiously.

A powerfully built guard in a long pleated kilt opened the door. His head was shaved and he bowed deeply as Kate stepped inside. AP, feeling encouraged, followed her lead, but didn't get beyond the entrance.

"*Wabs* have no right in here!" he snapped, and pushed AP back so hard he almost fell over. "You should know that priests must be four times pure to enter the sanctuary of the god. Be gone!" With that, he shut the door in AP's face.

27

Wab World

A stunned AP stood outside the door, wondering what to do. They'd soon discover Kate was an imposter, so he decided to wait. Minutes dragged by like hours. Eventually, he had to accept that Kate wasn't coming out. Worried and confused, he made his way back to the open courtyard. How would he reconnect with Kate?

AP noticed several other boys, shaved and dressed like he was, doing jobs around the temple. One had just reported to a bald man wearing a long white robe. AP guessed the man was a priest, and was close enough to hear what he was saying.

"Take those offerings to the proper place." The priest pointed to a pile of loaves stacked against a column. Then, seeing AP, he called out, "You, boy, lend a hand."

AP did as he was told.

"You're new," said the other boy, looking AP up and down. "I haven't seen you here before. Just start today?"

"Er...yes," replied AP.

"My name's Nekhti. What's yours?" The boy, who was about a year older than AP, was a head and shoulders taller, and much broader.

"I'm called AP."

"Aypee," Nekhti repeated. "I've not heard that name before. You're not from here."

"No, not exactly." Then, changing the subject, "Where's all this stuff got to go?"

"We take it as far as the hypostyle hall." Seeing the blank look on AP's face, he added, "Wabs are not sufficiently pure to enter the offering vestibule."

AP still looked lost.

"You have no idea what I'm talking about, do you?" Nekhti sounded puzzled, though there was nothing threatening in his voice. "You must be from the desert," he concluded, as if that explained everything. "I've heard desert people do everything differently."

AP nodded.

"So you know nothing of how our temples work?"

"Not really. Temples in the desert are so different from yours."

"And you don't know the ways of our priesthood?"

"I know it's a *bit* like ours," AP improvised.

"Where you come from, is a wab the most junior priest, as it is here?"

AP nodded, hoping the questions wouldn't get harder.

"And wabs work part-time at the temple?"

Again, AP nodded.

"Do you want to learn more about the priesthood, like I do, and reach the next level of purity?"

"Yes," said AP, not sure what that might involve.

"Good," said Nekhti, bending down and picking up an armful of loaves. "Let's make a start by getting all this over to the hypostyle."

Minutes later, they arrived at the hypostyle, the roofed-in area at the far end of the courtyard that AP and Kate had explored. Nekhti led the way to a small room that was half filled with food and jugs of wine and beer.

"Most offerings to the gods are made by the temple itself," Nekhti explained. "Like other large temples, we've got our own farms. During special festivals like today, though, the common people bring offerings too."

AP picked up a small pottery figure of a crocodile.

"There are lots of ornaments like that—they've become quite popular as offerings."

"So what happens to all this food and drink?"

"The same as happens to all temple offerings."

AP looked puzzled.

"Surely you have daily offerings to the gods at your temples?"

"Well, yes—"

"Right," he shot back. "So when the food and drink has been offered, and the god has taken his fill, the rest is shared out among the priests and temple workers."

AP nodded.

"Come on," said Nekhti, stepping out of the room. "There's a lot more to be moved."

The boys were on their way back through the courtyard to pick up their last load of offerings when they heard a loud commotion behind them. Turning around, AP saw a procession heading straight for them. At its center was a gold ceremonial boat—the very one he and Kate had glimpsed through the golden door. Twelve priests were carrying it on their shoulders. Each wore a stiff kilt, reaching almost to his ankles. Three more priests walked on either side, each carrying a large fan of ostrich feathers.

"Do you see who's in the boat?" asked Nekhti, pointing to the wooden box in the middle of the vessel. Elaborately carved, the open-fronted box was almost as big as a phone booth.

"It's a statue of Horus," said AP.

"*Statue?*" gasped Nekhti. If AP had said the priests were carrying a hippopotamus, he couldn't have been more shocked. "It's not a *statue* of Horus, it *is* Horus."

"Yes, yes of course," said AP, realizing he'd made a big blunder.

"Surely you desert people know that the god's spirit lives inside the statue, so the statue *is* the god?"

"Yes, we do," said AP, blushing.

The priest leading the procession carried a rod shaped like an outstretched arm. The cup in its hand held burning incense. The sweet-smelling smoke wafted through the air.

AP was too engrossed in the spectacle to notice at first. Then it hit him like a collapsing column: Kate, walking immediately behind the leading priest, was part of the procession.

"Who's the one behind the leader?" asked AP, trying hard to sound casual.

"She's a *shemayet*," said Nekhti. Seeing AP's blank expression he added, "Maybe you say priestess."

"Priestess?" repeated AP in disbelief.

"Yes, and there's another one right behind her."

AP recognized the second priestess as the young woman who had entered the golden door just before Kate. Aside from being dressed alike, they each carried a rattle, which they shook and banged against their free hand. "What do *you* call the thing in their hand?" asked AP, as if he had a different name for it.

"We call it a *sistrum*. Priestesses always carry them. What do you call it?"

"Oh, the same."

As the procession went past, Kate spotted her brother and made eye contact. She tried mouthing a message, which he couldn't understand, so he gave an exaggerated shrug of his shoulders.

Musicians playing flutes, harps and cymbals followed the ceremonial boat. People in the crowd joined in behind them, singing and shouting and thoroughly enjoying themselves.

"So what happens now?" asked AP, wondering how he could contact Kate.

"The procession will make a circuit around the temple, then thread through the town before returning."

"Where do the priests and priestesses go afterwards?"

"The priests live on the temple grounds, so they'll carry on with their duties. As for the priestesses—they looked wealthy, so they'll probably return to their big houses."

"Do all priestesses live at home?"

"No. Some live in a special part of the temple." Nekhti paused. "Why are you so interested in the priestesses?"

"I'm not. I just wondered whether it's the same as back home."

AP had no time to figure out how to connect with Kate because as soon as he and Nekhti delivered the last of the offerings, the priest sent them on another errand.

After making its way along the main street, the procession came to a halt, and the priests set down the ceremonial boat. Kate, stressed out from playing the role of a priestess, wondered what would happen now. She was also wondering how she would ever find her brother.

A dozen wabs appeared, carrying jugs of water. Kate was grateful for the drink, and the break gave her the chance to continue her conversation with Tamit, the other priestess.

"You *must* come and stay at my home," insisted Tamit. "My parents wouldn't hear of your staying at the temple."

"I'll be fine," said Kate, knowing the temple was her only link with her brother. "I can't just turn up at your home."

"It happens all the time! My father's the royal scribe in charge of the treasury. He's *always* entertaining guests."

"All the more reason not to bother your mother with me."

"My mother *won't* be bothered. We have a huge house full of servants—it makes no difference how many guests come to stay."

Kate knew Tamit would never take no for an answer. But how would she contact AP if she went to her house? And how long would it be before she was exposed as a fake, anyway?

Meanwhile, AP was learning a lot about his new friend. Nekhti was the youngest of four brothers and two sisters. They lived with their parents in a small house, not far from the temple.

"My father expected me to go into the family business like my brothers," Nekhti explained. "But I didn't want to."

When AP asked what sort of business that was, Nekhti was vague.

"Let's just say I've tried it and don't like it. I still work there when I'm not at the temple, but it's the priesthood that really interests me. I spend the mornings with my father and brothers, and the afternoons at the temple."

The Egyptians, AP discovered, divided their day into twenty-four hours too, and Nekhti spent the last three hours of each afternoon at the temple's school.

They finished their errands before the procession returned, and Nekhti was about to go off to his class.

208

Before leaving, he turned to AP. "You've got nowhere to live, have you?"

"I planned on staying at the temple."

"No need," said Nekhti, "you can come and stay with us."

Just then, a loud trumpeting sounded throughout the courtyard. "That's the call for afternoon class," said Nekhti, and before AP had a chance to reply, his friend dashed off.

An hour dragged by, and AP wondered if the procession would return before Nekhti's class ended. Fortunately, it did.

Catching Kate's eye, AP pointed to himself and then to the ground. She nodded, knowing he was going to stay put.

AP had to wait ages before she finally appeared.

"I've only got a few minutes," Kate began, grabbing his arm and leading him behind the nearest column. "I've got to talk fast."

He had seen his sister agitated before, though never like this. She quickly told him how Tamit was pressuring her to stay at her home. "I can't go and leave you to fend for yourself."

When AP explained how Nekhti had invited him to stay at his house, she was so relieved she hugged him. Unfortunately, her other problem had no solution. "Tamit and those priests think I'm a *priestess*!" she blurted out, almost in tears. "They'll soon find out I'm a complete fraud—I've no way of stopping them."

"Hang on," said AP, "there must be a way out of this."

After pondering for a while, he started smiling. "Dreams!" he exclaimed. "The Egyptians are great believers in the meaning of dreams—I read about it in one of Dad's books."

Kate stared blankly.

"All you've got to do is tell Tamit you've been having this strange dream. Exactly the same dream every night." He paused, thinking up a suitable story. "I've got it! Say one of the gods speaks to you—choose one whose name you'll remember. This god predicts you're going to forget everything you know about being a priestess. That's okay because you've been chosen for greater things." Then, with a grin he added, "Be sure to say the god hands you a loaf of white bread after telling you this."

"This is no time for jokes," Kate snapped. "Can't you see I'm in *real* trouble?"

"I'm not joking. When someone gives you white bread in a dream, it's a sign things are going to work out well."

"You're sure?"

"Of course. I'm trying to help, not make things worse."

"Okay, but if I tell Tamit this story and she believes it, I'll just be buying extra time. If I've been chosen for greater things, I'll have to *prove* it sometime, won't I?"

"Exactly. And that's where I come in. I'll think of something you can do to show your new powers."

"Like what?"

"I don't know yet."

"That's just great! I'm going to convince Tamit I'm about to have special powers, and then—"

"Listen Kate," AP interrupted, "the idea of having a dream will work for sure. In the meantime, I'll think of something that'll show everyone you're a powerful priestess."

She looked unconvinced.

"Remember the soap bubbles at Camelot? You have to admit, they blew everyone away."

"You're going to make more *soap*?"

"No, of course not. I've got to think of something appropriate for ancient Egyptians."

"How are we going to keep in touch?"

"We'll meet right here at a certain time each day," said AP.

"Suppose one of us can't make it?"

"We'll have a backup time. How about we always meet when the temple class starts—you'll hear the trumpeting sound. If we miss that rendezvous, we'll meet again as the sun goes down."

"And if something still goes wrong and we miss each other?" asked Kate.

"Then we'll leave a note—any ideas where?"

"How about the stone with the baby holding the snakes?"

AP nodded.

"We can tuck it beneath a corner of the stone," said Kate.

"So we've got it all sorted."

"Seems like it." Kate, for the first time, looked calm.

"One last thing. Which god are you going to use for your dream?"

"Hathor," she replied without hesitation. "She's the goddess who made the *sistrum* a sacred instrument. Hathor got me into this mess—she can get me out of it!"

They would have talked for longer, but Kate saw Tamit waiting. "Got to go," she said, giving her brother another hug. "Thanks for sorting me out. Take care."

"No problem. I'll come up with something that'll make you the queen of priestesses!"

28

Mummies

I'm not sure about this," AP told Nekhti some time later. "I can't just arrive at your house and say I've nowhere to stay."

"It'll be okay. My mother and father are very friendly—you'll see. If I didn't bring you home, I'd be in big trouble."

After leaving the temple grounds, they crossed the avenue and began threading their way through the town. Even Kate would have found it challenging navigating the winding roads and alleyways. "They're made of mud brick—the same as yours in the desert," said Nekhti, nodding toward the small square houses which stood so close together it would have been a tight squeeze walking between them. All had flat roofs and some had a second story. "I expect your houses have tiny windows to keep out the sun too?"

AP nodded absentmindedly, totally engrossed in his new surroundings. With suppertime approaching, the air was filled with enticing aromas. Most were unfamiliar, though he recognized the smell of charcoal.

"We've got a big house," Nekhti announced proudly, "with upstairs rooms. And father has a garden out back where he grows all sorts of things."

When they arrived, Nekhti led the way through the narrow front door. This opened into a dimly lit room occupying the full width of the house. The floor was covered with rush matting. Nekhti's mother, Nefret, was busy preparing a meal in the kitchen area at one end of the room, helped by her two daughters. An open side door was letting in the delicious smells of baking from an oven standing just outside. When Nekhti explained AP's situation, Nefret stopped what she was doing to greet him. "You're welcome to stay with us for as long as you want," she said enthusiastically. "You'll be much more comfortable here than at the temple."

Her two daughters—both about Kate's age—were equally welcoming. Like their mother, each wore a simple long dress of thin, cool linen.

"Now the weather's getting hot, you two boys can sleep on the roof," Nefret continued. Then, turning to Nekhti, "Go and show Aypee around. You've both got time to bathe before supper."

AP hung back, fascinated by what was going on. Nefret stepped outside to the oven, which looked like a giant upturned flowerpot. After she had peered through the opening at the front to check on the bread, one of her daughters added more charcoal to the fire at the bottom. Meanwhile, her other daughter was kneeling at a low table on the kitchen floor, cutting up a huge fish with a knife. AP started feeling hungry.

"This is where we bathe," said Nekhti, nodding toward a small room beside the kitchen area. "And the one next to that—well, I'll show you later." He led the way to the other end of the main room to show his guest the eating and living area. Instead of one large dining table, there were several small ones, and AP was surprised at how low they were—hardly higher than his shins. For seating, there were many low stools, and two chairs with small backs and no arms. "Let's bathe," said Nekhti, heading back to the small room.

There was no door, just a knee-high wall. Seeing AP hesitate, Nekhti said, "I'll go first."

The walls and floor were lined with stone—mud brick would have washed away. A tall table stood in one corner, with a large hand basin and two small bowls. One bowl contained a white powder, the other a greasy-looking gray cream. Beneath the table was a tall water jug. Nekhti filled the basin from the jug, adding some of the white powder. "You must use natron for washing in the desert too," he said, adding a pinch more.

"Er, yes," AP replied. He knew the Egyptians used natron in mummification, but didn't realize they used it for washing too.

Slipping off his kilt without any embarrassment, Nekhti gave himself a good wash-down, splashing water everywhere. Once he'd dried himself with a linen towel, he rubbed some of the cream into his skin. Then he put on a clean kilt. AP, feeling distinctly uncomfortable, had kept his eyes fixed on the floor.

"You must use a lot of this in the desert," said Nekhti, rubbing in more of the greasy cream. "That desert air must dry out your skin."

"Oh yes," said AP, "I slap it on!"

"Here," said Nekhti, handing him a clean kilt. "You can use one of mine. Leave your dirty one in the basket—the washing gets done tomorrow."

"I can't expect your mother to do my washing."

"Mother?" repeated Nekhti. "Washing may be women's work in the desert, but it's men's work in this part of Egypt."

AP looked puzzled.

"Clothes are washed in the Nile." When AP still didn't understand, he explained. "Crocodiles live in the Nile. Sometimes they *eat* people."

"Oh, I see. Well, that's one thing about the desert—no crocodiles!"

Blushing brightly, AP bathed himself as fast as he could and got dressed.

Fortunately, the room next to the bathroom did have a door, though it was barely shoulder-high. Nekhti swung it open so AP could look inside. The toilet seat was made of limestone and supported on four blocks. Beneath was an earthenware pot filled with sand. Standing beside it were a water jug, several hand basins and a bowl of natron. "When you're finished," said Nekhti, glancing down at the toilet, "the pit's in the garden. I'll show you in a moment."

AP nodded, as if this was all familiar to him, but he was desperately trying to work out the details of using an Egyptian toilet.

"That's my parents' bedroom," said Nekhti, pointing to a narrow doorway leading off from the main room. "My sisters share the one beside it."

"And through here is the garden." Opening a narrow door, he led the way to a patch of green no bigger than AP's patio back home. "See, we've got a date palm and a fig tree, and father's growing onions, garlic, beans and melons."

AP was surprised at how much had been crammed into such a small area.

"We've got a well too." Nekhti pointed to a deep hole in the ground. "And over there, behind the palm, is the pit— for the toilet."

They reached the second floor by a mud-brick stairway built against the back wall of the house. "This is the bedroom I share with my brothers," said Nekhti, stepping inside. The windows were tiny and close to the ceiling, like the ones downstairs. The beds were simple wooden frames, criss-crossed with woven strips of linen and supported on four short legs. Several thick linen sheets were piled on top, to keep out the cold night air. Instead of a pillow, there was a wooden headrest that looked extremely uncomfortable.

"We're going to sleep on the roof," said Nekhti enthusiastically. He clambered up a flimsy wooden ladder leaning against the rear wall, and disappeared through a small opening in the ceiling. "Come on up," he called down to AP.

From their vantage point on the rooftop, they could look over the neighborhood. The sun was sinking fast, and the first star was shining in a sapphire sky. Off in the distance, AP could see the temple of Horus. As he stood there gazing across the ancient skyline, an idea popped into his head—the perfect thing for Kate to demonstrate her new powers.

"Let's go downstairs," said Nekhti, rousing his friend from his thoughts. "My father and brothers have just returned from work."

The evening meal with Nekhti and his family reminded AP of childhood birthday parties. Everyone was talking at once, and the noisiest of them all was Shedou, Nekhti's father. Beer was the regular drink, for adults and children, and the more beer Shedou drank, the louder he became. AP didn't like the taste, and surprised everyone by sipping from the bowl of water beside his plate. All too late, he realized it was for washing his fingers. Nefret set a jug of water and a cup beside him, and the embarrassing incident was forgotten. AP ate his fill of Nile perch, flatbread and leeks.

"So what are we going to do with you, young Aypee?" roared Shedou toward the end of the meal. "How about coming to work with me and the boys?" Then, turning to Nekhti, he added, "My youngest son doesn't want to join the family business, though he still works with us when he's not playing at the temple!" He guffawed with laughter, and his three older sons joined in.

"I don't *play* at the temple," Nekhti protested. "I go there to learn about the priesthood. One day I'm going to become an important priest, then you'll all see."

This made them laugh all the louder, but it was all good-natured. Shedou leaned across from his table and patted Nekhti on the shoulder. "I'm sure you will. Then I might have to start visiting the temple myself!

"So, young Aypee, are you going to come to work with us tomorrow morning?"

"Of course," said AP, "though I still don't know what work you do."

For the first time that evening, the room fell silent.

"Nekhti hasn't told you?" asked Shedou. Nekhti shook his head. "Well, in that case, we'll keep it as a surprise until we get there."

Soon after clearing away the meal, everyone started getting ready for bed. AP was surprised at how early ancient Egyptians retired.

AP gazed up at the slimmest crescent moon—a luminous C in a black sky of stars. "There'll be a new moon tomorrow," he thought, and drifted off to sleep.

There was a private guest house on the edge of town. Visitors could stay there in seclusion, safe from prying eyes and inquisitive ears. The latest arrival was a man on a mission. From his well-dressed appearance he might have been a nobleman—someone above suspicion. Important people would have accepted him as one of their own. Lesser people would have bent to his will in an effort to please. He had traveled far that day, and retired early. But sleep did not come easily to Robert Drew. His mind was too busy planning his next move. There must be no mistakes this time. Mordax's brats had to be stopped and the chronoverser recovered.

"Not much farther," said Shedou next morning, as they walked past the entrance to the temple grounds. "It's around the back, on the far side."

AP noticed the smell as soon as they rounded the second corner. He thought it might be the drains, and then wondered whether these even existed in ancient Egypt. Nekhti exchanged guilty glances with his friend.

"That's our workshop over there." Shedou pointed to a large single-story building standing some distance away from the back wall of the temple compound. Several smaller ones surrounded it.

"Welcome to the House of Embalming and Purification," Shedou proudly announced.

The words hammered into AP's skull. Seeing mummies in museums never bothered him, but he'd never seen a "real" dead person before.

"Don't worry, Aypee," said Shedou, draping a large arm across his shoulder, "you won't have to see anything you'd rather avoid. Nekhti's never got used to handling bodies, so we give him other jobs. Just stay with him, Aypee, and you'll be fine."

Nekhti had given AP a pair of old sandals to wear to work, and as he followed his friend into one of the small buildings, they crunched over the white powder covering the floor. There was a huge pile of the stuff at the far end, with a stack of empty baskets nearby.

"We've got to fill them with natron and carry them to this end," Nekhti explained, "then line them up beside the door."

They walked to the other end. "Here," said Nekhti, passing AP an empty basket, "you hold it steady while I shovel."

Although it was hot and dusty inside, Nekhti said it was far better than being in the workshop. AP had no wish to visit the embalming room, but was intrigued to know what went on there, so Nekhti explained.

"First, they give the body a good washing with natron and water—the beginners get that job. After that, they coat the face with hot resin."

AP looked puzzled.

"The sticky stuff from trees," Nekhti explained. "It goes hard when it sets."

AP nodded, recalling the sticky beads he'd seen on tree trunks.

"Next, they have to remove all the internal organs, starting with the brain." At this point Nekhti paused—the basket was full, and they carried it to the far end.

"When they've got all the brain out," Nekhti continued, "they fill up the braincase with strips of linen dipped in resin." He purposely avoided giving details of how they removed the brain through the nostrils, after hammering a hole through the skull with a chisel. "Then they pull out the intestines and things, and wash out the space with wine and spices. The embalmer does the same with the chest, but he leaves the heart in place."

"Why?"

"The dead person needs his heart so he can still think."

AP nodded—ancient Egyptians believed thinking took place in the heart.

Swapping jobs, AP took a turn at shoveling.

"The embalmers have to pack all the empty spaces in the body," Nekhti began again, "to keep its natural shape. They use rags, straw, wood shavings—anything will do."

AP listened intently.

"Once that's been done, they heap the body with natron and leave it for forty days. That draws out all the water. Burying a body in the desert does the same thing, but it gets too shriveled. Embalmed bodies look more lifelike, so it's easier for the person to go on living in the afterlife."

Nekhti paused. "I forgot about the organs. They cover them with natron too. Then they're wrapped in linen, scented with oils, and put into four special stone pots called canopic jars."

After shoveling for two hours, Nekhti said they'd filled enough baskets. Other workers had already collected most of these, but before starting their next job, they delivered one themselves.

Setting the basket down outside the embalming room door, AP couldn't resist a peek inside. The dimly lit workshop was crammed with tables, each with a body at a different stage in the process. He saw several gruesome sights, but the picture that stayed in his mind was of the jackal-headed Anubis, bending over a body to perform some mystical rite. Although AP knew it was only an embalmer wearing a mask, the experience was unsettling.

The second building was smaller than the first, and much cleaner. Nekhti pointed to a wide roll of bandage material, attached to the wall like a giant toilet roll.

"We've got to cut long strips," he said, pulling on the free end of the roll. "Here, you hold while I cut." Once he had cut one strip, he rolled it into a bandage. As they cut and rolled together, Nekhti explained the final stages of mummification.

"After the forty days in natron, the embalmers have to restuff the body and sew up all the openings. Then they rub it all over with oils and spices, paint on hot resin and it's ready for bandaging."

When they swapped jobs, AP discovered that cutting a straight edge was harder than it looked.

"The wrapping is the most difficult part of embalming," Nekhti continued. "After dipping the bandages in resin, the embalmers bind the body, wrapping each finger and toe separately. They include special charms in the bandaging to help the journey to the afterlife."

"What about the outer casing?" asked AP. "Aren't there several?"

Nekhti nodded. "The first is the smallest. Sometimes it's just made from strips of bandage dipped in plaster. The mask comes next, painted like the person's face." He gestured with his hands to show how it fitted over the head and shoulders. "This is really important because it allows the person's *ba*—their spirit—to find its way back to the body at night, after visiting the world during the day."

Egyptian beliefs were more complicated than AP had realized.

"The next mummy case is painted to look like the person dressed in their finest clothes. The outer box is also painted."

"What about the sarcophagus?" asked AP, thinking of the heavy stone boxes he'd seen in museums.

"The outer case *is* the sarcophagus."

"Oh, I thought the sarcophagus was made of stone."

"Sometimes it is, but that's only for pharaohs and other important people."

29

Conjuring up Magic

T he morning flew by, and the boys were soon on their way to the temple. Nefret had packed them a lunch—some flatbread, olives and figs, with a flask of water for AP instead of beer. AP didn't think he'd have any appetite, but he munched away with his friend as they walked around the perimeter wall.

After reporting to the priest, AP and Nekhti spent the next two hours running errands around the temple. Then it was time for Nekhti's class. They agreed to meet outside the temple entrance at sunset, then the two boys went their separate ways.

AP squinted up at the afternoon sun. He had been waiting at the rendezvous for some time since the temple trumpet had sounded, and still there was no sign of Kate. He was about to check whether she'd left a note when he saw her.

"Sorry," she said, slipping behind a column. We had a late start."

"How long have we got?"

"Plenty of time." Kate sounded remarkably relaxed. "Tamit's meeting someone. She was being mysterious, so it could be a boy. Anyway, we're not getting together for an hour."

AP expected her to tell him all about her "dream," but she had other things on her mind.

"You should *see* where Tamit lives. It's more like a palace than a house—a great hall, stone columns, rooms everywhere, a huge garden and a *pool*. The servants' building is like a mansion." She barely paused for breath. "And the servants do absolutely everything! Tamit has a servant to help her bathe and get dressed, and another to put on her makeup. I've got this amazing room, with my own bathroom."

"You won't want to go back home."

"I could certainly get used to living in ancient Egypt. How about you?"

"I'm not living in *quite* such luxury. They're really nice people, though, and they've made me feel like one of the family." Then, changing the subject, he asked about her "dream."

"It worked like magic. Especially when I mentioned the white bread."

"So you're not suspected of being a fraud?"

"No way. When I told Tamit about the dream, she said I should be resting. She's already spoken with the priests, and they agree. They say I can attend the ceremonies if I want, though I don't have to perform any duties. So I can get up to speed without raising suspicions."

After chatting about the priesthood and Egyptian beliefs, he said he had an idea for her magical trick.

"What is it?"

"I'd rather wait until I've had a chance to build the thing and try it out."

"How long will that take?"

"Half an hour. But I'll need your help getting all the stuff."

"What do you need?"

"First, a piece of really thin white linen—you must be able to see light through it—about the size of a sheet of paper."

"No problem."

"I also need some black cloth, about this large." He stretched out his arms. "If you can't get black, any dark material will do, as long as it keeps out the light."

"Done."

"Then I need some sort of container—about the size of a shoebox. Wood is best, but that's scarce. Pottery would work." Then he had an idea. "I guess I could use a flower-pot, provided there's a hole in the bottom."

"Is that it?"

"Just about. The other things I need are string, some gum for gluing, a needle, a small piece of papyrus—that thick paper scribes write on—and some of that black stuff you use on your eyes."

"Kohl," said Kate.

"Oh, one last thing, though this could be difficult. I need somewhere quiet where I can experiment. There's no way I can do anything where I'm staying."

Kate said she would see what she could do. They arranged to meet at the same time the next day—she hoped she would have everything he needed by then. Just before he left, AP asked her if she was still wearing the abacus. "It's safe," she said, patting her chest.

AP spent the rest of the afternoon exploring. After a long walk, he found himself in a fashionable neighborhood of luxury homes. The narrow streets where Nekhti lived were always crowded with people, but the broad avenue he was on was deserted. Remembering the lesson from Talking Cloud, AP turned around several times to make sure nobody was following him.

225

AP had not expected to see ruins in ancient Egypt. He was therefore surprised to come across the relics of an old temple, in the middle of an open space. Intrigued, he decided to take a closer look. All that remained were a few columns, part of the floor and a colossal statue lying in several pieces. He was so intent on clambering over the largest piece that he didn't hear the approaching footsteps. One moment he was crouching on the statue's massive shoulders. The next instant he was slammed down hard against the stone. Before he could struggle to his feet, he felt a hand patting his kilt—searching. Then he fell to the ground, knocking his head hard against the temple floor. Everything went black.

AP lay there for several seconds trying to remember what happened. Feeling the lump on his forehead, he remembered. Somebody had just attacked him. It was Snakebite—it *had* to be him. That explained the uneasy feeling of being watched when they had first arrived. Snakebite must have seen him slip the abacus into his kilt, which is why he searched him. But wouldn't he have wanted to know where the abacus was when he didn't find it? Maybe he just panicked when he saw his victim knocked unconscious.

By suppertime, the lump on his head was much smaller. Nefret still insisted on treating it with herbs.

Wild duck was on the menu that night, and Shedou was tearing handfuls of meat from the carcasses for everyone. "I've finally found the seeds I've been looking for," he proudly announced. "There's not enough daylight to plant them tonight, but I'll put them in the ground first thing in the morning, before work. And you, young Aypee, will have the honor of giving them their first water from the

Nile." He made a sprinkling gesture with his greasy fingers.

To AP's surprise, Kate was on time for their rendezvous the following day. As soon as she saw the bruise on his forehead, she wanted all the details.

"So Snakebite's back on our track," she said at the end of his story.

"Yes, which means you've got to be especially careful."

"You can be sure of that! But it's *you* I'm worried about."

"I'll be fine," said AP. Then, changing the subject, "Did you get the things I needed?"

Kate patted the large bag on her shoulder. "I've also found the perfect place for your experiments. I'll show you."

They left the temple and set off across the grounds, passing the artificial lake which reminded AP of a large swimming pool. "They call it the Sacred Lake," Kate explained. "The priests bathe there each dawn to purify themselves for morning service."

"You get there *that* early?"

"I decided to miss that particular ceremony," she said, smiling. "Just while I'm resting for my new role."

"Sounds like you're enjoying yourself."

"I'm having a ball! Tamit's good fun, and I'm being treated like a princess."

"Priestess," he corrected.

"Her parents are having a big dinner party tonight. Their dressmaker created a gown especially for me. You should just see it!"

"Here we are," said Kate a few minutes later. They had arrived at a small mud-brick building, well secluded from all the others. "The priests sometimes use it for silent meditation, though it's now reserved for my private use."

When they stepped inside, it took several moments for their eyes to adjust to the dim light. The great thickness of the walls made the room feel deliciously cool.

"Look, there's a table and chair, even a bed."

"It's perfect. But what happens if someone comes along and finds *me* here instead of you?"

"All taken care of," she said proudly. "I had another one of my "dreams." There was a wab, about your size, standing by my side. Hathor came along, holding a loaf of white bread. She broke it in two, and gave one half to me and the other to the little wab."

"Not so much of the 'little'," AP interrupted.

"Hathor smiled and then departed."

"That's *good*. I bet Tamit loved it."

"She said there must be a very special wab looking after my interests."

"Okay, let's see what you've got."

Ten minutes later, they stepped out into the sunshine and said their goodbyes. As Kate headed toward the temple, AP called out after her, "Same time and place tomorrow."

AP would have preferred a smaller flowerpot, though this one would do. The first job was to make the pinhole. Tearing off a piece of papyrus the size of a Post-it note, he painted both sides with black kohl. When he held it up to the tiny window, he was pleased to see it did not let through any light.

After pricking a hole in the center with the needle, he glued the papyrus over the hole in the bottom of the flowerpot. While waiting for this to dry, he held the linen up to the window to make sure it was thin enough to let through the light. Draping the material over the top of the flowerpot, he tied it in place with string. Then, pulling it tight like a drum to form the screen, he trimmed off the surplus material with a knife.

"Now for the scary part," he said to himself. "Will it work?"

He couldn't risk being seen outdoors, so he stood on the chair and aimed the bottom end of the flowerpot through the window. Then, looking like an old-time photographer, he draped the black cloth over the flowerpot and over his head, making sure it didn't cover the screen. Holding the device at arm's length, he moved it from side to side, focusing his eyes on the screen. The faint image that appeared on the screen was not the bright picture he had expected. Maybe the pinhole was too small. He enlarged the hole and tried again.

At first, he saw only a blue haze. Then AP tilted the flowerpot down. "Yes!" he shouted, as a perfect upside-down image of the temple jumped onto the screen. He spent several minutes scanning the terrain, identifying the miniature images that paraded across the screen. Satisfied with the results, he stepped down from the chair and set the camera on the table. He decided to spend the rest of the afternoon exploring the town. If he kept to well-populated areas and stayed alert, there'd be no chance of Snakebite attacking him again.

AP met Nekhti at sunset, and they had a leisurely stroll home.

Nefret met them at the door in a terrible state. "Something awful has happened," she said, wringing her hands. "Come and see for yourselves." She led the way to the garden. "Your father will be so upset."

Nekhti and AP stared down in disbelief. In the patch of soil where Shedou had so carefully planted his seeds that morning there was now a gaping hole and mounds of soil.

"Who would do this?" she asked, completely bewildered. "And why?"

AP asked if she and her daughters had been at home all day.

"No. We visited the temple just before noon, as we do every day."

"Has anything been touched inside the house?" he continued, sounding like a police officer.

"Not as far as I know, though I haven't checked the roof yet. I thought I'd wait until you boys came home."

"What a mess!" said Nekhti, moments later.

Somebody had turned both beds upside down, scattering linen everywhere. They'd pulled everything else apart too, leaving no doubt they were searching for something. AP knew exactly what the intruder was after, but said nothing.

"Whoever it was," said a gloomy Shedou at supper that night, "they were after my seeds."

Nefret suggested the seeds were probably still there in the mounds of soil, but he couldn't be consoled

"I wouldn't be surprised if it was Merab," he said, naming someone he knew from the tavern. "He's been searching for some of those seeds for ages."

❀ ❀ ❀

While AP ate boiled fish and cabbage, Kate had the choice of beef, antelope, wild goose and quail, with a wide assortment of vegetables. Dessert was a selection of fresh fruits and a tempting array of pastries. Serving girls darted between the small tables throughout the meal, making sure everyone had all they wanted. And while musicians played and sang, a troupe of acrobats performed remarkable tricks.

Like all the women at the party, Kate wore a cup-sized cone on her head, held in place with a string. Made of perfumed beeswax, it melted and ran through her wig during the evening, scenting the air all around. Kate enjoyed the most amazing night of her life.

AP lay awake long after Nekhti had fallen asleep. He had gone over the events of the last few days so many times, but he still came up with the same answers. Snakebite must have followed him to Nekhti's house on the first day and been spying on him ever since. He could easily have hidden in the garden and watched him and Nekhti climb up to the roof to sleep. Discovering how many people lived there would have been easy, and when he saw Nefret leaving with her two daughters, he had seized his opportunity to search the house. He probably noticed the freshly dug soil from the roof, so when he didn't find the abacus upstairs, he must have thought it was buried in the garden.

What would Snakebite do next? Would he realize Kate had the abacus?

AP was up at first light, and while everyone else slept, he set to work in the garden. First, he sifted through the soil until he found the seeds—fortunately, they were large and easy to spot. Then he replanted them in rows, the way Shedou had done, and gave them a good watering. Everyone was still asleep when he crept into the bathroom to wash.

Although AP made no mention of the seeds at breakfast, the family soon realized who had replanted them. Shedou was overjoyed.

"I can't thank you enough," he told AP yet again. "My garden and those seeds are so important to me."

AP felt embarrassed by all the attention, especially as he was the reason for the damage in the first place.

AP's third morning working with Nekhti was like the others—natron-shoveling followed by bandage-making— little wonder his friend was so keen to succeed in the priesthood. As they worked away in the heat and the smell, AP asked, out of interest, whether they ever embalmed anyone important.

"We've got one in there now," said Nekhti, jabbing a thumb toward the workshop. "His name's Nehy, the vizier for Upper Egypt. You must have heard of him—he was the second most powerful man after the Pharaoh."

"Yes, of course," AP fibbed.

When Kate failed to show up for their afternoon rendezvous, AP suspected the worst—Snakebite must have attacked her. But suppose she just couldn't get away from Tamit? If that were the case, she would have left a note. AP hurried to the healing stone. There was no note. What to do now? Without knowing where Tamit lived, and unable to search the innermost parts of the temple, he could do nothing.

AP spent an agonizing afternoon in his secluded workshop, trying to think positively. With Kate's busy new social life, there could be many reasons why she hadn't shown up. What if Snakebite *had* captured her, though? At best, he would have taken the abacus, leaving them stranded. At worst? AP didn't want to think about it.

The sun was low in the sky when AP emerged from his seclusion. Maybe Kate had now left a note. He checked the healing stone. Still nothing. Would she be at their sunset rendezvous? He dashed across the courtyard.

"Hey, where are you going?" shouted a familiar voice. "What's the rush?"

AP swung around, bewildered.

"You went straight past me, just as if I wasn't here!"

"Oh, sorry, Nekhti. I didn't see you. I...I was miles away."

"What's wrong?"

"Nothing. Nothing's wrong at all."

Nekhti was unconvinced.

"I've got a bad headache, that's all. I get them some-times."

"My mother will have something for that. Come on, you can take it before supper."

"You go ahead," said AP. "I'll be along in a while."

Nekhti hesitated.

"Go on, I'll be fine. I just need a bit of quiet time while the sun goes down. Then the headache will go away."

Darkness had fallen long before AP left the temple and headed for Nekhti's house. He wanted to stay longer but knew it was hopeless. Something terrible had happened to Kate—he was convinced of that now.

Silent at supper, AP spent a sleepless night staring at the stars, wondering what to do. He must find Tamit and see if she knew what had happened to Kate. That would be diffi-cult because Tamit spent so little time in the public part of the temple. He had to find a way of getting into the inner parts of the temple. Sleep finally came shortly before sunrise.

"You're very quiet," said Shedou as they walked to the House of Embalming and Purification that morning. "Still got your headache?"

"Yes," said AP. "Sometimes they go on for days."

"There's a healing stone at the temple. You should offer a prayer when you go there today."

"Maybe I will," AP replied.

On the remotest chance Kate had left a message overnight, AP headed for the healing stone. There was no note. Mind racing, he wandered over to his hideaway.

Just as he approached the building, he saw the most incredible sight—Kate, heading straight for him. "Where have you been?" they sang in unison. After expressing relief at seeing each other, they worked out what had happened.

"The day before yesterday, we'd agreed to make *this* the rendezvous," said Kate, nodding toward his workshop.

"I thought we were still using the *old* one," said AP. "But the important thing is you're safe. I thought you'd been… hurt."

He then told her how Nekhti's house had been ransacked. "Snakebite must realize you've got the abacus now," he said grimly. "He's going to come after you, Kate."

"Well, he won't be able to get into Tamit's house. It's surrounded by a high wall, with a gate that's manned 24–7."

"He'll likely try when you're out on your own, like he did with me."

"But I'm *never* alone. Tamit's always there—or I'm in the temple, surrounded by priests."

"Okay, but you must be *extra* careful now."

Kate promised she would be. Then she had an idea.

"Snakebite's already frisked you and searched Nekhti's house, so he knows for certain that you don't have the abacus. The smart thing now is for you to take it back. We can fix it so it won't slip from your kilt. Let's go inside and do it right now."

After taking care of the abacus, AP wanted to tell her about the device he had built, but Kate was too preoccupied with the other night's dinner party. AP listened patiently.

"I wish I'd had a camera—you wouldn't *believe* some of the things I saw."

"You could've taken one with you." AP grinned. "I've made one for you—a pinhole camera. Come and take a look."

"This is *so cool*," said Kate a few minutes later. She was standing on the chair with the device pointing through the tiny window. "I can see a perfect picture of the temple, all upside down. Can you make it the right way up?"

"No, that's it."

"Do you have to use the black cloth?"

"Yes, the picture's too faint otherwise. And it can only be used to see things outdoors, in bright sunlight. There's not enough light indoors."

"So how should I announce my new powers?"

"I'd start with another dream." He paused, thinking. "I've got it. Hathor pays you a visit. She's wearing a black cloth over her head and is holding this strange device. She tells you it's how the world is seen in the afterlife—upside down and in miniature."

"That's *good*," she said, beaming. "And they'll be blown away when they see this. It's so neat!"

"We just need some cloth to cover up the pot and make it look more mystical."

Before leaving, they agreed to always meet at AP's hideaway. Aside from avoiding further confusion, they could talk freely without being seen.

30

Ramesses the Great

Within hours of Kate's demonstrating the camera in the temple, word of the new priestess's miraculous powers had reached the ears of the most supreme being in Egypt—the Pharaoh. Tamit's father was duly summoned to the Royal Palace. After a brief consultation with the senior member of the Pharaoh's council, the decision was made that the new priestess would attend the palace to demonstrate her celestial device to His Majesty.

"I can't believe it!" Kate blurted the following day. "I'm actually going to meet a real living pharaoh, *the* Pharaoh, in his Royal Palace—in three days' time!"

AP had never seen his sister so excited. "That's absolutely fantastic! I'm really happy for you. I'd give a lot to be going too."

"So come along!" she said enthusiastically.

"How can I? The Pharaoh's asked to see you, not me. There's no way I can tag along. You're not visiting a friend's house—you're summoned to see Ramesses II!"

"I can fix that! I'll tell the High Priest I had another vision. Hathor told me I must take a certain wab to the palace when I see the Pharaoh."

"So how's this mysterious wab going to appear on the scene?"

Kate thought for a minute. "What if I said he'd walk up to me at some particular time and place, on the day of the visit?"

"Okay," said AP, "and suppose I were carrying something special that I handed to you?"

"Hey, I like that. What could it be?"

"Um…something simple. How about a bunch of papyrus? I can collect some down by the Nile."

"Sounds good to me."

"You'd better bring me something to wrap it in. I don't want anyone seeing it until the right moment."

"Okay."

"What time have you got to be at the palace?"

"Three o'clock. I'm being driven in a chariot. Tamit's father has a fleet of them. We're going to leave from the Temple of Amun—he's the main god. It's on the other side of the town."

"I'll be there! All you've got to do is find out when you're leaving."

"I'll do that tonight and tell you tomorrow."

"Talking of telling," said AP, "you haven't told me how you demonstrated your magical device to the priesthood."

"I put on a performance, like you did at Camelot."

AP smiled.

"Tamit was taking part in the early morning ceremony, and I went along, just to watch. So there was this great procession through the temple, led by a chanting priest, with all these others carrying offerings of food and drink for the god. People had been up for hours baking bread, and cutting up meat and stuff. I was following along with all the priests, and we were heading for the altar room, the room with the golden door. It was a *wild* scene.

"While all this was going on, a high priest went inside the sanctuary—that's the small room where the god's statue lives—and he opened up its shrine, which is a special cabinet. He then washed the statue, sprinkled it with oils and perfume, dressed it and put on its jewelry. Can you believe that? Now the god was ready to receive the offerings."

"How can they get all that food and drink into the sanctuary?" asked AP. "It's so small."

"They don't. They just take in a selection on a tray. Once the god has 'taken' what he wants, they share out all the rest."

"You still haven't said about your magical device."

"I was just getting to that. Well, there I am at the heart of the temple, surrounded by all the priests, and I'm thinking, 'I can't do this.' But I've *got* to. So I take a deep breath and start talking in this mystical voice about my dream of Hathor. I say I want to show them this wondrous device."

"Did you have the camera with you?"

"No, I didn't want to carry a heavy flowerpot through the temple."

"Good point."

"I left it in your workroom. I would have chosen somewhere special, like the Sacred Lake, except I was afraid someone might find it. So I told them they must follow me. It was amazing, having all those high-powered priests trailing behind me, like I was taking a bunch of kids to the zoo!"

"So what did you do when you got there?"

"I brought out the camera, all mysteriously, went up to the most senior priest, put the cloth over his head and pointed the camera at the temple. Fortunately, he saw the picture right away."

"What did he say?"

"Nothing at first. But I could tell he was impressed."

"Did the others try it?"

"They didn't get a chance because he wouldn't put it down! He just kept panning around, every so often letting out a great whoop. I eventually persuaded him to let somebody else have a go, but that was it."

❋　❋　❋

On the appointed day, AP went off to work, the same as usual. Word of the new priestess and her celestial device had spread throughout the town—it was the sole topic of conversation on the walk to work.

"They say that when it's held up to the night sky you can see all the gods in the universe," Shedou announced solemnly. "Imagine that! And it can even see into the future."

"You could use it to see how your seeds turn out!" joked his eldest son, but Shedou wasn't amused.

Just to be safe, AP arrived at the Temple of Amun well before the rendezvous time. Choosing a spot in the shade, he sat down and waited.

The first indication something was about to happen was when six priests swept from the temple, looking very grand in their fresh white robes. Lining themselves up outside, they scanned the faces of the gathering crowd like security guards. AP's heart began to race.

Moments later Kate appeared, carrying a large bag made of linen and accompanied by a priest.

Holding the papyrus before him, AP strode up to his sister and placed it in her hand. The effect on the priests was electrifying. Unbeknownst to AP, Hathor was often shown as a cow among the papyrus. He could not have chosen a more appropriate symbol.

For several seconds the priests just stood there, staring at him. Then a distinguished man in elegant robes stepped forward and escorted him and Kate to the first chariot—he was Tamit's father. The chariot driver, bowing respectfully, helped them aboard, and they set off at a gallop, followed by a fleet of chariots.

Arriving at the palace, Kate and AP, accompanied by Tamit's father, were escorted to the chamber of the Pharaoh's senior adviser.

"There are some important things I must explain before I take you to see His Majesty," began the adviser pompously. Then, sneering down at AP, he asked, "Is this the wab Hathor spoke of in your vision?"

Kate nodded.

"First," he said, pausing for emphasis, "when you enter His Majesty's presence, you will approach His throne with your eyes cast down. You will then fall on your knees, with your head touching the ground, and remain there until He bids you to rise."

Kate and AP exchanged indignant looks.

"Second, you will not address His Majesty unless he first speaks to you."

He paused to let the words sink in.

"Third, you will not presume to tell His Majesty *anything*. The Pharaoh is the living descendent of Amun, the supreme ruler of Upper and Lower Egypt, the knower of *all* things.

"Fourth, you will under no circumstances touch His Majesty, nor will you allow anything you are holding to touch Him."

The adviser's gaze shifted from Kate to her wab, and he gave him such a disapproving look that AP felt even more insignificant than before.

If Kate and AP had been free to gaze around the throne room, the gold ceiling and the vibrant battle scenes on the walls would have overwhelmed them. Instead, they had to study the highly polished stone floor.

Ramesses II was a striking man. He could have walked into any room, dressed in ordinary clothes, and everyone would have noticed him. Surrounded by servants and officials, he sat on an ornate gold throne beneath a canopy of red and gold fabric. Looking like a picturebook illustration of a pharaoh, he wore the traditional striped cloth over his head and shoulders. In the center of his forehead was a raised cobra's head of gold, and he wore a heavy gold necklace. A long white gown of the finest linen covered his chest and most of his stifflypleated kilt. Kate judged him to be about the same age as their father.

Completely ignoring AP, he spoke only to Kate. "Have I the new priestess before me, the one with the celestial device?"

Kate had intended to sound mystical, but when she answered "Yes," her voice was barely a croak—she was *so* nervous.

"Bring it here so I may witness its powers," he said, beckoning her to stand beside his throne.

Remembering AP's dire warning to use it only outdoors, Kate took a deep breath.

"As your Royal Majesty knows in all his wisdom," she began in a confident voice she hardly recognized as her own, "the celestial device only has eyes when it is outside, beneath the Pharaoh's clear blue sky."

"Way to go!" AP wanted to shout, but all he could do was slip her an approving glance.

Ramesses II, smiling regally, arose from his throne and led the way outdoors, closely followed by Kate and an army of advisers, scribes, officers, bodyguards and fan-bearers. AP tagged along behind, completely ignored by everyone.

To avoid contact with His Royal Majesty, Kate demonstrated how to use the device by example. The Pharaoh gave her his full attention. He then resolved her dilemma of how to hand it over by taking it from her. Moments later, Ramesses II, head and camera draped in black, scanned the nearby buildings. Everyone waited expectantly.

The Pharaoh remained ominously quiet. Then he uttered, "Nothing!"

Kate, recognizing the seriousness of the situation, moved to his side and immediately saw the problem. Because he was holding the device too close to his face, the black cloth had fallen in front of the screen. Without even thinking, she pulled the cloth taut, hoping this would do the trick.

The Pharaoh stood in silence for more than a minute, slowly scanning the buildings. Kate's heart was pounding. AP shuffled nervously. Then the Pharaoh announced, "I can see! This is miraculous!"

His advisers cheered, along with his scribes, officers, bodyguards and fan-bearers. Kate and AP gave a silent sigh of relief.

From that moment on, Kate could do no wrong in the eyes of Ramesses II. After spending some time gazing at familiar landmarks, he invited her to accompany him to his chambers. AP was not sure whether the invitation extended to him, and nor was Kate. The two exchanged anxious glances, which the Pharaoh noticed.

"I suppose your wab should come too," he said, sounding quite unconcerned whether he did or not.

Then, placing a hand on her shoulder, the Pharaoh led the way back, pointing out places of interest along the way. Kate, now entirely at ease, talked away as if she had known him for ages. AP tagged along behind, feeling completely unimportant. Meanwhile, Tamit's father was escorted into another room to await their return.

The Pharaoh's favorite topic of conversation was himself, and it wasn't long before he was reliving his heroism at the battle of Kadesh.

"The Hittites, that war-like rabble to the east, had been troubling Egypt since long before my father's reign." He settled down in a comfortable chair for what promised to be a long story. Kate sat opposite him. "Then, during the fifth year of my reign, they formed an alliance with our other enemies." He leaned forward, bringing his face within inches of Kate's. "It was time to march on the city of Kadesh and destroy them all!"

He explained how he had set off with 20,000 men, and how enemy spies along the way had convinced him the city had been abandoned. "So we camped on the outskirts of Kadesh, waiting for the rest of my army to catch up. But it was an ambush!" he said, raising his voice. "The hordes swept upon us like locusts."

AP, who always enjoyed a good story, was listening to every word, though he knew his sister must be totally bored. But Kate—sitting on the edge of her chair looking enthralled—was doing a convincing job of hiding it.

"The Hittite king had twice as many men as me, and my soldiers, seeing them charging down in their chariots, turned and fled! They all deserted me, except my loyal bodyguards."

"That's *terrible*," cried Kate, sounding genuinely shocked. "What happened?"

"The enemy's chariots surrounded us. Then I saw one spot where they were fewer. So I charged at that weakness and my bodyguards followed. The sight of such outstanding courage rallied my men, and a glorious battle followed."

From his account of events, Ramesses II was the bravest of them all, and it was entirely due to his great leadership, and to the support of his father, the God Amun, that they had defeated the enemy.

AP, unimpressed by such bragging, lost interest. But Kate sat spellbound, nodding and smiling at all the right times, asking the occasional question, and flattering the Pharaoh at every turn.

Ramesses II seemed as interested in her as she appeared to be in him. "You are a very special young lady," he said thoughtfully, "and a most powerful priestess. Such gifts as you possess must be treasured and protected. You will have one of my personal bodyguards to watch over you."

Kate didn't know what to say, so she just smiled and shyly lowered her eyes. Her brother had no idea whether she was intentionally leading the Pharaoh on, or whether she was the one being led.

"Your celestial device works in the light of the sun," the Pharaoh mused. "Maybe you can summon an equally wondrous instrument to work in the darkness of the tomb."

He went on to explain how Nehy, his loyal vizier, would soon be making his long journey to the afterlife. "It would give me great joy to send him on his way with a celestial guide in the darkness."

Kate glanced desperately at her brother. AP just shrugged his shoulders, so she lowered her eyes demurely and said nothing.

Over the years, Tamit's father had witnessed many remarkable things at the palace, but what took place that day was unique. Kate, a complete stranger, had been with the Pharaoh for more time than he spent with his most senior advisers. Even more extraordinary was the Pharaoh's gift of a personal bodyguard. Therefore, when Kate apologized for keeping him waiting so long, he said it was nothing at all.

"It is a great honor and pleasure for me to help you in any way I can," he said with a bow. "I, my household, and my humble home are at your complete disposal."

After that, Kate knew he wouldn't mind her spending a few minutes alone with her wab.

Kate and AP took a stroll around the palace gardens.

"I'm not sure what to call you now," AP began with a grin. "I can't call you Kate anymore. What should it be—Your Priestess, Your Eminence?"

"Okay, cut that out! It wasn't my idea to become a high-powered priestess."

"He'll come in handy," said AP, pointing back to Kate's new bodyguard. Massive, muscular and menacing, he was prowling behind at a respectful distance. "Snakebite will keep his distance now!"

"For sure," said Kate. "So, what do you think of the Pharaoh's request? Could you make a device to work in the dark?"

"I'll have to think about." AP shook his head. "Ideas don't appear like magic."

31

Black Magnet

While Kate was being treated like a celebrity, AP's life continued as before. Every morning he worked with Nekhti, and most afternoons he spent at the temple. Between the two, he was learning a great deal about Egyptian burial ceremonies and the priesthood. Sometimes he did odd jobs around the temple with his friend, and occasionally attended some of Nekhti's classes. He also spent time alone, experimenting in his workshop. Aware that Snakebite could attack at any time, he kept a watchful eye out for him, but never caught a glimpse.

The idea for a device that would work in the dark came to AP from something Nekhti had mentioned. "One of the oldest beliefs," Nekhti had explained, "is that the afterlife is spent in a special place, far off to the west." Mummies were buried with all kinds of things to help them in the afterlife, so what better than a magnetic compass that pointed west? The idea was simple enough, though it could prove difficult to make.

AP's first problem was finding a piece of iron to make into a magnet. "There's lots of copper and gold around," Shedou said on the way to work one morning, "but iron..." He rubbed his chin thoughtfully. "That's hard to find. There's *some* about. It comes from the east—the Hittites use it for making swords."

When Kate met AP that afternoon, she was bursting to tell him her latest news. "The Pharaoh's invited me to his palace again!" she exclaimed. "This is so amazingly awesome. Just imagine."

"Right now I'm imagining old Ramesses when you can't come up with another magical device," he said gloomily.

"You can't think of anything to build?" she asked, feeling deflated.

"I've got an idea that *might* work, but you'll have a hard time finding the things I need."

"Fire away."

"First, I need some iron. Preferably small pieces, like needles or nails."

"You've got it!" she said. "What's next?"

"Finding iron will be *difficult*—but that's your problem, not mine." AP sounded uncharacteristically cranky.

"What's up?"

"Nothing."

"I know my little brother well enough to tell when something's bothering him."

"Why do you always have to go on about my size?" he snapped.

Suddenly it occurred to Kate what the problem might be. "Listen, I know that guy, the Pharaoh's adviser, was really snooty with you the other day. And the Pharaoh pretty well ignored you altogether."

AP remained silent.

"I realize you're doing all the work, and I'm having all the fun, but I didn't want it to be this way. You know that."

AP nodded. "It's not your fault, but I did have a bad time at the palace. They made me feel like I didn't count."

"I know," she said, putting an arm around his shoulder. "They were horrible to you. And I didn't help by sucking up to the Pharaoh like I did."

"That's okay," he said, sounding more like his old self. "You obviously impressed him." Then, smiling, he added, "Maybe he *likes* you!"

"No way!" Kate protested. "He's old enough to be my father. Besides, he's got such a big nose!"

They both laughed.

"So, getting back to your shopping list, what else do you need beside iron?"

"Just some thread and a hammer."

"What are you going to make?"

"A compass."

Kate looked puzzled, until he explained about the journey west. "How do you make a magnet?"

"There are two ways—hammering and using electricity. The second way's easy, and I've done it many times. The only snag is you need a battery. So I've got to use the hammering method, which I've never tried before."

"How does it work?"

"It's quite simple. You line up your piece of iron so it's pointing north and south, then you start hitting it with a hammer. That lines up all the mini-magnets inside the iron, so they point the same way."

"How hard do you have to hammer?"

"No idea. I'm not sure how long to hammer for either. I'll have to experiment."

After several days of searching, Kate managed to find some small pieces of iron. AP set to work.

Finding north and south was easy because the temple faced north. He also checked this for himself by watching the setting sun. Choosing a piece of iron the size of a small nail, he hammered away for several minutes. This flattened the rod slightly, but when he tried using it to pick up a small scrap of iron, nothing happened. AP was puzzled—he knew he had lined it up properly. Maybe he hadn't hammered it long enough. He carried on hammering until his arm ached, yet the rod still didn't act like a magnet. "What can I *do*?" he muttered in desperation.

Everyone noticed how quiet he was at supper that night. "Are you sick?" asked Nefret, sounding concerned.

"Just another headache," he said, anxious to avoid attention. "It'll be gone by morning."

"You should go to bed early," she suggested. AP, glad of the opportunity to be alone, took her advice.

He lay awake, thinking. "If only I had a battery," he said to himself, "it'd be so easy." Then he realized he could make one.

"Tell me you're kidding," said Kate the next day when he told her the bad news.

"I wish I were."

"This is serious. I saw the Pharaoh again yesterday—I've seen a lot of him lately. He keeps dropping hints about the device. Well, he began with hints, but yesterday he came right out with it. That Nee guy—"

"Nehy," he corrected.

"Whatever. Well, he's going to be buried next week, and Ramesses wants the device before then."

"Talk about pressure!" AP groaned. "There *is* a chance I can do it using the electrical method, but first I have to make a battery."

"You can't do that," she challenged. "*Can* you?"

"Sure, anyone can. Haven't you seen that trick where you stick a paper clip and a coin into a lemon, and feel the tingle of electricity when you put your tongue across them?"

"Can't say I have," said Kate.

"Okay, I've got a new shopping list. I need some more iron, but big bits this time." He cupped a hand to show the size. "I also need some copper—that'll be easy. I need thin sheets, the thinner the better, about as long as my arm and as wide as my hand. I'll make…" he paused for a moment, "say, three batteries, so I'll need three sheets of copper— three chunks of iron too."

"Hang on, I'll never remember all this."

After repeating the list, he started on the other items.

"I need some copper wire." He stretched out his hands. "About twice this length. I'm sure they use it for making necklaces and things. And I'll need some insulation— strips of linen dipped in oil should work."

"Is that it?"

"Nearly. The only other things I need are three bucket-sized pots and lots of vinegar, enough to fill them all."

"I'll need a donkey cart for that lot."

"How *are* you going to carry it all?"

"No problem. After my star performance for the Pharaoh, everyone's falling over themselves to be helpful."

"I almost forgot. I'll need a sheet of papyrus, something nice and fancy. And some ink and paints—bright colors would be good—and a brush."

"That's really it?"

"Absolutely. Unless you can find some chocolate bars."

It was a race against time, and AP wasn't sure he would win. Making each of the batteries was easy enough. First, he rolled one of the copper sheets into a scroll, attached a length of wire and lowered it into a pot. Then he attached a second wire to a piece of iron and placed this in the pot beside the copper, making sure they didn't touch. Next came the acid.

He poured in just enough vinegar to cover both pieces of metal. To check if the battery was working, he touched the ends of the two wires against his tongue. "Good," he said, feeling the tingle. He then made the other two batteries, but delayed adding the vinegar.

The piece of iron he chose to magnetize was the size of a toothpick. The difficult part was winding the wire around it to make a coil. This would have been easy using insulated wire, but he had to keep stopping to wrap the wire in oily linen. It took forever!

AP knew the strength of the magnet increased with the number of turns of the wire, so he wound the loops close together, building up several layers. Once that was finished, he filled the remaining batteries with vinegar, connected them together and then connected them to the coil. The current was only a fraction of what he'd get from a regular battery, so he decided to leave the coil connected for a whole day.

"I can't do anymore," he thought, looking over his handiwork. "Let's hope we've got a magnet by morning."

Kate was already waiting for him when they met the following day, which was unusual.

"*There* you are!" she said, sounding stressed. "Did it work?"

"I haven't had a chance to check yet."

"But do you *think* it worked?"

"There's only one way to find out."

AP hesitated before disconnecting the coil. Should he wait a bit longer? What difference would it make anyway? He disconnected the coil and pulled the rod free.

"Here goes," he said, lowering the rod toward a small scrap of iron.

As soon as the rod made contact, he knew it wasn't going to work, and when he raised the rod, the iron stayed where it was.

"Oh *no!*" gasped Kate. "What's happened?"

"It's a total failure." He stood back, shaking his head. "The current must have been too small."

"What are we going to do?" Kate was desperate. "And what will I tell the Pharaoh?"

Suddenly AP had an idea—a tiny glimmer of hope. Tying the rod to a piece of thread, he adjusted the position of the knot so it hung level. Then he attached the other end of the thread to the edge of the table. After spinning this way and that for a while, the rod stopped.

"What are you doing?" asked Kate.

"Hang on a sec." He gave the rod a small nudge. Swinging back and forth several times, it stopped—in the same position as before. He tried a second time, with the same result. "This is looking better."

Kate was bursting to know what was happening, but AP wasn't ready to explain.

"I just want to try the same experiment with the rod I hammered yesterday."

Tying the hammered rod to a second length of thread, he suspended it from the other end of the table. When it stopped spinning, it was pointing in the same direction as the first rod.

"Yes!" he shouted jubilantly. "We've done it!"

"It's working?"

"Absolutely! See? They're both pointing in the same direction—north and south!"

"You said it was a failure."

"I *thought* it was. When the rod didn't pick up the iron, I figured it wasn't magnetized. I was wrong. It *was* magnetized—just too weakly to pick up anything."

Kate looked blank.

"Just watch this," he said, untying the hammered rod and holding it close to the other one. The suspended rod immediately started turning, bringing their two ends closer together.

"See that, Kate? These two ends attract each other because they're opposite poles. Now watch what happens when I use the other end of the hammered rod." The free magnet now swung away, increasing the gap between the two ends.

"Is that ever neat! You're driving the other magnet away."

"That's because the two ends have the same polarity— similar poles repel, opposite poles attract."

"Here, let me try that."

"Well this is a first," he said, handing over the magnet. "Kate's doing a science experiment!"

"Okay," she said a couple of minutes later. "How do we get from an iron rod that points north and south to a celestial device that points west?"

"That's where you and your artistic talents come in!" He handed her the papyrus and the painting supplies. "Cut out a disc, big enough to cover the rod. Then decorate it with a fancy arrow pointing to the setting sun."

"Are we going to just hand it over to him on a piece of string?"

"Of course not. While you do the artwork, I'm going to make a fancy stand from these bits of wood I scrounged from Shedou's workshop."

The topic of conversation changed from celestial devices to their nemesis—Snakebite.

"He's still around," said AP ominously, "spying on us from a distance. And we know from our last trip that he never gives up."

"But he won't get past my bodyguard!"

"Where's the big guy now?" asked AP. "I didn't see him when I arrived."

"Oh he's out there, prowling around—never lets me out of his sight. It's kind of creepy, but I feel safe."

Before leaving, AP dismantled the batteries, poured away the vinegar and washed out the pots—they might come in handy later.

32

Tomb Robber

Nehy's funeral was the highlight of the social calendar, and everyone who was anyone received an invitation. Naturally, that excluded mere wabs, but AP was the priestess's wab, so there were no objections to his attending. Nor were there any objections to his being at her side throughout the ceremony, even though many important people wanted to be seen in her company.

"That's the Celestial Priestess," whispered one guest. "They say her powers are greater than those of the entire priesthood put together."

"See how she wears the Pharaoh's gold," whispered another, referring to Kate's stunning new necklace.

The necklace was one of many gifts the Pharaoh had given her to show his appreciation for the magnetic device. Visits to the palace were now commonplace, and Ramesses II had become so attentive that Kate was beginning to feel uncomfortable in his company. Maybe she was being overly sensitive—any woman in Egypt would have gladly swapped places with her.

The funeral procession had set out from the Nehy estate just after sunrise. Tamit's house was in the same neighborhood, and AP had spent the previous night there so that he could attend. Leaving Tamit's house just before dawn, the Celestial Priestess and her wab were escorted to a special viewing platform reserved for the most important guests. Not even Tamit's father, the royal scribe, had been invited.

Dozens of servants led the procession, carrying refreshments for the guests. There were trays of bread and cakes, baskets of fruit and racks of roast duck and beef. Thirsty guests could choose between water, beer or wine. Some servants carried bouquets of flowers, adding splashes of color to the spectacle. Behind the refreshments came men carrying large boxes containing the vizier's provisions for his journey to the afterlife. Others followed carrying ceremonial items for his tomb.

"See that painted box?" asked AP, pointing toward one of the servants. "That contains the *shabtis*."

"What's that?" queried Kate. They had to whisper to avoid being overheard. Anyone watching probably thought they were exchanging spiritual thoughts.

"*Shabtis* are small figures of servants. They're left in the tomb in case the dead person has to labor on the land in the afterlife—the *shabtis* do the work for him!"

"So what's with all the furniture those guys behind him are carrying? They've even got a chariot."

"Those are the things he needs in the afterlife. The Egyptians believe the person comes back to life in the other world and carries on doing the same things as before."

Kate nodded.

"That's why those scribes are carrying all those scrolls and writing supplies. Nehy was the vizier, dealing with the law and government."

Mourners followed the scribes—family members, friends, fellow officials and servants. Behind them came two teams of men pulling on ropes, hauling a wooden sled with Nehy's stone statue. A priest walked in front of the life-size figure waving an incense burner, with two more priests on either side. Meanwhile, men darted between the priests with flagons of water, which they poured onto the road ahead to help the sled to slide.

"That's got to be hard work," whispered Kate "Why not use a wagon?"

"Maybe they can't build wheels strong enough to take such heavy loads. They use sleds for hauling massive statues across the desert too."

Nehy's sarcophagus, the last and most important part of the procession, followed behind. Shaped like a person and elaborately painted with symbols and hieroglyphs, it lay on a ceremonial boat that was being hauled on a second sled.

The priest walking in front of the sarcophagus had a leopard skin draped over his shoulder, showing he was a sem-priest.

"He's in charge of the burial ceremony," said AP. "Sem-priests spend a lot of time at the House of Embalming and Purification. They're responsible for performing all the mummification and tomb rituals."

"That explains why I've not seen one at the temple."

Following closely behind the sled were a dozen young women, weeping and wailing hysterically. Their cries could be heard above the noise of the hundreds of spectators lining the route.

"Who are *they*?" asked Kate.

"They're professional mourners. When they've finished here, they could be going on to another funeral."

The Celestial Priestess and her wab, together with the other special guests, followed along at the end of the procession, which took over an hour to make its way through the town and down to the Nile. There, a fleet of boats was waiting to take everyone across to the other side. Getting the people aboard took some time. Meanwhile, the heavy sarcophagus was loaded onto a ceremonial boat filled with flowers.

"I bet Mum and Dad's trip along the Nile will be nothing like this," said AP under his breath. "Have you ever seen anything like it?"

They gazed across at the bobbing flotilla of boats, all loaded to capacity with people and goods. One boat even had a team of oxen aboard for hauling the sleds when they reached the other side. Every so often, the professional mourners broke out into a somber chant, which carried across the still air. The crossing was slow, and the boatmen had to pull hard on their oars.

"Look at all that silt," said AP, pointing at the brown water. "That comes all the way from Africa." Kate wasn't listening.

As the west bank drew closer, they noticed there were far fewer buildings than on the other side. Rolling hills filled the foreground, shimmering in a heat haze. And beyond the hills—which they would soon have to climb—were mountains.

❉ ❉ ❉

"How much farther?" Kate complained. "And how much steeper is it going to get?"

Some of the older people looked too exhausted to continue. Servants moved up and down the column with jugs of water. Some of the guests had already started into the wine and beer. A troupe of dancers and musicians led the procession, their lively antics and music standing in contrast to the solemnity of the occasion.

Eventually, the procession came to a halt. They had arrived at the necropolis. Generations of workers had labored for years cutting tombs into the cliffs for the burial of important people.

"Now what?" asked Kate.

"It's time for the Opening of the Mouth ceremony."

"Does that mean lunch?"

"Afraid not," said AP, whose stomach was also rumbling. "It's going to be performed on the mummy."

"What happens?"

"The sem-priest will touch the mummy's face with a special forked rod. That allows the dead person to do all the things they did before, like eating, speaking and moving."

As Kate and AP made their way forward for a better view, people dropped back to let the Celestial Priestess pass. Everyone bowed, and some even reached out just to touch her.

The priests had removed the mummy from its outer cases and propped it, upright, beside the tomb. Forked rod in one hand, incense burner in the other, the sem-priest slowly approached, as if afraid the mummy might come to life. He then began chanting and reciting prayers, after which he tapped the mummy's face with the rod. He did this twice more, and the ceremony was complete.

"Once the mummy's back in the sarcophagus, it'll be placed in the burial chamber, along with all the other stuff," AP began. "Then the priests will take the family members down there."

"Us too, remember," added Kate.

"I'm not likely to forget that! What a fantastic opportunity. If you hadn't become so famous, there's no way we'd see inside an Egyptian tomb."

"And if you hadn't conjured up the magic, I wouldn't *be* famous. I'd have been exposed as a fraud."

Using ropes, a group of men lowered the sarcophagus into the burial chamber through a vertical shaft. Then servants began carrying all the other items into the tomb, using a spiral staircase cut into the side of the shaft. Meanwhile, family members, accompanied by specially invited guests, viewed the aboveground part of the tomb.

"Imagine doing this with hand tools," said AP, gazing at the huge cavern chiseled out of the rock. "The walls and ceiling are perfectly flat and smooth."

Kate was marveling at the mystical paintings. "Thoth," she said, pointing to the ibis-headed god of wisdom. "And the goddess with the round headpiece and horns is Hathor."

"You won't forget her!" said AP, smiling. Then, glancing around, he asked if she was feeling lonely.

"What?"

"I just thought you might be missing your bodyguard, that's all."

"Oh, I see what you mean," said Kate. "He was *really* upset when they told him the tomb visit was strictly by invitation. Anyway, nothing can happen to me in here."

Soon people began making their way toward the spiral staircase leading to the tomb. Kate and AP wanted to explore some more.

"We'd better get back," said AP some minutes later. "We mustn't miss the tomb."

The staircase was poorly lit and the steps steep, so they had to watch their footing. The farther they descended, the dimmer it got, and when they reached the bottom, they were in darkness. A guide appeared with a burning torch and led the way to the burial chamber. As their eyes grew accustomed to the gloom, they realized they were alone. The other visitors had all left.

The tomb was smaller than they expected and was so crammed that they had to pick their way slowly to avoid tripping over things. A lone torch was mounted on the opposite wall. In its flickering light, they could see a mystical painting at the far end, above the sarcophagus.

"Let's check it out," said Kate. She was no longer whispering because the guide, probably out of respect for their privacy, had disappeared.

"That's Anubis, the jackal guy," she said, recognizing the god of the dead. "But what's he doing with that set of scales?"

"He's weighing the dead person's heart against a feather. The feather represents the truth, and it's a test to see whether the person lived a truthful life. This is his day of judgment."

"What about that ugly-looking thing crouched beneath the scales? It looks like some sort of crocodile monster."

"That's exactly what it is," said AP. "If the person fails the test, it chomps down their heart. Then they can't go to the afterlife."

Kate noticed four large containers in front of the sarcophagus. Made of stone, they had carved animal heads for stoppers. "What are they?"

"Canopic jars. They contain the organs removed from the body."

Kate groaned. "It's all so spooky," she said, watching the shadows flickering on the walls. "Let's get out of here."

Turning their backs on the painting and the sarcophagus, they started groping their way back toward the shaft.

"I'll go first," said AP, taking the lead. "I'll feel my way. Just stick close behind me."

Kate never saw the bony hands that reached out from the shadows. Grabbing her from behind, they dragged her down. She would have screamed, except one of the hands was clamped tightly across her mouth. Her legs were still free though, and the scuffling of her feet on the stone floor alerted her brother.

"Kate!" he shouted. "What's happening?"

"Stay just where you are!" snapped a voice from somewhere near the sarcophagus. "Do as I tell you, and your sister will be safe." AP immediately recognized the voice.

"Let her go!" shouted AP, trying to sound intimidating. "She's done nothing to you."

"Oh, but I think she has," the voice replied calmly. "If I'm not mistaken, she has my chronoverser."

"No she doesn't!" yelled AP defiantly. "I've got it. And if you want it back, you'll have to come and get it!"

"You're lying," replied Snakebite, still sounding relaxed. "I've already checked you over, and the house where you're staying. I didn't find it, did I?" He chuckled. "No, I'm quite sure your big sister has it, probably around her neck. Let's just see." The struggling sounds became frantic.

"Here's proof I have it," shouted AP. "Look!"

While Snakebite had been holding his sister, AP had pulled the abacus from his kilt and tied it to a chair. He now pressed the white button, illuminating the screen with the world map.

That got Snakebite's attention! AP then ducked behind an ebony cabinet and started feeling his way back toward the sarcophagus—he didn't have far to go.

"Stay where you are, and *do not* let go of the chrono-verser. Remember, I have your sister." Snakebite's disembodied voice sounded quietly menacing. Then, turning to Kate, he hissed, "If you ever want to see your brother again, stay where you are and be quiet. Understood?"

Kate nodded, and her attacker was gone.

Lying on the cold hard floor, eyes and ears straining into the gloom, she could hear Snakebite's footsteps—and his curses as he bumped into things. Then everything went deathly quiet. All she could hear was her own breathing.

Several things then happened in rapid succession. There was a dull thud and a loud groan, followed by a crash and the sound of breaking pottery. Moments later the air was filled with the most disgusting smell.

"Come on, Kate!" shouted AP, grabbing her hand. "Let's get out of here."

The bottom of the staircase was in complete darkness, so they had to grope on all fours to find the first step. Kate kept glancing over her shoulder, expecting to see Snakebite, but all she saw was blackness.

"We'll never find our way out of here," she whimpered. "He's going to get us!"

"No he won't," said AP resolutely.

Then he found the first step and they threw themselves up the stairs.

Half a minute later, they were standing in the courtyard, panting and blinking in the sunlight.

In their absence, the servants had set out a magnificent buffet. Everyone was too busy feasting to notice their belated arrival—everyone, that is, except Kate's bodyguard. He looked enormously relieved.

"That was close," said AP, still breathing heavily. After explaining what he had done with the abacus, he said what happened next. "When he told you to stay where you were, I was already beside the sarcophagus, and fully armed. So, as soon as he made his way toward the abacus, I let him have it from behind!"

"What was that terrible smell?"

"Maybe an overripe intestine. I hit him with one of the canopic jars, and it smashed onto the floor." He paused. "Let's get some food—I'm starving."

"I've just lost my appetite."

As AP gorged and Kate picked halfheartedly, their conversation changed from their tomb ordeal to the events of the day.

"This is amazing," said Kate, looking around. "The ancient Egyptians seem to spend more time building tombs and planning for the afterlife than thinking about the present."

"I know what you mean," said AP, taking another helping of roast duck. "And while most people live in simple mud-brick homes, their temples are colossal buildings made from stone. We've seen only a few of them too—you can imagine the temples and pyramids the pharaohs built for themselves."

"Ramesses is *always* talking about his tomb," said Kate. She was about to continue when she noticed some activity around the tomb. "What's going on over there?"

Gangs of workers were hauling baskets of rock toward the courtyard.

"They're going to fill in the shaft," AP explained. "Once it's full of rocks and rubble, they'll cover it over with blocks of stone."

"Why go to all that trouble?"

"To stop the tomb robbers."

"People rob the tombs?"

"Big time. Think of all the valuables rich people have buried with them—or the treasures of a pharaoh."

"Wouldn't robbers be too afraid of being caught? Imagine what the officials would do to someone who robbed a *pharaoh's* tomb."

AP smiled. "Most of the officials are involved themselves. The robbers pay them to look the other way."

"I thought a pharaoh's tomb had all sorts of secret passages so nobody knew where he was buried."

"The robbers are usually the ones who help *build* the tombs!"

"What a scam!"

"That's why so few treasures have ever been found. There are King Tut's treasures—they're *really* impressive, and he was only a minor king. Imagine what your friend Ramesses is going to leave in his tomb."

Then AP had a terrible thought. "The shaft!" he gasped. "What if Snakebite didn't get out?"

"He had plenty of time—at least an hour before they started filling it in. I'm sure he got out, unfortunately!"

"*Unfortunately*? I don't like him any more than you do, but I wouldn't want to be responsible for his—"

Kate didn't let him finish. "Listen to me AP, what happened down there was entirely his fault. *He* attacked *us*, remember? Someone like that deserves everything that's coming to him. But I bet you all the gold in Egypt that he slithered out in time to save his miserable skin."

33

Fleeing the Pharaoh

I can hardly disappear, just like that," protested AP as they headed down toward the waiting boats. "They've been so nice to me—they treat me like one of the family. I couldn't leave without saying goodbye."

"There's no choice. You have to come and stay with me. Look at the facts. Snakebite knows you have the abacus, and he's going to come after you. He's probably somewhere in that crowd right now, following us."

"*If* he got out."

"You can count on it!"

"So I'll be extra careful from now on and won't go *anywhere* alone. I'll tag along with Nekhti."

"And how's he going to help if Snakebite decides to attack you?"

"He's taller and stronger than me."

"Big deal. So now you've got your own bodyguard, only he's a kid."

"I know judo."

"Get real, AP. You might be able to toss your little buddies around at your judo club, but this is a full-grown man. All the time you're with me, you've got the protection of a *real* bodyguard. And when I'm not around, you'll be safe inside a home that's built like a fortress. End of discussion."

✳ ✳ ✳

AP had been living at Tamit's house for several days. Aside from one trip to the countryside with Kate, he had not set a foot outdoors since the funeral. On the plus side, his new home was luxurious, and he had his own room close to Kate's. Regardless, without any projects to work on and with nowhere to go, he was bored.

All that changed on the evening of the fifth day. Kate had been at the Pharaoh's palace since early afternoon—she seemed to spend most of her time there these days—and had not returned before her brother went to bed.

AP was sound asleep. Suddenly, his door slowly opened and then closed. Someone was in his room. The next instant he was wide awake.

"It's you!" he whispered, sitting bolt upright. "You scared me."

"Sorry, I didn't mean to. I'm sorry for waking you...I just...I..." Kate's voice was quaking.

"What's wrong?"

"We've got to get out of here."

"Right now?"

"No, not tonight, but as soon as we can."

"What's happened?" asked AP. "Does it have anything to do with the Pharaoh?"

"It has *everything* to do with the Pharaoh." She took a deep breath. "He wants to make me one of his wives."

"One of his *wives*?" AP was as stunned at the thought his sister was old enough to get married as he was by the idea that the Pharaoh had asked her. "How many wives does he *have*?"

"Two principal ones—he married them when he was fifteen—and many others."

"Wouldn't you like to be one of the queens of Egypt?" he asked with a grin. "It sounds like a promotion from Celestial Priestess!"

"This isn't funny AP, it's deadly serious. The Pharaoh *always* gets what he wants. Nobody ever says no to the supreme ruler of Egypt—you've seen the way people grovel like he's a god. If I said no, I hate to think what would happen."

"Okay, I'm ready for a change anyway. Where do you want to go?"

"As far away from the Pharaoh as possible."

"Let's head north and check out the marshlands around the Delta region."

"How do we get there?" asked Kate.

"Like everyone else, we take a boat down the Nile. That's the easy part." He paused. "The difficult bit is getting away from here, especially giving your bodyguard the slip."

"How will we do that?"

"We'll think of something." He stifled a yawn. "Let's talk about it in the morning."

They'd gone over the plan a dozen times, and their preparations had gone without a hitch. However, when the day of their escape arrived, they were both on edge.

"There's nothing to worry about," he tried to convince her. "Everything will be fine. How could a plan worked out by two great minds possibly go wrong?"

Kate forced a smile.

The plan was a good one, though AP was still unhappy with the role Kate had created for him. After finishing a late breakfast, they told Tamit they would be home by early afternoon. Kate, like AP, carried a large bag over her shoulder, on the pretext of delivering old clothes to a needy family in town. When Tamit offered to take the chariots and go along too, Kate said she'd had a dream where only she and her wab had appeared, on foot.

"This is it," said AP, pointing across the narrow street to the tavern. "Do you think he'll be shocked when he sees us going inside?" AP nodded toward Kate's bodyguard, who was following closely behind. With so many people on the street, he wanted to keep Kate in sight all the time.

"We should invite him in for a drink," she joked, though she was feeling anything but jovial.

"So this is where Shedou spends so much of his time," said AP, looking around the crowded bar. "I wonder whether it's ever quiet in here?" He was almost shouting to be heard above the din. "I'd better order some beer, otherwise it'll look suspicious."

"You go first," said AP some time later. Neither one had drunk much of their beer.

"I'll see you in a few minutes," said Kate, picking up her bag and heading for what passed as the "ladies' room" in ancient Egypt.

AP watched her bodyguard pushing his way through the crowd. But when he saw where she was going, he relaxed a little, and was content to stand a discreet distance from the door while she went inside. As he waited, several other young ladies went through the same door. Meanwhile, AP picked up his bag and made for the men's room.

After several minutes, Kate's bodyguard was becoming anxious. He'd seen several young women coming out of the room, though none as elegantly dressed as she was. He waited a few minutes longer. Then, accompanied by howls of protests, he barged through the door. The Celestial Priestess wasn't there. Knocking people flying, he dashed from the bar and onto the street.

A young lady, seemingly accompanied by her younger sister, hurried through the main entrance of the temple grounds. Each carried a large bag. Their simple dresses indicated they were not wealthy. Instead of heading toward the temple with everyone else, they veered toward the Sacred Lake. Several minutes later, they arrived outside a small building. Glancing around to make sure nobody was following, they disappeared inside.

The pots used for the batteries were still stacked against the far wall where AP had left them. After feeling inside to check they had not been disturbed, he turned to Kate. "I can empty them while you do the packing." Kate nodded and they both got busy.

For the past few days, they had been smuggling things that they needed for the journey from the house, and hiding them inside the pots.

"That dress suits you," said Kate, sniggering. "Though you didn't do a very good job with the kohl."

"If any of my friends saw me now…"

"You have to admit, it was a brilliant idea," said Kate. "They'll be looking for a priestess and a wab, not a couple of underprivileged girls."

"Snakebite's been fooled too."

AP, familiar with the town after all his exploring, led the way to the quay. "Let's be quick," he urged. "We must put as much distance between us and the Pharaoh before your bodyguard reports back."

"I'm going as fast as I can," she puffed. "This bag's heavy."

"So's mine—remember, I'm carrying all the valuables."

AP did the negotiations for their boat passage while Kate looked after their bags.

"How did it go?" she asked when he returned.

"We can't get a boat to take us all the way to the Delta— it's four hundred miles away—we've got to do it in stages. I've arranged for the first part, but I must improve my bargaining skills! It cost one pair of gold earrings, a bracelet, a copper mirror and four wooden combs."

Their boat was a cargo vessel, and the wooden deck was piled high with boxes and containers. A small cabin amidships was for the use of the passengers, though there was only one other person traveling besides them.

"Why are we zigzagging across the river?" asked Kate.

"I'm not sure," said AP, who didn't know much about sailing.

"It's because of the wind," explained their fellow passenger, a kindly old man wearing corn-colored robes. "The wind blows from the sea, to our north." He pointed toward the prow of the boat. "Can you feel it blowing in your face?" They both nodded. "We can't sail directly into the wind, so we have to tack from one side to the other. Sailing south is much easier and quicker because the wind's always behind you."

Kate asked him what the man with the big oar standing at the back of the boat was doing.

"That's the steering oar. See how it's painted with the head of Hathor? Protecting travelers is one of her duties."

Kate caught AP's eye and smiled. Hathor was doing a good job. Having escaped from the Pharaoh and Snakebite, they could relax and enjoy the rest of their time in Egypt.

The banks of the Nile were lush and green, with marshlands stretching into the distance. Water lilies blanketed the surface, their white flowers radiant in the sun. Tall stands of papyrus and reeds fringed the marshes like a dense jungle, forming secluded worlds for the many birds and other animals living there.

A small boat with two fishermen aboard slipped into view, gliding among the reeds.

"It looks like it's made of straw," said Kate.

"Papyrus," corrected the old man. "The locals make them by tying bundles of stalks together. In this part of Egypt, papyrus is used for building houses too."

Crocodiles, hauled up on the riverbank like logs, lay basking in the sun. Later that afternoon, they saw their first hippopotamus, wallowing in the shallows.

As night fell, they had the magical experience of floating beneath the stars.

"Just look at that moon," said AP casually.

"Left, last, less," Kate replied in a flash.

"We've been here almost a month. That means we can use the abacus again in a few days."

"I'm in no rush," Kate said lazily.

Their journey down the Nile took two weeks, with frequent stops along the way to look at the countryside, visit towns, and change boats. Each of the towns had its own temples to the gods. One of the most impressive buildings turned out to be a royal palace, used by the Pharaoh when he visited the area. Just to be safe, they kept well clear of that.

They decided to do something special for their last day. Arriving at a picturesque town overlooking the sea, they spent the day sightseeing. Then, as the sun began to set, they changed into their finest clothes and checked into the most expensive guesthouse they could find. After enjoying a sumptuous dinner delivered to their room, Kate put on all of her jewelry, including the magnificent gold necklace Ramesses II had given her.

"*Very* impressive," said AP, and he meant it.

"Thanks," said Kate. "This trip's been an absolute blast. But the time's gone so fast—it seems like we've been here a week."

AP pulled out the abacus and rechecked the settings. His face lit up in the glow from the screen. "There's still time to change your mind if you want."

"No," she said dreamily, slipping her arm through his. "This has been absolutely fantastic, but it's time to go."

"I didn't mean about going home," he said with a grin. "I was talking about accepting the Pharaoh's offer of becoming a queen!"

Before she could reply, there was a dazzling flash, and they tumbled to the floor in AP's room.

"Okay, it's only me," shouted a familiar voice from downstairs. "Dad only got to the end of the driveway when he realized he'd left his wallet on the hall table." Moments later, the door closed and they were alone again.

"You've lost your tan," said AP. "The Celestial Priestess is as pale as a ghost."

"The wab's white too!" said Kate. "It's *so* weird the way things change instantly. We arrive in ancient Egypt, we're both brown and bald, and we speak the language. Then, ZAP, we're home again as if it never happened."

"Like that holiday in Florida when we took off in a snowstorm and arrived in a heat wave."

"What about that creep Snakebite?" said Kate, sounding serious. "He's been on all the trips. How come he happens to be there at that particular time?"

"He must be able to tell that we're there."

"How?"

"The abacus gives off that bright flash. Maybe Snakebite can detect it, the way the TV used to pick up interference from Dad's old lawnmower."

"What if he could do that when it's *not* being used? He could come here and attack us!"

"No need to worry about that," AP assured her. "The thing's been sitting here for months and nothing's happened."

"Let's hope you're right. I'd hate to wake up in the middle of the night and find *him* staring down at me."

"Changing the subject, what did you think of ancient Egypt?"

"Awesome."

"As good as I said it would be?"

"Way better. I had the time of my life!"

"The Celestial Priestess." He said the name slowly. "Sounds pretty impressive."

Kate smiled. "The name I really liked was Gold Butterfly Woman."

"You really hit it off with Talking Cloud, didn't you?"

"He was a lovely old man. He reminded me so much of Granddad."

"Was that your favorite trip?"

She thought for a while before answering. "Yes...yes I think so—apart from that battle! Egypt was definitely the most fun. Medieval England was...different. But life on the Great Plains with the Sioux was special. It was like watching a wonderful movie. You're all involved and never want it to end, then suddenly the credits start rolling. And you sit there in the dark because you don't want to break the spell."

AP nodded without saying anything.

"How about you? What was your favorite trip?"

"Probably the first one. I really connected with Arthur, like you did with Talking Cloud. I was really sorry when we had to leave."

"I was sorry to leave Egypt too. I had a good thing going there!"

"So, are you ready for another trip?"

"What, right now?" asked Kate.

"No. But sometime in the next few weeks."

"What've you got in mind?"

"There are so many interesting times and places. After 'Camelot' I'd like to see some *real* castles—with armor and jousting. Maybe the next trip should be to the Mesozoic, to see living dinosaurs."

"What about Snakebite?"

"He's just the price we have to pay for all the fabulous things we see. Besides," AP broke into a grin, "he may not be so bad when you get to know him!"

Kate pulled the pillow from his bed and hit him with it.

❋ ❋ ❋

On the other side of the world, and forty-seven years into the future, Robert Drew was developing an apparatus to detect the abacus when it was not in use. The device he'd built for tracking it during activation—first tested in

Medieval England—had taken over two years to perfect. He hoped the new equipment would be ready much sooner.

Further Reading for Young People

MEDIEVAL BRITAIN AND THE ARTHURIAN LEGEND

Although many books have been written about King Arthur, most are fiction and are not included. The ancient Britons, unlike the ancient Egyptians, left few written accounts of their times, which is why we have so little reliable information about them.

The Discovery of King Arthur. Geoffrey Ashe, 1985. Henry Holt, New York, 224 pp.

Everyday Life in Roman and Anglo-Saxon times. Marjorie and C.H.B. Quennell, 1959. B.T. Batsford, London, 236 pp.

PLAINS INDIANS AND CUSTER

Atlas of Indians. Gilbert Legay, 1995. Barron's Educational Series, Hauppauge, New York, 95 pp.

Indians of the Plains. Elaine Andrews, 1992. Facts on File, New York, 96 pp.

Plains Indians. Fiona MacDonald, 1993. Barron's Educational Series, Hauppauge, New York, 56 pp.

The Plains Indians. Colin F. Taylor, 1994. Crescent Books, New York, 256 pp.

ANCIENT EGYPT

Egypt (Ancient World Series). Jane Shuter, 1999. Steck-Vaughn Company, Austin, Texas, 63 pp.

Egyptian Mummies: People from the Past. Delia Pemberton, 2001. Harcourt, San Diego, 48 pp.

Life in Ancient Egypt. Thomas Streissguth, 2001. Lucent Books, San Diego, 93 pp.

Lost Civilizations: The Ancient Egyptians. Allison Lassieur, 2001. Lucent Books, San Diego, 96 pp.

People Who Made History in Ancient Egypt. Jane Shuter, 2001. Steck-Vaughn Company, Austin, Texas, 48 pp.

Pharaohs and Priests. Jane Shuter, 1999. Heinemann Library, Des Plaines, Illinois, 32 pp.

Further Reading for Parents and Teachers

MEDIEVAL BRITAIN AND THE ARTHURIAN LEGEND

See **Further reading for Young People** p. 279

PLAINS INDIANS AND CUSTER

Atlas of the North American Indian. Carl Waldman, 2000. Facts on File, New York, 385 pp.

Bury my Heart at Wounded Knee. Dee Brown, 1972. Bantam Books, New York, 458 pp.

Black Elk Speaks: Being the Life Story of a Holy Man of the Oglala Sioux. John G. Neihardt (editor), 1979 (first published 1932). University of Nebraska Press, Lincoln, Nebraska, 298 pp.

Crazy Horse and Custer. Stephen E. Ambrose, 1996. Anchor Books, New York, 527 pp.

Everyday Life of the North American Indian. J. Manchip White, 1979. Dover Publications, Mineola, New York, 256 pp.

The Indians of the Great Plains. Norman Bancroft-Hunt, 1981. Orbis Publishing, London, 128 pp.

Indians of the Plains. Robert H. Lowie, 1982 (first published 1954). University of Nebraska Press, Lincoln, Nebraska, 222 pp.

My People the Sioux. Luther Standing Bear, 2006 (first published 1928). University of Nebraska Press, Lincoln, Nebraska, 288 pp.

The Story of the Little Big Horn. W. A. Graham, 1988 (first published 1926). University of Nebraska Press, Lincoln, Nebraska, 178 pp.

ANCIENT EGYPT

Chronicles of the Pharaohs: The Reign-By-Reign Record of the Rulers and Dynasties of Ancient Egypt. Peter A. Clayton, 1994. Thames & Hudson, London, 224 pp.

The Complete Temples of Ancient Egypt. Richard H. Wilkinson, 2000. Thames & Hudson, London, 256 pp.

Egypt and the Egyptians. Douglas J. Brewer and Emily Teeter, 1999. Cambridge University Press, Cambridge, 218 pp.

Egyptian Mummies: Unraveling the Secrets of an Ancient Art. Bob Briar, 1994. William Morrow, New York, 352 pp.

Everyday Life in Egypt in the Days of Ramesses the Great. Pierre Montet, 1981 (first published 1958). University of Pennsylvania Press, Philadelphia, 365 pp.

Gods of Ancient Egypt. Barbara Waterson, 1996. Sutton Publishing, Stroud, Gloucestershire, 227 pp.

The Hieroglyphs of Ancient Egypt. Aidan Dodson, 2001. New Holland Publishers, London, 144 pp.

The Horizon Book of Daily Life in Ancient Egypt. Lionel Casson, 1975. American Heritage, New York, 128 pp.

Introducing Egyptian Hieroglyphs. Barbara Watterson, 1993. Scottish Academic Press, Edinburgh, 152 pp.

Kings and Queens of Ancient Egypt. Various contributors, portraits by Winifred Brunton, 1924. Hodder and Stoughton, London, 160 pp.

Mummies: Death and Life in Ancient Egypt. James Hamilton-Paterson and Carol Andrews, 1978. Collins, London, in association with British Museum Publications Ltd., London, 224 pp.

The Priests of Ancient Egypt. New Edition. Serge Sauneron, 2000. Cornell University Press, Ithaca, New York, 215 pp.

Notes

These notes explain some of the facts in the story, and give some background information about the real historical events and how they compare to what Kate and AP saw.

p. 38 **Fishermen in medieval England** used a rod and line, without a reel. Claudius Aelianus, a Roman writer of this period, says feathers were attached to the iron hook to lure the fish, instead of bait.

p. 45 A **quill pen** is made from the wing feather of a large bird, like a chicken, by cutting off the end at an angle. When the hollow quill is dipped in ink, some of the ink runs up inside the quill (by a process called capillary action), and the quill acts as a reservoir.

p. 56 A **league**, a unit of distance used in Roman times, was about 1.5 miles (just over 2 kilometers).

p. 75 **Parchment**, made from the inside layer of sheep skin, was used for writing upon long before paper was developed.

p. 84 **Enchanter's nightshade** (*Circaea lutetiana*)—not to be mistaken for deadly nightshade (*Atropa belladonna*), which is a poisonous plant—was once used for cleaning wounds.

p. 87 **To find the North Star** (Polaris), find the Big Dipper (or Plough). Draw a line through the last two stars at the "cup" end. Polaris lies along this line, about one Big-Dipper-length away. You can find a star map online using the keywords "North Star" and "Big Dipper."

p. 138 Although hook-and-line fishing was used by Indians, **spearfishing** was more common.

p. 143 **General Crook** had 260 Indians under his command, mostly Crows and Shoshones.

p. 143 **Black Hawk**, the warrior who brought word from Sitting Bull and Crazy Horse, is a fictional character.

p. 144 Indians at that time would have called the Little Bighorn by its Indian name: **Greasy Grass**.

p. 145 AP and Kate would have been lucky to be picked up on the **Bozeman Trail** as it was not being used by settlers until shortly after the Battle of the Little Bighorn. The trail did not lead directly to the Black Hills.

p. 164 While **General Crook** was heading north along the Rosebud River to find the Sioux, Crazy Horse and his warriors were heading south to find the soldiers. Crazy Horse spotted them on the morning of June 17. He took them by surprise while Crook and his soldiers were letting their horses graze. Crook took such a beating that he retreated back to his fort. (See *Crazy Horse and Custer*, pp. 420–4.)

p. 168 About a week before the Battle of the Little Bighorn, Custer ordered that all of the **sabers** be crated, so it is unlikely he wore one on June 22.

p. 168 Bloody Knife, like the other scouts, did think there were **too many Sioux** for the Army to handle.

p. 169 **Custer** would have addressed his men sometime before the battle, but there is no record that he did so before setting out on June 22.

p. 170 Custer usually had the band playing, and their most popular tune was **"Garryowen."** However, Custer left the band behind sometime around June 16.

p. 170 The comment by **Gibbon** as Custer rode off is in his own words. (See *Crazy Horse and Custer*, pp. 427–8.)

p. 171 Bloody Knife really did say that **Custer couldn't hit a tent from the inside**! (See *Crazy Horse and Custer*, pp. 365, 378.)

p. 172 There was a real conversation between two officers after the Council of War meeting on June 22, 1876, where one said he thought **Custer was going to be killed**. (See *Crazy Horse and Custer*, p. 428.)

p. 175 **Sitting Bull** did have a vision of **soldiers falling** with their heads down. (See *Crazy Horse and Custer*, p. 47).

p. 176 **Bloody Knife warned Custer** there were more Sioux than they had bullets for, but it is not known whether he suggested they wait until Gibbon arrived.

p. 177 Custer did shout out, "**We've caught them napping**," but not until his detachment was in position at the north end of the Indian camp.

p. 177 Custer sent **Reno's orders** by messenger because Reno was already some distance away. Custer said his detachment would support him, but instead of following Reno into the attack, Custer took his men to the north end of the camp.

p. 180 The twenty-minute length estimate for **Custer's battle** is from *Crazy Horse and Custer*, p. 443.

p. 181 Reno almost lost his nerve at the start of the fighting when **Bloody Knife was shot dead**, and his brain splattered across the Major's face.

p. 214 **Natron**, which the ancient Egyptians called *netjeryt*, is sodium carbonate.

p. 232 Ramesses II did have a vizier named **Nehy,** but the stories told here of his death and later burial are fictitious.

p. 247 AP knew that **steel was better than iron** for making a permanent magnet, but he also knew that steel had not yet been invented.

p. 251 AP calls each of the pots with copper and iron in them a battery, but that's not quite right. The individual containers with their copper and iron electrodes should have been called **cells**. When cells are joined together, they form a battery (of cells).

p. 272 AP had to trade goods for their journey down the Nile because **ancient Egyptians did not use money**.

How to Repeat the Experiments in the Book

If possible, do these experiments with a partner so you can talk about them and help each other. You **MUST** have an adult helper for some experiments.

MAKE SOAP (CHAPTER 5)

Making soap is easy but it involves boiling a liquid which soon becomes caustic. This activity therefore requires adult supervision and great care. For these reasons the instructions will not be included here. This would be an ideal project to do at school. Visit our website at www.abacusadventure.com to see how to get the instructions.

USE A SMALL HOLE TO IMPROVE VISION (CHAPTER 8)

This simple experiment only works for people who have to use glasses to read. So, if you don't use reading glasses, find someone who does: maybe an older family member like a grandparent. This person will be the subject of your experiment.

You'll need:

- a square piece of paper, 2 × 2 inches (5 × 5 cm)
- a needle or pin
- a subject: someone who needs reading glasses

1. Ask your subject to try reading something, like a newspaper or the small print on a cereal box, without wearing glasses. Do this indoors, without a reading lamp. The print will look blurry and your subject will probably be unable to read it.

Can your subject read small print without wearing glasses outdoors in bright sunlight (or indoors, using a bright lamp)? The answer is probably yes. This is because the pupil—the black hole in the center of the eye—gets smaller, or contracts, when bright light falls on it.

2. Use the pin to make a small hole (about 1 mm in diameter) in the piece of paper. Ask your subject to hold the paper up close to one eye, so he or she can see through the hole. If your subject can't see properly, try making the hole a little bigger. The print should no longer look fuzzy, and your subject should be able to read it.

MAKE A PINHOLE CAMERA (CHAPTER 29)

You'll need:

- an adult helper
- an empty tin can, open at one end
- a hammer and a nail
- wax paper or a white plastic bag
- an elastic band

- a piece of thick, dark cloth large enough to cover your head
- a small piece of aluminum foil (the size of a postage stamp)
- Scotch tape
- a needle or pin
- a sharp pencil or round toothpick

1. Ask your adult helper to punch a small hole in the center of the bottom of the can using a hammer and nail. Prick a hole in the center of the aluminum foil. Tape the foil to the bottom of the can, lining up the pinprick with the hole. Hold it up to the light to check the alignment.
2. Using a sharp pencil or round toothpick, enlarge the hole in the foil to a diameter of 1/16 inch (1.5 mm). Use a twisting action while you do this to make sure the hole is round.
3. Cut off a piece of wax paper or plastic just large enough to cover the open end of the can, with an overlap of about 1 inch (2 cm). Secure the paper or plastic with the elastic band, pulling it tight like a drum. This is the screen of your pinhole camera.
4. Go outside, preferably on a bright day, and point the pinhole toward a distant object, like a tree. Place the cloth over your head and drape it around the screen end of your pinhole camera. Make sure the cloth cuts out most of the light but doesn't cover the screen. Your face should be about 9 inches (23 cm) away from the screen. Focus your eyes on the screen and move the camera from side to side. You should see an upside-down image of the object on the screen.

GENERATE ELECTRICITY WITH A LEMON (CHAPTER 31)

You'll need:

- a lemon
- a knife
- a copper coin (1 cent or 1P or 2P)
- a paper clip (the silver-colored iron kind, not the gold-colored brass or colored kinds)

1. Wash the coin thoroughly—you're going to lick it!
2. Use the knife to make two small slits in the skin of the lemon, ¼ inch (5 mm) apart.
3. Push the coin into one of the slits so that only a few millimeters protrude. Repeat for the paper clip.
4. Touch your tongue across the coin and the paper clip. You should feel the metal-taste sensation of the electricity that this simple cell generates.

MAGNETIZE A SEWING NEEDLE, USING A AA BATTERY (CHAPTER 31)

You'll need:

- an old AA battery (don't use a new battery!)
- 6 feet (2 m) of insulated wire (You can buy reels of wire from an electronics shop. They come in different colors according to thickness. The green one works well.)
- sandpaper or an emery board
- 2 large darning needles
- Scotch tape
- a length of thread about 1 foot (30 cm) long

1. Leaving 2 inches (5 cm) of wire free at the end, wrap the wire around the needle, starting 1/4 inch (1/2 cm) from

one end. Make sure each coil touches its neighbor. The easiest way to do this is to wind 4 coils at a time—spreading them out along the needle—and then push them together so they touch. Don't wrap the wire too tightly because you need to remove the needle! When you are 1/4 inch (1/2 cm) from the other end of the needle, continue wrapping over the top of the first layer of wire. This time, instead of making each coil touch its neighbor, just get them as close as you can. Continue until you have 6 or 7 layers of wire. Snip off the wire, leaving 2 inches (5 cm) free at the end.

2. Strip the colored insulation from the two ends, over a length of about 1 inch (2 cm). Do this by rubbing the wire with sandpaper or an emery board. Otherwise, get an adult to scrape the wire with a knife. Hold the two bared wires to the two terminals of the battery. **Warning:** The coil will get warm, and if the battery is too fresh, the coil will get too hot to touch. If that happens, disconnect and allow the coil to cool down before reconnecting.

3. Try picking up a paper clip while the battery is still connected—you have made an electromagnet. When you disconnect one of the wires, the paper clip falls.

4. Using tape, connect the coil to the battery and leave for 1 minute to permanently magnetize the needle. If the coil gets too hot to touch, disconnect one of the wires and allow it to cool before reconnecting. Disconnect the coil from the battery, and then remove the needle from the coil. Try picking up a paper clip—the needle is probably too weakly magnetized to do this.

5. Using a small piece of tape, attach the needle to one end of the thread so it hangs horizontally. Attach the other end to the edge of a table or bookshelf so the needle

swings freely. **Important:** Choose a place with no metal nearby! When the needle stops swinging, make a note of its direction. Gently prod one end of the needle. See if it returns to the same position when it stops swinging (it should be pointing north and south).

6. Make a second magnet by slipping a second needle into the coil and connecting to the battery for 1 minute. Disconnect the battery and remove the needle from the coil. Slowly bring one end of the second magnet toward one end of the first magnet. The suspended magnet will either be attracted or repelled. If you switch ends and try again, you'll get the opposite reaction: like poles repel, opposite poles attract.

MAKE YOUR OWN BATTERY AND USE IT TO MAGNETIZE A NEEDLE (CHAPTER 31)

You'll actually be making just one cell of a battery. If you made two or more such cells and joined them together, this would be called a battery (of cells).

You'll need:

- an adult helper
- 25 feet (8 m) of steel strapping (not galvanized)

> Strapping is a narrow strip of metal, ½–¾ inch wide (15–20 mm) perforated with holes, which is used in plumbing for securing pipes. You can find it in hardware stores.

- pliers
- 2 copper dish scourers
- a large bottle of white vinegar (1 gallon or 4 L will be plenty)
- 1 plastic bucket
- 2 feet (60 cm) of twin-flex wire (speaker wire from a radio shop works well)

- the wire coil from the previous experiment (see p. 294)
- 2 large darning needles (don't use any you've already magnetized!)
- some paper towel
- a length of thread about 1 foot (30 cm) long
- Scotch tape
- an old knife

1. Join the two dish scourers together—side by side—by pulling out loops of copper and twisting them tightly together.
2. Carefully remove the coil of steel strapping from its box, making sure it doesn't unravel.
3. Separate the two strands of twin-flex wire at either end, so that each free end is about 4 inches (10 cm) long. Ask your helper to strip 1 inch (2 cm) of the plastic insulation from each strand, at each end, using the knife.
4. Connect one of the bared wires to the outer end of the steel coil. Connect its neighbor to one end of the joined scourers.
5. Position the steel coil and copper scourers side by side on the bottom of the bucket. Loosely wrap the scourers in a sheet of paper towel so they don't touch the coil. Make sure the two connecting wires are separated by paper towel too. **Warning:** if the copper and steel—or their connecting wires—touch, your battery cell will not work. Drape the rest of the twin-flex wire over the side of the bucket.
6. Carefully slip one of the needles through the center of the wire coil from the previous experiment so that most of it is covered by the coil. Connect each end of the coil to one of the two free ends of the twin-flex wire. Do this by wrapping each one tightly around the bared wire.

Important: if you don't make good contacts between the wires, your needle will not be magnetized.

7. Ask your helper to pour vinegar into the bucket so it covers the top of the copper scourers. **Warning:** Immediately wash off any splashes—vinegar can damage your clothes. Using a pencil, jiggle the steel coil to remove any air bubbles. Leave the wire coil connected overnight.

8. Disconnect the coil and remove the needle. Suspend the needle by the thread so that it swings freely, as in the previous experiment. Notice the direction in which it settles. Check to see if it returns to the same position after prodding one of the ends.

9. Add about 1 pint (1/2 L) of fresh vinegar and then magnetize a second needle, the same way as before. Keep the coil connected for about 24 hours. Holding the second magnetized needle, use it to attract and then repel, one end of the suspended one, as in the previous experiment.

CPSIA information can be obtained at www.ICGtesting.com
Printed in the USA
LVOW121540020613

336538LV00004B/73/P